# WHAT'S IN A NAME?

## RESIDENTS OF ASHWICK HALL BOOK 1

### A REGENCY ROMANCE

## JENNY HAMBLY

# CHAPTER 1

*October 1817, Ashwick Hall, Somerset*
O         Emma awoke to the familiar rattle of rain against the windowpanes. It had poured incessantly for the past week, and she was heartily sick of it. She sighed and turned on her side, her gaze going to the empty bed pushed against the far wall of her chamber. It had been nine months since it had been slept in, and then only for a few short weeks.

Emma had spent two of them nursing its occupant, and although no confidences had been exchanged, she had gleaned much of what had troubled Nell Marsdon from her fever induced ramblings. She had never questioned her about them; it was not done. All the ladies at Ashwick Hall had a history, but in return for the safe haven Lady Westcliffe offered them, they agreed not to enquire too closely into anyone's circumstances.

It might have been supposed that the lack of such confidences and the varying characters of the residents would make it difficult to form friendships, but there was a bond between them, nonetheless. They each had some degree of gentility, but whatever rank or position they had held before they entered was left at the gates to the estate along with their true names. Only women who had suffered some extraordinary misfortune were sheltered by Lady Westcliffe, and this united them as surely as their differing positions in the outside world would have divided them.

Emma was happy that Nell had only been a resident for three weeks before she had found her happiness and future place in society, and as the Marchioness of Eagleton no less, but she missed her. In those few short weeks, they had formed a bond which had not since been broken by Nell's exalted circumstances. Emma looked forward to her monthly letters. She smiled sadly. It could only be a friendship conducted by letter, of course, and she doubted she would have even that much longer. The time was fast approaching when she must leave Ashwick Hall.

Emma felt the urge to huddle under her blankets, instead she threw them off. She would not give in to such weakness. She had always known the day would come when she must face the task ahead. It would be unpleasant, but she would do it; it was not only her future she was protecting, after all.

Her lips twitched as a maid, her cap askew, poked her head around the door.

"Come in, Lizzie. As you see, I am awake."

The girl grinned and pushed open the door with her hip before walking over to the washstand in the corner of the room, the tip of her tongue protruding from her lips an indication of her determination not to spill a drop of warm water from the jug she carried.

Steam rose from the wash bowl as the water collided with the cool air in the room. Emma made no comment as she observed the damp stain on the girl's apron when she turned from the washstand.

"I thought you would be, Miss Wynn. You're always up with the lark. It's a shame it's raining again. I know you like to walk before breakfast."

"I do," Emma agreed.

"May I lay out a dress for you?" Lizzie asked.

Emma smiled. From the girl's eager expression, you would have thought she had a glittering array of silks and satins to choose from, but this was far from the truth. There were only a handful of gowns in the wardrobe, and all of them were practical rather than elegant.

"You may," she said, walking over to the washstand.

Lizzie had grown up in the wing of Ashfield Hall that housed orphans. Most of the girls went into service or were apprenticed to a respectable trade, but Lizzie had been difficult to place. It was not her clumsiness that put prospective employers off as much as the dark red stain that had covered half of her face and neck since birth. Now, at seventeen, she was one of the household servants, and Emma had a soft spot for her. Lizzie was always so eager to please.

She thought it unjust that the girl should be prevented from achieving her ambition of becoming a seamstress merely because of her blemish. She might not be trusted to dust valuable ornaments or carry the best china, but she was an excellent needlewoman. It was true that the orphans benefited from her talents, and Lizzie never complained about the mundanity of mending or making their clothes, but Emma knew that although her ambition may have been thwarted, it had not waned. Lady Westcliffe made a variety of periodicals available to her ladies so that if and when they re-entered the world at large, they would not do so in ignorance. Emma had caught Lizzie several times poring over discarded copies of *La Belle Assemblée* and sighing over the fashion plates.

The girl pulled a grey dress made of fine wool from the wardrobe and smiled a little uncertainly. "I hope you don't mind, Miss Wynn, but I brightened it up a bit yesterday afternoon. I think it's a shame that someone as young and pretty as you should dress so plainly."

Emma did not think of herself as pretty. She was passable, but her nose was a little too long and her brown hair flecked with tints of blond and auburn as if it couldn't make up its mind what colour it should be. She finished drying her face and glanced at the dress the maid held. She had added a lilac ribbon to the high waist of the gown and lace to the hem and neckline.

"Lizzie, that was so kind of you. Where did you get the ribbon and lace?"

The girl beamed. "It was nothing, miss. I have a basket of bits and bobs various ladies have given me over the years."

Emma was sure she treasured every item and felt touched at the maid's thoughtfulness and generosity.

"I wish I could stay to dress you, miss, but Mrs Primly will box my ears if I don't get back downstairs to take the other ladies their water."

Emma frowned at the thought. The housekeeper

was a formidable woman, but then she had to be. Besides the five ladies at present resident at Ashwick Hall, fifteen orphaned girls were housed in the west wing and half a dozen boys of various ages lived elsewhere on the estate. All had to be fed along with the servants necessary to cater to their needs and keep the house and grounds in order. Still, she did not like the thought of Lizzie's ears being boxed.

"That is quite all right. I have been here for the best part of a year now and have become quite used to dressing myself."

Only Flora, who was both the eldest and most longstanding resident at the hall, was assigned a maid to help her dress. Nell had been an exception because she had arrived with a maid. As they had shared the nursing of her mistress, the lively Italian girl had extended her services to Emma. Never had she encountered a lady's maid so outspoken or inquisitive as Maria. Whilst staying very close lipped about her mistress's predicament, she had repeatedly tried to prise information from Emma about hers. Eventually, she had thrown her hands up in frustration.

"Bah! You need not tell me. You hide from an unwanted suitor or a cruel husband, no?"

"No," Emma had said quietly but firmly.

The maid had been brushing her hair, but at that moment their eyes had met in the mirror and something in Emma's had given Maria pause. She had shrugged.

"Very well. I will ask no more. I only wished to help."

She had been as good as her word, something Emma had been profoundly grateful for. However well-meaning she had been, it would have been futile to confide in her or anyone else as well as unwise. Lady Westcliffe had been very clear on this point.

"When the time comes you shall have my support, Emma, of that you may be sure. In the meantime, Lord Westcliffe will set some enquiries afoot, although it will likely be some months before he discovers anything of use, if that is, there is anything to be found." She had smiled apologetically. "I am afraid that I must insist you do not correspond with anyone who was previously known to you outside these walls, nor confide your unfortunate situation to anyone within them. Your safety is my primary concern, and we must not run the risk of it being compromised, however unlikely that prospect."

Emma had, at first, been too relieved to chafe at these restrictions, but she had grown increasingly restless. Perhaps that was why Lady Westcliffe had relaxed her rule and permitted her to correspond with Nell.

"I do not think it can do any harm, although I still counsel you to put nothing in writing that might reveal either your whereabouts, identity, or circumstances. Letters have been known to go astray, after all."

Emma felt the advantage of this arrangement was all hers. The world had so long been denied her that she lived vicariously through Nell's experiences, sharing her excitement at the life growing inside her, the development of her stepdaughter, Lady Francesca, and the happiness and frustration life with her husband brought her. Emma could only dream of the joy to be had from being loved to distraction by someone you in turn loved and felt the frustration of being so closely watched over by that person must be a small price to pay.

As she dressed, her eyes repeatedly strayed to the window, an action she knew to be futile. The rain would hardly stop merely because she wished it to. Yet she could not help it. Her walks in the large grounds were important to her. They gave her an illusion of freedom. Whilst meandering through the park and looking at the countryside beyond she could forget her confinement for a short while and imagine that she was otherwhere, until, at least, she retraced her steps. She shook her head and walked quickly towards the door. She must not be ungrateful or so impatient. In only a month, she would leave whether or not Lord Westcliffe had discovered anything further to aid her. She dared not wait any longer.

As she stepped onto the landing, Lizzie hurried out of Flora's room. The old woman was a trifle deaf, and her booming voice followed Lizzie through the open door.

"You'd best change before Mrs Primly catches sight of you, Lizzie."

Emma saw what she meant. The apron was no longer merely damp but saturated, as was the dress beneath it. Tears started to the girl's eyes as she saw Emma.

"I try so hard not to have these accidents, miss. I really do, but it's no use. No use at all."

"Perhaps you should not try so hard," Emma said calmly. "If you are constantly thinking about not having an accident, the more likely you are to suffer one because you are distracted. Now, do as Flora... Mrs Marley suggests and go and change."

Lizzie bravely suppressed a sob. "Yes, miss, but I'll be late and then I'll have to explain why."

Emma smiled reassuringly. "You may say that I detained you to help me dress."

Relief flooded the maid's eyes. "Thank you, miss. I was a little distracted and in a hurry for I have a message for you. Lady Westcliffe is in the book room, and she wishes to speak with you."

"Oh," Nell said, her stomach churning as she wondered if Lord Westcliffe's enquiries had finally borne fruit. "Then perhaps it would be better if you said that you could not immediately find me, for that is something that might well happen and you could not be blamed for."

The girl cast her a grateful glance and hurried away.

"You should not encourage her to tell lies."

Flora stood in her doorway, wrapped in a voluminous puce dressing gown, wisps of grey hair escaping from beneath her cap. A glint that was difficult to interpret brightened blue eyes that were remarkably keen despite the old woman's assertions that her eyesight was not what it once was. Emma blinked, surprised that she should have overheard their conversation.

"Would you rather I allowed her ears to be boxed for something she really cannot help?"

Flora evaded this question. "You have a soft heart, Emma. You must harden it if you are to survive in the outside world."

Emma lifted her chin a little. "You may be sure it shall be as flint when I need it to be."

The old woman laughed dryly. "Flint can be

chipped; granite would be better."

Emma wondered, not for the first time, what Flora's history was.

"Don't stand there daydreaming. You must not keep Lady Westcliffe waiting."

Lady Westcliffe was the only person Flora accorded any noticeable respect. As she turned to go, Flora added in gruff tones, "By the way, I like what Lizzie has done with your dress."

This was as close as Flora would come to a compliment. Emma looked over her shoulder, a slight smile on her lips. "Did she tell you of her intentions?"

"No, but it is I who gave her the fripperies."

She stepped back into her room and shut the door with a decided snap, as if annoyed or embarrassed by the admission. Emma wondered if she had put the idea in Lizzie's head. For all her brusqueness, Flora was not unkind, and she had a startling array of colourful dresses adorned with an overabundance of frills and furbelows. Whatever had caused Flora to leave the sanctity of her home had not precluded her bringing an extensive wardrobe, unlike Emma, who had arrived without so much as a portmanteau.

She shivered at the memory and hurried to the book room eager to hear Lady Westcliffe's news. The tall, elegant lady rose gracefully from her chair and came around the desk to greet her, a warm smile on her lips. She was a breathtakingly beautiful woman in her mid-thirties, with an abundance of raven hair and slate grey eyes.

"Good morning, my dear. I have news that I think will please you."

Emma's heartbeat quickened. "Lord Westcliffe has discovered something?"

Lady Westcliffe's smile turned wry. "His enquiries are not yet complete. It takes months for a letter to reach India, and months more for a reply to reach England."

Emma felt a stab of disappointment. "That is unfortunate, but I shall act whether or not he discovers anything to strengthen my case."

Lady Westcliffe sighed. "Emma, sit down and allow me to pour you a cup of tea."

She perched on the edge of a wingchair set before the fire, her hands so tightly clasped in her lap that when Lady Westcliffe held out a cup, she had to consciously unfurl her fingers to take it.

"I understand your desire to act, but I still ask that you wait a little longer."

"For how long?" Emma winced. "I am sorry. I sound like a recalcitrant child."

"You do not," Lady Westcliffe assured her, a glimmer of humour in her eyes. "And I understand your impatience, but if there is to be a delay, it should only be a short one. You will be one and twenty in a little over a month, and Lord Flint expects a reply within two at the most. One more month cannot make any great difference."

Although it was not what she wished to hear, Emma knew that Lady Westcliffe was right.

"Very well. But if he has not heard by then, I must act. You know what troubles me."

"Indeed, I do," Lady Westcliffe said gently. "But I can assure you all is well in that quarter."

It frustrated Emma that she could not speak more

openly, but Lady Westcliffe exercised caution even within the walls of Ashfield Hall.

"I hope my servants know better than to listen at keyholes," she had explained soon after Emma's arrival, "but it is better to err on the side of caution."

"Now," she said smiling, "I hope you will find the rest of my news more palatable. I have a proposal to put to you. I have talked it over at length with Lord Westcliffe and we agree that you might benefit from a change."

Emma's eyes widened and her heart beat a little faster. "Do you mean... could you mean...?"

She broke off, fear of disappointment making her reluctant to voice the thought that had come into her mind.

Lady Westcliffe laughed softly. "Yes, I do mean a change of place. Flora has informed me that you escape into the grounds whenever possible, which is perfectly understandable, but she is concerned lest the temptation to explore farther might overcome you."

"I have occasionally wondered if it could do any harm to wander just a little farther," Emma admitted ruefully. "But I would never go against your wishes for so trivial a reason as curiosity or..."

She paused, not wishing to utter words that might be deemed ungrateful or complaining.

Lady Westcliffe understood, however. "Boredom? Restlessness?"

Emma coloured. "Not boredom for there is always something for me to do, but I will admit to feeling rest-less. A change of scenery would be most welcome, but I cannot imagine where I am to go. Unless... are you perhaps going to invite me to Westcliffe Park for a short time?"

"No, my dear," Lady Westcliffe said. "My husband has many visitors and so it would not be wise. It is better that you go somewhere a little quieter." She raised her fine eyebrows, a teasing look in her eyes. "To someone who is not receiving visitors, perhaps, and is in need of the companionship of a friend. One who understands your situation and so will not pry."

Emma felt a bubble of happiness rise within her. "You mean I am to visit Nell?"

"I do. Lady Eagleton wrote to me and begged me to allow you to come to her. It appears that Lord Eagleton wishes the baby to be born at his smaller estate, Pengelly, which lies on the banks of the River Lynher in Cornwall. It is a secluded spot so you should be quite safe there."

"Thank you!" Emma cried. "I wonder why Nell did not mention anything to me in her last letter?"

"She would not raise your hopes until I had agreed to the visit. She would like you to stay until the baby is born. Indeed, it is my hope that you will not need to return to Ashwick Hall at all. My carriage will take you as far as Okehampton. You shall go on the morrow, and tonight we shall hold a farewell dinner for you."

"I can hardly believe it," Emma murmured. "And if Nell is not receiving visitors, then my sparse wardrobe and lack of a lady's maid matters not a jot."

"I would not put you in so awkward a position," Lady Westcliffe said gently. "You will find a trunk in your room containing a variety of day and evening wear, and I have a mind to send Lizzie with you. She will need a little training, particularly with the arrangement of your hair, but I feel sure Lady Eagleton's maid will be willing to help her."

Emma surged to her feet. "You are so kind, so good, Lady Westcliffe. I hope I may one day be able to repay you."

Lady Westcliffe rose gracefully and took Emma's outstretched hands. "There is something you can do, Emma. If Lizzie conducts herself well, when matters are resolved, I would ask that you keep her as your lady's maid."

Emma nodded. "It would be the very thing for her."

# CHAPTER 2

Oliver Carne pulled at the oars, ignoring the burning ache in his arms and the sweat sheening his brow. There were only two hundred yards to the bend in the river, his newest target. It had been almost a year since he had arrived at Carne Castle a wreck of a man with the strength of a gnat. It had taken six months of constant coaxing by Steen, the valet he had acquired with the property, and Oliver's manservant, Hurley, who now acted as his butler, to put any flesh on his bones or instil in him a wish to recover his strength.

He had begun with walks about his garden and then had discovered the boatshed. It housed a small yacht and a rowing boat. From that day forth, he had walked down to the river before launching the rowing boat. Every week he pushed himself to row farther, which at first had meant going no more than twenty yards. Now, he could row hard for two miles before returning in a more leisurely fashion.

He allowed the oars to rest on his knees and

sucked in deep breaths, his head bowed as he reached the curve of the bend. It was early, and mist swirled in patches above the water. A small smile tilted his lips as he heard the raspy call of an egret. It seemed to be telling him to go away, protesting that this was his domain and he an unwelcome visitor. He understood the sentiment. He felt much the same about his estate. Carne Castle was built on a slight rise, at the centre of a finger of land that protruded into the river. Surrounded by water on three sides, and with many acres of farm and woodland protecting its rear, the house had become his hidden oasis from a world he had forsaken. The four square towers and crenellated roof of the fortified manor house could only be glimpsed from the river, a circumstance which suited him. He valued his privacy.

As he raised his head, the sudden warmth on the back of his neck told him that the sun had risen from the thickly wooded bank behind him. His eyebrows rose as he glanced at the unexplored stretch of water in front of him. The mist arched over the river, forming a gossamer bridge. Intrigued by the phenomenon, Oliver began to row slowly towards it, his fanciful imagination suggesting that the odd wisp above it was an ethereal figure crossing over, perhaps to the realm of the fae.

A soft laugh escaped him. Perhaps Hurley was right, and he spent too much time locked up in his library. He had been reading *A Midsummer Night's Dream*, which no doubt accounted for his absurd thoughts. The words of the mischievous fairy Puck came into his head. 'Lord, what fools these mortals be!' His lips twisted. He was in complete agreement.

He caught a movement out of the corner of his eye and turned his head. On a shingle beach to his left, a dark-haired man bent and picked up a pebble. With a flick of his wrist, he sent it skimming across the water. So expert was he that it skipped ten times across the filmy surface before striking the side of Oliver's boat and sinking into the river's murky green depths. He called an apology, but Oliver ignored him; the last thing he wanted was to give him any encouragement to visit.

His gaze strayed to a honey-coloured house that sat on a hill a few hundred yards from the riverbank. Another attraction of Carne Castle was that several miles of narrow winding lanes separated him from his neighbour, who rarely visited Pengelly Manor. Indeed, he had not been in residence since Oliver's arrival. It irritated him that he was now. He shivered as a cloud covered the sun, suddenly aware of the damp shirt clinging to his back. He glanced once more down the river, but the gossamer bridge had disappeared along with the magic of the morning.

It transpired that his new neighbour did not need any encouragement to visit. In itself, this was hardly surprising. It had seemed to him that any man with a claim to gentility within a twelve-mile radius had called when he first arrived. Perhaps it was his lack of a title that had emboldened them, or perhaps rampant curiosity, either way, they had been disappointed.

His illness had provided the perfect excuse for Hurley to turn them away, but he would have seen them off regardless. Oliver was therefore considerably surprised when his trusty servant held a small tray under his nose with a card placed exactly in its centre.

He waved it away irritably, his gaze returning swiftly to the book he held.

"That is unnecessary, Hurley. You know what to do."

When the butler did not immediately withdraw, he glanced up, steel in his dark, blue eyes.

"Hurley. Do not try my patience if you wish to remain in my employ."

These words were softly uttered but implacable, and yet the butler did not quake, nor did he withdraw. Rather he stood as if rooted to the ground, a stubborn tilt to his chin. He knew them to be an empty threat.

"If you expect me to accept all your whims and crochets without pointing out how... how block-headed they are, then perhaps I should go. It's one thing to ignore the vicar, Squire Roberts, or Doctor Ramsey, but quite another to treat a marquess with such disrespect."

Oliver's eyes narrowed, annoyance and reluctant amusement warring for prominence.

"Hurley, I did not think you the man to be influenced by a title."

"I'm not," he said gruffly. "I'm influenced by common sense. I didn't keep you alive all those months to see you throw that life away by burying yourself in seclusion forever. You should look to the future, sir. It wasn't the marquess's title that made an impression on me so much as the man. There is something about him that suggests he is not someone to be trifled with. It would be better that you befriend such a man than make an enemy of him."

A drawling voice Oliver did not recognise came from the doorway.

"You should listen to him. A good butler develops instincts that allow him to judge a guest in a heartbeat."

Oliver's fingers tightened on his book as a tall, strikingly good-looking man with unfashionably long hair and piercing green eyes stepped from behind Hurley. It was the man he had seen on the riverbank. Oliver had not needed to read the name on the card to know who he was. He had made it his business to know who his closest neighbours were. Pengelly Manor belonged to the Marquess of Eagleton, but if he thought his rank would make him any more acceptable to Oliver than anyone else, he would soon learn his mistake. The book tumbled to the floor as he surged to his feet.

"You are not a guest, sir, but an intruder."

The marquess's eyebrow winged up. "And you, Mr Carne, are a mannerless boor. You resemble your uncle in looks, but you certainly have none of his charm."

Oliver's fists clenched by his sides, the temptation to spoil the perfect symmetry of the handsome face before him almost overpowering. He took a deep, calming breath; a mannerless boor he might be, but he was not a savage.

"I have no wish to resemble my uncle in any way," he said, his jaw tight.

"You re-assure me," the marquess drawled. "Charm was his only virtue." His eyes fell to Oliver's clenched fists. "He certainly did not possess your self-restraint. I applaud you for overcoming the under-standable but unwise impulse to plant me a facer."

"Understandable?" Oliver said, thrown off balance.

A wry smile twisted the marquess's lips. "Certainly. I too shut myself up on my estate for a considerable time, and I also would have objected if anyone had had the temerity to ignore my wishes."

The sympathetic gleam in the marquess's eyes spoke of the veracity of his words and Oliver's anger dissipated a little.

"Then why did you come?" he asked, bemused.

The marquess glanced pointedly at a chair.

"Very well," Oliver said. "Take a seat."

This ungracious invitation could only cement the marquess's opinion of him, but Oliver cared not a jot. He was supremely indifferent to what the marquess might think of him and made no attempt to continue the conversation. He had asked a reasonable question and he would wait for the answer. He had no time for small talk. In his opinion, if someone had something to say they should speak, if not, they should remain silent. He found the convoluted ramblings of polite society difficult to navigate; what was left unsaid was often as important as what was uttered, and to his cost, he knew that he had no talent for reading between the lines.

He met and matched the cool, assessing gaze of his unwanted visitor, but as the moments stretched into minutes, it became increasingly difficult to hold the penetrating green eyes and he fought the urge to look away. He was grateful when Hurley returned with a tray bearing two glasses of claret, enabling him to do so without appearing to concede any ground.

The marquess accepted the glass offered, took a thoughtful sip, and then his lips twitched.

"You are not as uncivilised as you appear, Mr Carne. This is a fine claret."

"It was laid down by my predecessor," he said curtly.

"Ah," the marquess said dryly, "I should have guessed, of course."

Oliver's lip curled. "I expect you have sampled my uncle's wine cellar before. No doubt he would have been flattered to number a marquess amongst his acquaintances."

"I, however," the marquess said softly, "would not have been flattered by the association. I did once, many years ago, accept an invitation from Mr Cedric Carne to dine here." His lips twisted disdainfully. "It was not the sort of party I enjoy, and I did not repeat the experience."

Oliver winced, a dull flush creeping into his cheeks. His uncle had indulged in so profligate a lifestyle that he was rumoured to have kept a mistress in each of the four towers of the house. That was nonsense, of course, but wine, food, and women had certainly been his raison d'être. Which of these indulgences had killed him was unclear.

"You are also not flattered by the association, I see," the marquess said, the sympathetic gleam back in his eyes. "You should not regard it. None of us are responsible for the excesses of our relatives. It is certainly no reason to hide yourself away."

Oliver's fingers curled tightly about his glass. "It is not that... not just that."

He blinked, shocked that this stranger had managed to get even that much out of him. The marquess had a commanding presence, and yet he did not make an effort to impose himself. He possessed the confidence of one born to privilege, but it was not this that impressed Oliver. It was the quiet intensity of the man and the understanding he had read in his gaze on more than one occasion even though Oliver's behaviour had been calculated to provoke. He had the uncomfortable feeling that those green eyes could penetrate the mask of stony indifference he had tried so hard to cultivate.

"Why did you come, Lord Eagleton?" he asked, wishing to deflect the conversation.

The marquess put down his glass and crossed his legs, his fingers tapping on the arm of his chair.

"It was not to pry into your private affairs, Mr Carne, nor to satisfy my curiosity. We all have our secrets, and I would no more ask yours than I would offer mine. I will admit, however, that this is not merely a courtesy call."

His lips curled with sardonic amusement, effectively reminding Oliver of his lack of that commodity. To his surprise, he felt a little ashamed. Lord Eagleton could be no more than ten years his senior at most, and yet he felt like an errant schoolboy who had been caught in an act of crass stupidity.

"Then what may I do for you?"

The marquess laughed softly. "What you would like to do is tell me to go to the devil."

Involuntarily, Oliver's lips quirked in response. "True, but that would be futile, and I hate to waste words."

"How well we begin to understand one another. Neither do I."

Oliver felt strangely drawn to this stranger who offered him no flummery.

"I came, Mr Carne, because I wished to know what sort of a man you are."

Oliver felt a stab of disappointment. The marquess had lied to him. He despised liars, and himself for still being such a poor judge of character.

"Then it *was* curiosity that prompted your visit," he said, his tone flat.

Lord Eagleton's gaze hardened. "Not only do I not waste words, Mr Carne, I choose them carefully. It was not curiosity but necessity. My wife is with child. It is only two months before she is brought to bed, and I will allow nothing and no one to upset her."

Oliver stiffened. "I may be mannerless when my privacy is invaded, but I am not a brute, sir. I would never intentionally injure either a lady's feelings or her person, especially when she is in a delicate condition."

"No," the marquess said ruminatively, "I don't think you would."

"If that is what you came to discover, your trip was wasted," Oliver said, frowning. "As I rarely leave the estate, it is extremely unlikely that I will ever meet your wife."

"My trip has not been wasted, Mr Carne. I do not know why you hide yourself away…"

"I am not hiding," Oliver snapped. "It is simply that there is no one I wish to see and nowhere I wish to go."

The marquess ignored the interruption. "What I do know, Mr Carne, is that you are direct to the point of rudeness, irritable, and lacking in social graces. You are also determined to the point of stubbornness, not above getting out of bed in the morning to take your exercise, and possess a sense of humour, however deeply buried. You are not impressed by rank, in fact, I think you might despise it. You are not a man to be easily swayed and you do not lack courage. You are certainly nothing like your uncle, and I expect the only thing your towers hold is cobwebs and mice."

Oliver got to his feet. "It seems you have the measure of me, Lord Eagleton. And now, if you will excuse me, I have things to do."

The marquess leant forwards and picked up the book that lay on the floor between them before rising to his feet. He glanced at the title and quirked an eyebrow. "You have a fondness for Shakespeare, Mr Carne?"

"Not particularly," Oliver said. "But I thought I might find his comedies amusing."

"And do you?"

Oliver's lips thinned. "They rely too much on trickery and farce for my taste."

The marquess handed him the book and then withdrew a card from his pocket.

"You are clearly in need of amusement. My wife asked me to deliver this to you. She very much wishes to make your acquaintance, but as she tires in the evening, the invitation is for luncheon rather than dinner. Only my family will be in attendance and so you need not fear inviting familiarity from your other neighbours."

Oliver stared at the gilt-edged invitation as if it were a snake about to bite. "You must know that I won't accept. Please offer Lady Eagleton my apologies."

"I will do no such thing," the marquess said, dropping the card onto a nearby table. "We will expect you on Friday at one o'clock."

"You will be disappointed," Oliver said flatly.

"I am not at all disappointed, and I doubt my wife will be either. She has a sharp tongue but a kind heart. You must not fear her disapproval."

"You know that is not what I meant," Oliver said through gritted teeth. "And if you think I will oblige you…"

"I don't," the marquess said. "It is not me you will oblige but my wife. You said that you would never intentionally injure a lady's feelings, and I will hold you to it, Mr Carne. I will allow nothing to make Lady Eagleton unhappy."

"But, surely my refusal would not…"

"It would make her discontented, at the very least."

The vision of a spoilt beauty whose every whim was indulged came into Oliver's mind and his stomach twisted. He knew the type and also knew that he was unlikely to get any peace until he capitulated.

"I will come," he said reluctantly, "but only on the understanding that you will then leave me alone."

The marquess held out his hand. "I can almost guarantee it. Let us shake on it."

# CHAPTER 3

I t was still dark when Emma left her room the following morning. Knowing she would be making an early start, she had taken her leave of her fellow residents the evening before, but as she made her way towards the stairs, a door farther along the corridor opened. The youngest resident of Ashwick Hall stepped onto the landing. With her long, dark brown hair falling in a plait over the shoulder of her dressing gown and her bare toes peeping beneath it, she looked even younger than her nineteen years. She was a shy girl with large pansy eyes that seemed perpetually sad.

"Lucy," Emma whispered, "I did not expect you to get up at such an hour. We said our goodbyes last evening."

"I know," the girl said. "But I wished to give you something."

She brought a hand from behind her back, revealing a fine, gold chain with a pendant containing three topaz stones set one beneath the other. It was of unusual design, each stone larger than the one before, with the medium-sized gem surrounded by an intricate pattern of delicately inter-woven gold.

"Lucy," Emma said. "It is beautiful, but I cannot take it. I am sure it means a great deal to you—"

"It does." Lucy came to her and took her gloved hand. She turned it and dropped the necklace into her palm. "And I am only lending it to you. My godmother gave it to me, and I like to think it brings the wearer good luck."

Emma looked at her questioningly. The girl gave a half-smile.

"I was clutching the pendant in my hand when Lady Westcliffe found me. I do not know where you are going, but I think you might need some luck."

Emma glanced down at the necklace, her throat suddenly tight. "Yes. I think I might."

"Then take it," Lucy said softly, closing Emma's fingers around it.

"Thank you. I will keep it safe, and you may be sure I will return it to you when I no longer need it."

Tears shimmered in Lucy's eyes. "I know you will. I think it will be some time before I leave Ashwick Hall. I don't mind, but I shall miss you, Emma. You are the closest to me in age and understand me better than the others, I think."

Emma felt a twinge of guilt. Lucy had arrived only a few days before Nell, and she had kept to her room for much of the first few weeks. When she had emerged, she had said little, only talking when she had been spoken to. The air of melancholy that had surrounded her then had lessened, but its tendrils still clung to her. In truth, Emma felt she understood very little about the girl. She had certainly had no idea that Lucy had grown so fond of her.

"I wish I had done more for you, Lucy."

"You have done many things for me. You shield me from Flora's abrasive tongue——"

"Her bark is worse than her bite," Emma said, smiling.

"I know, although it took me several months to stop quaking every time she spoke to me. But it is not just that. You have never told me to cheer up or to stop dwelling in the past, or a dozen other things that were said with the best of intentions but were ultimately unhelpful."

"No, I did not do that," Emma agreed. "We must all come to terms with our situation in our own time, and I would never have presumed to offer you advice when I am ignorant of the circumstances that brought you here."

"That is precisely what I mean," Lucy said. "You never treated me differently merely because I was so young. You respected my feelings even if you could not fully understand them."

"I am sure everyone respects your feelings, Lucy. They just want you to feel better."

"I am improving," she said. "Lending you the necklace is proof of it. I could not have parted with it before."

Emma slipped it into her reticule and leant forward to kiss the girl's cheek. "Thank you, Lucy. I shall treasure it."

She was surprised to find Lady Westcliffe waiting for her in the hall, a basket at her feet. She picked it up as Emma descended the stairs.

"There you are, Emma. We will enjoy breakfast in the carriage. The rain has stopped, but after so many days of it the roads are likely to be treacherous in places which is why I insisted on so early a start."

"We?"

"Yes, we," Lady Westcliffe said. "The thought of you spending a night alone at an inn has been troubling me. However, Lord Westcliffe suggested that it is quite possible for you to make the journey in three days rather than four. It will, unfortunately, mean long hours shut up in the carriage. I shall come with you as far as Wellington and return the following day. You will spend your second night at Eagleton Priory, before continuing to Pengelly Manor in one of Lord Eagleton's carriages."

"Thank you," Emma said, "for everything. I never meant to be so much trouble."

Fear mingled with the anticipation of finally stepping back into the world beyond the gates of Ashwick Hall. Lady Westcliffe seemed to sense this.

"You have nothing to worry about," she assured her. "As always, I am overly cautious, but we are a long way from your old home, and it is highly unlikely you will meet anyone who might recognise you."

"No, of course not."

"And I do not consider protecting any of my ladies irksome. Now, we must be away."

Two carriages, each pulled by four horses awaited them. The lanterns hanging from them illuminated the steam rising from the horses' nostrils and Lizzie's face almost pressed against the window of the second carriage. She grinned and offered Emma a little wave, but then turned away, a look of chagrin crossing her face.

"Her exuberance is understandable," Lady Westcliffe said. "It is quite the adventure for her. My maid has no doubt pointed out the inappropriateness of her behaviour, however. I asked her to advise Lizzie on what will be expected of her."

"Poor Lizzie," Emma murmured. "She will be quite overwhelmed."

"Quite possibly," Lady Westcliffe said, accepting the hand of the footman waiting to hand her into the carriage. "But she must learn, otherwise she will only humiliate herself, and her confidence, which is already sadly lacking, will be further diminished. You must be firm with her, Emma. Kindness is all well and good in its place, but it can do more harm than good if administered indiscriminately."

The footman turned to her and held out his hand. It was not unusual for a footman to be tall and well-built, but this one was huge. His stockings were stretched over bulging calves, his yellow knee breeches strained against muscled thighs, and his shoulders were so broad, his arms so thick, it seemed they might tear the seams of his dark blue coat at any moment. As Emma's hand was swallowed by his, she felt the rough, hardened skin of his palm. She glanced up and saw that his face was also weathered, and his nose bent as if it had been broken at some point. When he closed the door behind her, he did not stand back but climbed up next to the coachman.

"That is Finn," Lady Westcliffe said. "He will travel with you as far as Eagleton Priory."

"Is he truly your footman?" Emma asked as the

carriage lurched into motion. "He is unlike any I have seen before."

"He is whatever I need him to be," Lady Westcliffe said. "All that you need know, is that he is loyal and to be trusted. He will ensure you are not troubled on your journey."

Lady Westcliffe proved to be just as evasive when she tried to discuss her own circumstances.

"Emma, there is nothing to be gained from going over old ground. Nothing has changed since we last spoke. The people who most concern you are being watched very carefully, I assure you."

"The people who most concern me," Emma said, a touch of bitterness in her voice. "May we not mention names, even here, alone in a closed carriage?"

Lady Westcliffe touched her arm. "It is hard, I know, but it is better not to get in the habit of it."

Emma turned away and looked out of the window. The sky was lightening, and as they passed through Wells, she could just make out the formidable dimensions of a large cathedral. She had lived only a few miles from it for almost a year and never stepped foot inside it.

"What do the townspeople know of us?" Emma said. "Do they not think it strange that we never come into Wells to do our shopping?"

"Not at all. They know only that a few ladies who have fallen on hard times help with the running of Ashwick Hall. It is almost the truth, after all. You all help in some way."

A half smile touched Emma's lips. "Even Flora?"

"Especially Flora," she said gently. "She oversees

things in my absence. Did you not know that she meets with Mrs Primly regularly and gives advice to the warden of the girls' wing?"

"I thought that she was most likely complaining," Emma said ruefully.

Lady Westcliffe laughed softly. "I am sure she sometimes does, but she is vastly experienced at running a large household. She is also wise, and she watches over my ladies. I value her insights."

"Has she offered any about Lucy?" Emma asked, turning her head. "She said that she would miss me. I had not realised—"

"Lucy will do better now that you are gone."

"Better now that I am gone?" Emma repeated slowly, feeling rather hurt. "What can you mean?"

"She has come to depend on you in small ways. You answer for her on occasion, you deflect awkward questions, in short, you protect her. Lucy needs to learn to manage for herself. More than that, to be herself."

Emma was about to protest, but then she remembered Lucy's words. *You shield me from Flora's abrasive tongue.* "I thought I was allowing her to be herself by not badgering her or allowing anyone else to."

"Lucy is used to being overshadowed," Lady Westcliffe said gravely. "No, do not look so downcast; I did not mean by you. I was referring to someone who was very close to her, and who abused her good nature. She has become comfortable in that situation, used to it. But before she goes out again into the world, she must be able to hold her own. Flora can help her with that."

"Perhaps," Emma murmured, feeling a little

abashed. She suddenly felt she did not deserve the parting gift Lucy had given her. *I would never have presumed to offer you advice when I am ignorant of the circumstances that brought you here.* Lady Westcliffe was aware of those circumstances, and it seemed that however well-meaning Emma's actions, they had not been in Lucy's best interests.

"You did what you thought right," Lady Westcliffe said gently. "Indeed, it was right for a time. Lucy needs something different now, that is all, and it is Lady Eagleton who needs your support."

"I am happy to do anything I can for her," Emma said, a little uncertainly. "But I know nothing of bearing a child."

Lady Westcliffe smiled. "She requires your company not your expertise. You are level-headed, calm, and sensible, Emma. Those qualities will prove invaluable to your friend."

Emma thought she understood. "I suppose it is natural to become nervous when the time approaches."

"Indeed it is, but it is not only Lady Eagleton you may need to reassure."

"Oh, I see," Emma said. "You mean Lord Eagleton will also be anxious, of course. He watches over her like a mother hen."

Lady Westcliffe laughed. "He would not thank you for the comparison, but it is accurate, nonetheless." She frowned slightly as if considering something. "I do not like to share information without permission, but in this case, I think it only fair to warn you. Lord Eagleton lost both his mother and his first wife to childbirth. He may become quite irrational when the time comes."

"Irrational?" Emma said, faintly alarmed.

"Well, perhaps that is an exaggeration, but he will certainly find the waiting difficult to bear when his wife is brought to bed. He has his grandmother to support him through it, but I expect she will be with Lady Eagleton for much of the time."

Emma had only seen Lord Eagleton once from afar when he had come to Ashwick Hall to propose to Nell. She had somehow known instantly who the tall, aristocratic man was. Perhaps because Nell had once described him as beautiful. She had thought it an odd epithet for a man and put it down to the nonsensical ramblings of a woman in a high fever, but when she had seen him, she had understood. His expression had been austere, his face alabaster, and with his high chiselled cheekbones, straight nose and firm lips, she had been reminded of a bust of a Roman god she had once seen. She felt daunted at the prospect of having to support such a man.

"Now," Lady Westcliffe said, opening the basket that sat on the seat between them, "let us break our fast, and then we shall while away the hours by playing backgammon. I always carry a set with me."

The roads were as bad as Lady Westcliffe had predicted and flooded in places. It took them six hours to cover the first twenty miles to Bridgewater. It appeared the rain had not extended that far, and the town was buzzing with activity. Emma longed to get down from the carriage and stretch her legs, and her grumbling stomach reminded her that it was many hours since breakfast. She was disappointed when

Lady Westcliffe pulled down her blind and asked her to do the same.

"I had intended to stop here for refreshment, but judging by the number of people thronging the streets, it must be the Bridgewater races. We will continue on to North Petherton; it may be quieter there."

It was not, however, and Lady Westcliffe would not hear of them showing themselves.

"I am afraid horse racing attracts people from far and wide and so we must not take the risk. I will ask Finn to bring us some refreshments."

By the time they reached The Green Dragon in Wellington some three hours later, Emma was exhausted. She made a poor dinner and fell into a dreamless sleep. She parted from Lady Westcliffe after an early breakfast.

"Enjoy your time with Lady Eagleton, Emma," Lady Westcliffe said. "I know you will be as safe at Pengelly Manor as at Ashwick Hall for Lord Eagleton fiercely protects all those in his care."

The flat plains of Somerset soon gave way to the more dramatic scenery of Devon. Hills and valleys were traversed and rivers forded until they finally skirted the wilds of Dartmoor. The familiarity of gorse and fern brought a lump to Emma's throat, and she breathed a sigh of relief as they left the open expanse and seemingly never-ending sky of the moor and turned down a narrow, steep lane barely wide enough for the carriage. Lichen covered stone walls and burnt bracken marked the edges of the road and above, branches and leaves formed a fiery arch.

The horses slowed to a walk, no doubt finding it difficult to gain purchase on the treacherous carpet of yellow, gold, and red leaves beneath their hooves. The road widened before turning sharply, and a few hundred yards farther on the carriage came to a halt. Emma pulled down her window and poked her head out, interested to see what had caused the delay. She saw only high stone walls and one huge pillar surmounted by a round, stone globe. She sighed in relief. It must be the gates of Eagleton Priory. She glanced at Lizzie. The girl was pale, her expression wan, and her excitement at the journey long gone.

Lady Westcliffe's carriage was as comfortable as any Emma had been in, but no carriage, however well-sprung, could completely protect its occupants from being jolted over uneven, poorly maintained roads or from its sway as it turned steep bends. Poor Lizzie had grown quieter and quieter and had twice known the mortification of being sick in front of her mistress.

"We are here, Lizzie," Emma said gently.

The maid revived a little, and for the first time in many miles ventured to look out of the window. The carriage moved between the gate posts maintaining a decorous pace as it made its way along the driveway.

"Oh my," Lizzie said faintly.

Emma craned her neck to see what had provoked such a reaction. She caught only a brief glance of the abbey before they turned onto the gravel sweep in front of the house. Her impression was of a huge rambling structure of austere grey stone, of arched windows and tall chimneys set against the darkening sky.

"It gives me the shivers," Lizzie said as they

descended from the carriage. "It looks just the sort of place as would be haunted."

Emma had no time to answer her as an ancient oak door opened and a footman appeared. He bowed before coming forwards.

"If you will come this way, ma'am, I'll take you to Mrs Timberly, the housekeeper."

She followed him into a cavernous hall that was grand yet welcoming. The fading light that penetrated the huge windows was supplemented by several candelabra revealing highly polished wooden tables, colourful carpets, and thick mustard-coloured velvet curtains.

"I'm sorry I wasn't there to greet you, Miss Wynn. I wasn't expecting you until tomorrow."

Emma glanced up and saw a tidy lady of uncertain years descending an elegant, curving staircase.

"There was a last-minute change of plan," she explained.

"It's of no moment," the housekeeper said. "I'd already had your room prepared. I was just checking everything was in order when I saw the carriage. Now, you give James your cloak and hat, and I'll give you a brief tour whilst he shows your maid to your rooms."

Emma knew from Nell's letters that little of the original Priory remained, but it was still an old building, and as they traversed a seemingly endless succession of rooms, she felt the weight of history surrounding her. It was reflected in the furniture, the paintings, and the wall hangings, indeed, in the very fabric and design of the building. It was a far cry from the house she had grown up in, although that had been grand enough in its way. She was reminded that this impressive residence had been passed down the generations from father to son. No amount of new money could replicate the deep-rooted sense of belonging and privilege that such an inheritance must bestow on its caretaker, nor could it instil the sense of responsibility that such a position brought with it.

Now, she was to become the Marquess of Eagleton's responsibility for a short time. Her heart sank. She felt like an imposter. She had thought only of the pleasure of seeing Nell again, but she knew that in the normal way of things, she would never have been invited to step over the threshold of Eagleton Priory or Pengelly Manor.

# CHAPTER 4

A dog's frantic barking mingled with the sound of hooves clattering on cobbles as Oliver's mount skittered sideways across the stable yard. He drew in a deep breath, consciously relaxing his tight grip on the reins and the rigid muscles of his legs. He patted the horse's neck as it came to a halt.

"Good boy," he murmured.

"He's a little high strung today," his groom said. "You be careful how you go, sir."

Oliver nodded curtly and trotted out of the yard. It wasn't the horse that was highly strung; it was him. His nerves were wound taut and his mount knew it. It was not only the prospect of visiting his neighbours that had reduced him to such a state. That was an irritation, but parrying prying questions for a few hours could be borne if he would then be left alone. The problem was, he wouldn't be. He did not doubt either that Lord Eagleton would keep his word, or that Lady Eagleton would find that meeting him once was quite enough, but his father and brother were quite another matter.

He wanted nothing to do with them and the feeling, until very recently, had been mutual. His father had apparently discovered he had returned as well as the reason for it. He did not know if he really believed the malicious gossip that had seemingly followed Oliver to England, and he did not care. His lips twisted. His father had never been interested in the truth. He was only concerned with hiding it. The letter he had received that morning had been terse.

*London, October 15th, 1817*

*Oliver,*

*Will you never cease to be a cursed disappointment? Against my better judgement, I allowed you to train in a profession far beneath our dignity, and how do you repay me? By making a damned fool of yourself and creating a scandal into the bargain. I sometimes find it hard to believe that you are a Carne at all.*

*Just when your brother is hopeful of making a very creditable alliance, we discover that a potentially ruinous rumour concerning you is being whispered in certain quarters. At great inconvenience to us both, we will travel into Cornwall so that we may put our heads together and see what can be done.*

*Your exasperated father,*

*Painswick*

Oliver did not think that anything could be done, and he had no desire to discuss his unfortunate history with his father. He would be no less of a disappointment when he discovered the truth. His horse sidled beneath him, and he cursed under his breath.

"You are right," he murmured. "These reflections are pointless. Let us ride both of our fidgets out."

He turned from the narrow, tree-lined lane that led

from Carne Castle onto a grass track that would take him over the fields to Pengelly Manor. Not only would the undulating terrain and hedges require all his concentration, but it was far shorter a route than by road. If he had to endure this luncheon, he would get it over with as quickly as possible.

The weather in autumn was extremely variable in Cornwall, sometimes echoing the summer just gone, sometimes foreshadowing the winter to come. October had begun with mists and rain, but the past week had turned mild, encouraging bees to once more emerge and buzz among late-flowering shrubs.

This had apparently encouraged Lady Eagleton to turn her luncheon into an alfresco affair. Oliver was directed to the garden by the groom who took his horse, and he made his way around the side of the house. The lawn behind it descended to the river in a series of terraces. He had just begun to walk across the first stretch of grass when he heard a clear voice behind him.

"Good afternoon. You must be the elusive Mr Carne. Your timing is excellent."

He spun on his heel and saw a white-haired old lady walking towards him on the arm of a blond Adonis in the livery of a footman. She glanced up at the giant as they came to a stop in front of him.

"Thank you, Timothy, but Mr Carne will, I am sure, be delighted to escort me the rest of the way."

Two pairs of assessing eyes swivelled towards him. The footman's gaze held suspicion, and the lady's a hint of mischief.

Oliver bowed stiffly. "You have the advantage of me, ma'am."

"Undoubtedly. At my age I have the advantage over almost everyone. Don't let it concern you."

He did not know how to answer her and so said nothing. She gave a soft, slightly raspy chuckle.

"Forgive me, I should not tease you. I am Angelica Montovani, Lord Eagleton's grandmother."

Oliver had suspected as much. He had noted her resemblance to her grandson almost immediately. Her bone structure and clear, green eyes matched Lord Eagleton's almost exactly. He held out his arm.

"I will endeavour to deliver you safely to your family, ma'am."

"How very kind of you," she murmured, slipping her arm through his.

Again, he made no reply. They both knew it was not an act of kindness. She had given him little choice. As he led her over the second tier of lawn, she glanced up at him.

"It would be polite to attempt a little conversation," she chided gently. "Although with your jaw set so tightly, I can see that might be difficult. Is this really such an ordeal, Mr Carne?"

He saw the mischief in her eyes had been replaced by concern and compassion, and suddenly felt churlish.

"Forgive me…" He paused. "I am not sure how I should address you, ma'am."

"For many years I was addressed as Signora Montovani, but as I am English and once again reside in England, Mrs Montovani will do."

He thought Signora suited her better. There was something so commonplace about Mrs, and she was anything but. Despite her years, small stature, and

41

fragile figure, he sensed a strong will and something else; a quality he struggled to define. It was not the confidence that came with rank and privilege he realised but that which came with time, of storms weathered. Her eyes seemed both wise and kind.

"Signora Montovani, I meant no disrespect. I find small talk difficult."

She patted his arm. "I expect you are out of practice. You have spent too much time alone, Mr Carne."

He led her down a set of wide, shallow steps. To their left a small, ornamental temple nestled beneath a stand of trees. A blanket was laid out on the grass in front of it, and a wicker chair had been placed beside it. Lord and Lady Eagleton sat upon the blanket, a small child between them. As they approached, Lord Eagleton jumped to his feet and held his hand down to his wife. The child also stood and at sight of her great-grandmother, ran towards them with small, rapid steps. The girl was hardly more than a babe, and he was surprised how swiftly she could move. She had almost reached them when she stumbled and fell to the ground, issuing a surprised cry.

Releasing Signora Montovani, he moved swiftly forwards, went down on one knee, and set the little girl on her feet. Her tiny rosebud mouth quivered, and tears started in eyes that seemed overly large in her narrow face. It seemed green eyes were a family trait.

"You are very brave, my lady," he said, brushing a wisp of raven-black hair from her cheek with gentle fingers. "I am Mr Oliver Carne, your neighbour. I am delighted to make your acquaintance."

She studied his face solemnly for several moments and then held out her arms. "Up."

He glanced enquiringly over her head at Lord Eagleton and when he nodded, obeyed the peremptory command. It seemed that she was not satisfied for she placed her little hands on his cheeks and repeated her command. "Up! Up!"

When he looked confused, Lord Eagleton laughed softly. "My demanding daughter would like you to throw her a little way into the air and catch her," he explained wryly. "A game I, in a foolish moment, initiated."

"Up! Up!"

He complied and was rewarded with her delighted giggles. He did it again, and inch by inch a wide smile crept across his face. It felt exceedingly strange. He could not remember the last time he had experienced such simple, uncomplicated pleasure.

"You are honoured, Mr Carne," the marquess said. "Francesca is a most discerning young lady. Allow me to present my wife to you."

Oliver set the child down and turned his attention to Lady Eagleton. She carried her pregnancy well, the loose dress skimming over her rounded stomach the only sign of her condition. She was an undoubted beauty with flaming red hair, hazel eyes, and luminous porcelain skin, and she was clearly in the best of good health.

She was not quite what he had expected. In his experience, spoilt beauties did not enjoy the attention of visiting gentlemen being directed at anyone but themselves, even a child. In fact, such women did not generally display their children to their visitors, especially if they were not their own. Nor was Lady Eagleton's gaze either arch or flirtatious, on the contrary, it was direct and friendly.

"I am so glad to meet you, Mr Carne," she said, holding out her hand.

Oliver felt rather nonplussed. Nothing was going as he had planned. He had felt sure that Lord Eagleton would have repeated his assertion that Oliver was a mannerless boor to his family and had been quite prepared to live up to the description. What he had not expected was to be greeted with such amiability, nor to have his introduction to his neighbours interrupted by the innocent joy of a child not yet out of leading strings. It now seemed impossible to execute his plan, not only his breeding but his inclination argued against it.

He took Lady Eagleton's hand in a light clasp and bowed over it. "The pleasure is all mine, ma'am. I am glad to see you looking so well."

"And I you, sir. I believe you were very ill for some time."

He grimaced. It had not been a question, but it may as well have been. The prying had already begun. "Indeed, ma'am. A stubborn, recurring fever."

Again, she surprised him.

"How unfortunate. I can see you do not like to speak of it, and so I will not press you further. Let us sit and have some refreshment. It is most unladylike of me to admit it, but I am famished." She smiled impishly. "No doubt you are acquainted with Doctor Ramsey?"

"I have not had the pleasure."

For a moment she looked surprised, but then smiled. "Well, never mind. I know him only a little myself but can assure you that I am already a sore trial to him." She exchanged a fond, amused smile with her husband. "And to Eagleton, of course."

"I cannot imagine you being a trial to anyone, my lady," he said.

He meant it. She was not the spoilt, demanding creature he had imagined, but a warm, vibrant woman, who, it appeared, was not going to pry into what did not concern her.

"But the sorry truth is, that I am." She sank onto a bank of cushions and began emptying the contents of a basket. "My husband sent for Doctor Ramsey not long after we arrived. He is a very traditional practitioner and thinks I should benefit from laying in my bed all day, having my blood let, and reducing my diet. None of which I intend to do."

She popped a preserved cherry into her mouth as if proving her point.

"I cannot see the need for you to do so if you are feeling well," Oliver said.

Lady Eagleton sent her husband a triumphant look and he held up his hands.

"It was only the bed rest that I thought sensible," he said.

"It would drive me demented," Lady Eagleton said firmly.

"And I did not take to my bed until my pains began," Signora Montovani interjected.

The marquess sent Oliver a wry look. "As you see, I am outnumbered and outvoted."

"I must apologise, sir," Lady Eagleton said, not looking at all repentant. "I am fully aware that this is not accepted drawing room conversation. Have we shocked you?"

Oliver had been standing a little awkwardly by the blanket, but now he sat down, a faint smile on his lips. "Not at all. We are not in a drawing room, after all, and I think it as nonsensical to ignore a female's instincts in this matter, as it is to shy away from discussing something that is of real importance in favour of commenting on the weather or another topic just as trivial."

Lord Eagleton's lips quirked. "Your opinion is somewhat unorthodox."

"Mr Carne does not enjoy small talk," Signora Montovani said, smiling at him.

"I see," Lady Eagleton said. "Then we shall respect your wishes. What would you like to discuss?"

Oliver felt a moment's panic. He had not kept up with current events, knew nothing of what had been discussed in parliament, and could not think of a single topic that would deflect attention from himself. As he thought frantically, his eyes wandered towards the river. He breathed a sigh of relief. A small yacht was anchored just off the beach.

"I see you sail, Lord Eagleton."

"I do," he confirmed. "It gave me a sense of freedom when I most needed it."

"I have such a yacht in my boathouse," Oliver said. "But I have no idea what to do with it."

The marquess's eyes brightened as if a candle had been lit behind them.

"That is an entirely unsatisfactory circumstance. Allow me to show you."

"But the food," Lady Eagleton protested.

"The beauty of an alfresco luncheon," her husband said, "is that it is portable. Gather what you wish in a napkin, Carne, and we will be on our way."

"Well!" Lady Eagleton complained. "Of all the unhandsome things to do."

She looked as if she would have said more, but Signora Montovani forestalled her.

"Not at all, my dear. Alexander has been so patient with us both, he deserves a reward. And have you not been telling him for months that he ought to make some new friends?"

Lady Francesca chose that moment to stick her hand in the bowl of cherries, successfully distracting her stepmother.

"Come," the marquess murmured. "Now is the perfect time to make our escape."

As they strolled down to the river, Oliver glanced sideways at him.

"It seems that you lured me here under false pretences, Lord Eagleton. You claimed that you would allow nothing to upset your wife, yet if I am not much mistaken, she is not at all pleased at this moment."

"She is not upset," he said, a fond smile curling his lips. "She is piqued. There is a difference, and you may be sure I know just how to make amends. Besides, I took pity on you, Mr Carne. There is nothing so fatal to a conversation than to be asked what you would like to talk about. Either something entirely inappropriate comes to mind or you draw a complete blank." He raised an eyebrow. "Am I wrong?"

"No," Oliver admitted ruefully. "I am aware, however, that it is my own fault." He frowned. "I dislike falsehood, and I would not like to repay my warm welcome with evasive answers about my past."

"We all have a past," the marquess said, his lips twisting. "And I can tell you from experience that you cannot hide from it indefinitely. It is better to confront it, learn from it, and then move on. However, that is a personal matter, and there is no need that I can see for you to share your history with your neighbours unless you wish to do so."

Oliver bent and helped his host pull the rowing boat that awaited them on the shingle beach towards the water.

"You are very trusting," he said dryly. "You have invited me here knowing very little about me, and you are seemingly content to remain in a state of ignorance."

"I trust my instincts, Mr Carne; they are finely honed. If you were a danger to my family, I would sense it and make enquiries about you. As it is, I prefer to use my own judgement rather than listen to second-hand gossip." He laughed mirthlessly. "I have too often been the subject of it."

"And were the rumours about you entirely untrue?" Oliver asked.

"As is usually the case, some had an element of truth and some did not. They never worried me over-much unless they affected someone I cared about, and as there were so few that ever held any place in my affection, that was almost never. There is only one thing I would like to know about you at present."

Oliver's shoulders stiffened but he nodded. "Go on."

"Is the Earl of Painswick or the Reverend Thomas Carne your father?"

How Oliver wished he could claim his father's youngest brother as his sire. Tension coiled in his stomach as he considered how to answer without telling a falsehood. He met the marquess's eyes squarely. "As far as the world is concerned, I am the youngest son of Lord Painswick."

There was a flash of understanding in Lord Eagleton's acute gaze.

"Then no wonder you wish to bury yourself in Cornwall. He is a hypocritical, pompous ass."

This unvarnished description of Painswick took him off guard, and he laughed.

"That is better," the marquess said grinning. "Now, let us go sailing."

# CHAPTER 5

Lizzie did not fare much better on the last leg of their journey. The deeper they went into Cornwall, the narrower and more winding the roads became. It was mid-afternoon before they arrived at Pengelly Manor, an attractive, well-proportioned house of honey-coloured stone. The maid almost fell into the arms of the footman who opened the door of the carriage.

"Lizzie," he said, steadying her. "I am happy to see you, but you should have waited until I helped Miss Wynn out."

"I know," she said in a pathetic voice. "But, Timothy, I feared I was going to be sick again."

"You know each other," Emma said, surprised, accepting the footman's assistance to alight from the vehicle.

"Lord Eagleton has acquired several of his servants from Ashwick Hall," the footman explained. "I grew up there."

"How glad I am for you, Lizzie. You will feel more comfortable if you too have a friend here."

"Timothy always stood up for me when others made fun of me," the girl mumbled, swaying alarmingly.

The footman picked her up before she fell.

"Thank you," Emma said. "I am sure she will be perfectly well if she can only lie down for an hour or two. The journey has been very trying for her."

"Take her up to her room, Timothy. I will see to Miss Wynn."

Emma glanced at the door and saw a dignified man with greying hair. He walked forwards and bowed. "I am Manton, Lord Eagleton's butler, ma'am. Welcome to Pengelly Manor. We weren't expecting you until tomorrow, but I am sure Lady Eagleton will be delighted to see you. She is in the garden, at present. I shall inform her of your arrival after I have shown you to your room. I am sure you wish to freshen up a little."

"Thank you," Emma said, anticipation at the reunion driving out her weariness. "I do. But please don't disturb Lady Eagleton. I would like to surprise her."

"Very well, ma'am."

As he led her up the stairs, she saw Maria hovering at the top of them.

"Miss Wynn," she said, her dimples peeping as she smiled. "It is very good to see you again. I will help you change whilst your maid recovers."

"As I see Maria is determined to take charge of you," the butler said, a grimace of distaste momentarily disturbing his impassive countenance, "I will arrange for some refreshment to be brought to your room."

"Thank you, a glass of lemonade would be most welcome."

Maria pulled a face as he turned and made his way down the stairs in a stately fashion. "He does not like to call me Maria; it pains him." She grinned. "But he hates to call me Mrs Phipps even more!"

"Maria! You are married?"

"Si," she said proudly, waving her beringed hand before leading the way along the landing. "Timothy and I were married three months ago." She opened a door and led the way into a bright sunny room. "Manton disapproves of us keeping our positions, but as Lord Eagleton will not part with Timothy and Lady Eagleton will not part with me, he has to bear it."

"It is an unusual situation to be sure," Emma said. "But I am very happy for you."

Maria looked over Emma's shoulder, a glow of tenderness coming into her eyes. "I am happy for me too."

Emma turned her head and saw Timothy standing in the doorway with her trunk, a besotted grin on his face. He had eyes only for Maria, and she turned away before he realised she had witnessed his lapse of footmanly behaviour.

Some twenty minutes later, Timothy, his expression now suitably wooden, led her through a spacious drawing room and out into the garden beyond. She stood there for a moment, taking in the pleasant view before her. It was a very natural prospect, with neither fountains nor statuary disturbing the expanse of lawn that descended in neat terraces to a ribbon of water. A yacht glided over the river's glassy surface, its white sail flapping a little in the fitful wind, and on the far side of the water, the heavily wooded bank flamed with warm autumn colours.

"Shall I show you the way, Miss Wynn?" Timothy asked.

"Yes, if you please," she murmured, thinking how peaceful it was here.

She was surprised she could not see Nell as the garden was not huge, and it did not appear that there were any hidden alcoves. As they descended the flight of steps to the last tier of lawn, a burst of laughter to her left proved that she had been mistaken. An abandoned blanket, still laden with food, was laid out before an ornamental temple. Suddenly eager to see her friend, Emma hurried forwards and ran lightly up the shallow steps in front of it. She paused at the entrance, blinking as her eyes adjusted to the dimness within.

"Emma!"

The exclamation held a world of warmth, as did the embrace that followed it. Nell's bump and petite stature made the embrace a little awkward, but she managed to lay a hand on either side of Emma's waist and smile up into her face.

"You have come early, and in good time too. My husband has abandoned me to go sailing with our neighbour; a very reserved gentleman who does not like small talk, nor wishes to tell us anything about himself."

Emma laughed, the bubble of happiness inside her escaping. "Then he is in good company."

Nell stepped back, smiling wryly. "Very true. Allow

me to introduce you to Eagleton's grandmother and my stepdaughter."

A white-haired lady stepped out of the shadows, holding a small child by the hand.

"I am delighted to meet you, Miss Wynn." She smiled warmly. "I have never been one for formality. Would you mind if I called you Emma? Nell has spoken of you often, but always as Emma."

"Not at all."

"Thank you. And I would like it very much if you would call me Angelica." She laughed at Emma's surprised expression. "It may be vain of me, but I like my name. Nell addresses me as Angelica, and I have even persuaded my grandson to do so. Last names change, but we never lose our given name. It is who we really are."

Emma felt a stab of grief. She knew just what Angelica meant. It was why she had chosen Wynn as her last name. She should, perhaps, have chosen another, but she had been unable to bear losing her identity so completely.

"I understand, and Angelica is a beautiful name. I would be honoured to use it."

Nell sent the old woman an enquiring look. "I noticed that you did not ask Mr Carne to call you by that name."

Angelica gave a low, raspy chuckle. "The poor man was already finding it so difficult to come into company that I did not have the heart to befuddle him further."

Emma froze. She knew the name Carne. She was acquainted with two people who bore it, and she liked neither of them overmuch. It might prove disastrous if she were to be discovered here. She drew in a slow breath. It was most likely a coincidence; neither of the men she was acquainted with were shy of company. She was distracted as she felt a tiny hand tugging at her skirt. She glanced down and smiled at the small girl looking up at her, the child's serious expression seeming strange in one so young.

"Good afternoon. You must be Lady Francesca. I am very pleased to meet you."

The little girl held up her arms. Emma bent and lifted her onto her hip. The girl tugged at a curl of her hair and then smiled. "Itty."

"She means pretty," Nell clarified for her.

"Why, thank you," Emma said softly. "But you are far prettier than I."

The girl yawned as if she had heard such compliments before and was heartily tired of them.

"Timothy, perhaps you will take Francesca back to her nurse. It is time for her nap," Nell said.

"Of course, my lady."

He stepped forward and the girl went happily into his arms, snuggling against him and laying her cheek on his shoulder.

"Perhaps we too should return to the house," Nell said as he left the temple. "I do not think Lady Westcliffe would approve of me introducing you to Mr Carne, although I cannot think it could do any harm. He has lived for years abroad and has hardly stepped foot out of his estate since his return."

Nell's words dispelled Emma's anxiety. She had been right; it was just a coincidence, but her friend was also right. It would be better if she did not meet Nell's visitor.

It was too late. As they left the temple, Emma saw the Marquess of Eagleton and his guest striding towards them. She let out a slow breath. He bore little resemblance to the gentlemen whose name he shared.

He was not nearly as handsome as Lord Eagleton but striking in his own way. He was tall, almost of a height with the marquess, but although his shoulders were broad, he was extremely slender. Perhaps it was this slimness that made his face appear a little long and his cheeks hollow. His hair was of rich mahogany and his expression serious in repose, but as they neared, he suddenly laughed, his nicely moulded lips parting to reveal even white teeth. His skin was tanned as if he spent a great deal of time outdoors, and as he glanced towards them, she noted that his eyes were deep blue. The smile in them died as they met hers, and he turned and spoke quietly to the marquess.

"Oh dear," Nell said. "Mr Carne is something of a recluse, and he came today on the strict understanding that he would meet only the family. I hope he does not think we are matchmaking."

"I am sure Alexander is explaining the situation to him," Angelica said calmly.

Emma coloured, embarrassed to have upset their plans. "I am sorry. I would have sent word, but there was no time. I think I should make myself scarce. You are right, Nell. Lady Westcliffe would caution me against meeting anyone. She only agreed to this visit because she thought you were not receiving visitors. Make my excuses, will you? You may say I am tired after my journey or some such thing."

She hurried away, sudden unexpected tears blurring her eyes. She must be more fatigued than she had realised for she was not easily upset. It was true that she had been so looking forward to seeing Nell that to have their reunion cut short was something of a let-down, but that wasn't reason enough to turn into a watering pot. She blinked rapidly and wiped a hand across her eyes in an effort to clear them. She wished to meet a stranger as little as Mr Carne, and so it was ridiculous to also feel a little disappointed that he had looked at her with such animosity… no, not that, but there had been an element of hostility and wariness in his gaze. The hostility may not have been directed at her, of course, if he had felt he had been duped in some way, but it had seemed that way. It had been so long since she had gone into society that to be met with such a reception was unsettling. A ragged laugh escaped her. So much for being level-headed, calm, and sensible.

"Umph!"

This unladylike exclamation was swallowed up as Emma's face collided with the grass. She had fallen hard and lay still, a little stunned. She did not understand how she had come to do such a thing. She tried to push herself to her knees but screamed as a sharp, agonising pain that made her dizzy shot through her wrist. She sank back down, gasping. Even prone, her wrist still throbbed.

"Do not move!"

The deep, imperative voice was unknown to her, but she heeded the advice. She felt faint, a little sick, and completely humiliated. Not only had her early arrival disrupted Nell's luncheon, but she had now made a spectacle of herself into the bargain.

She felt a presence by her side, and attempted to lift her head to see who it was.

"Remain still, Miss Wynn, until I have determined where you are hurt."

She stiffened as she felt a probing hand on her ankle.

"It is my left hand, wrist, and arm," she gasped. "And my head aches a little."

"Very well," the voice said.

Its cool authority did much to calm the rapid beating of her heart. That organ seemed to stop altogether when two large hands spread themselves against her left hip and shoulder before gently rolling her onto her back, and she found herself staring up into deep, fathomless blue eyes. It was Mr Carne who had come to her rescue.

His gaze quickly dropped from hers to her hand.

"Your hand and I suspect your wrist are already swelling. We must get you inside and apply some ice to the area. It cannot be examined thoroughly until the swelling is brought down."

Lord Eagleton came up to them. "I shall send for Doctor Ramsey."

"I am sorry to cause so much trouble," Emma said, feeling utterly miserable.

"Not at all, Miss Wynn. I have long wished to meet the woman who helped nurse Nell back to health. Nothing I can do for you is too much trouble."

She struggled to sit up, but Mr Carne laid a restraining hand on her shoulder.

"You must lie still, Miss Wynn. I will secure your arm before I take you inside."

He began to tug at his neckcloth, clearly intending to use it as some sort of sling.

"Are your fingers tingling or even a little numb?" he asked.

"Yes," she murmured.

"I suspect you put your hand out to break your fall. Although you may feel pain in your hand and arm, it is more likely that it is the wrist that is damaged."

Nell and Angelica arrived on the scene.

"Oh, Emma," Nell said. "What an unfortunate accident. You must have tripped on the last step. Doctor Ramsey will be sent for, of course, but he generally visits his mother in Plymouth on a Friday. He does not usually return until evening."

"It cannot wait that long," Mr Carne said, pulling off his neckcloth. "I fear the wrist is either broken, dislocated, or both. Either way, the longer the ligaments and bones remain unaligned, the less satisfactory the outcome is likely to be."

"Bones?" Emma said faintly.

"The wrist has several small bones, Miss Wynn. If these are displaced, they put pressure on your nerves and ligaments as well as disrupting the supply of blood to your wrist."

He lifted Emma's arm as gently as he could, bending it at the elbow, and laying it across her chest so that her fingertips rested against her shoulder. She sucked in a deep breath and then bit her lip, stifling a moan of protest.

"I am sorry, ma'am. Such injuries are always painful. Try to keep your arm still whilst I lift you into a sitting position."

He slipped his arm under her shoulders as he spoke and raised her slowly, before efficiently placing his neckcloth over the arm, under her elbow, and tying it swiftly behind her neck. He then put one arm around her waist and another under her legs.

"Put your uninjured arm around my neck, ma'am."

Her instinct was to insist that she could walk, but common sense prevailed, and she did as she was bid. He lifted her easily.

"You seem to know what you are about," Lord Eagleton said, looking at him curiously.

"I do. Before I became a landowner, I practised as a doctor. I have worked closely with several eminent surgeons and know something of manipulating bones back into place. If you have some ice, procure it, along with several cloths and bandages."

Emma regarded the marquess, expecting to see him bristle at such peremptory commands, but he merely nodded and strode away.

Mr Carne turned his attention to Nell. "If you would show me the way to your drawing room, I would be grateful, Lady Eagleton."

"Of course," she said. "But perhaps it would be better if you carried Emma to her bedchamber. She will no doubt need to rest after you have done whatever it is you are going to do."

"No."

Emma glanced at the face so close to hers. Mr Carne's jaw was rigid and uncompromising.

"A sofa in the drawing room will do, and I would request that you stay with your friend the entire time. The manipulation that will be required will be painful.

If you have some laudanum in the house, I suggest you send someone to fetch it."

"No," Emma said, her tone as implacable as that of her rescuer. "I will not take it or any kind of sedative."

He gazed down at her for a moment and then nodded. "As you wish."

# CHAPTER 6

Oliver could not remember when he had enjoyed an afternoon more. The marquess was a competent sailor and a good teacher. It was a long time since he had learnt anything new, and he'd been fascinated by the technicalities of when to alter the sails to take advantage of the wind. Admittedly, it had been fitful, but that had only added to the challenge. They had sailed almost to where the Lynher met the Tamar River, and he had wanted to go farther when Lord Eagleton had said that from there it was a short sail to the open sea.

"Another day," he had said laughing. "My wife will not be as easily appeased if I return so late."

By the time they pulled the rowing boat up the beach again, Oliver felt unusually relaxed. He had enjoyed Eagleton's company. Hurley and Signora Montovani were right; he had spent too long alone. The marquess had a dry, acerbic wit that he appreciated. He could not imagine why Lady Eagleton thought her husband needed to make new friends.

As they walked towards the temple, he voiced the thought. "Surely, you have many?"

The marquess regarded him with a wry smile before saying, "*Words are easy, like the wind: Faithful friends are hard to find: Every man will be thy friend; Whilst thou hast wherewith to spend.*"

"You have a copy of *The Passionate Pilgrim*," Oliver said, a grin curling his lips. "That quote is from *Friends and Flatterers*, I believe. But you are cynical. Surely all your friends were not the latter?"

"Nearly all," the marquess said. "I knew it, of course. As I was not prepared to be a true friend either, it seemed a fair arrangement. I did not like anyone to become too close to me, and I certainly would never have invited any of my acquaintances to Pengelly, or taken them sailing."

"Then I am honoured," Oliver said. "Does Lady Eagleton hope that I will become your friend?"

"Undoubtedly."

A hint of colour rose in Oliver's cheeks. "And do you wish it, after the reception I gave you?"

The marquess gave a lop-sided smile. "You are certainly no flatterer, which is a point in your favour, and my daughter seems to like you, which is another. The clinching factor, however, is that my wife will stop nagging me if I befriend you." His mobile eyebrow rose. "The question is, will you befriend me, Carne?"

Oliver glanced at the man. Humour glimmered in the marquess's eyes.

"Yes," he said, an answering grin twitching his lips. "But only because I need several more sailing lessons before I dare take my own boat out."

They both laughed, but as Oliver glanced towards

the temple, he saw Lady Eagleton with a slender young woman on her arm. She was not as beautiful as the marchioness, but she was not unattractive. Her brown hair was streaked with blonde and hints of red, curling strands framing the perfect oval of her face. As her dark brown eyes met his, he instinctively stiffened. He had been assured that this was a family party, but it seemed that he had been misled.

"You assured me I need not fear inviting familiarity from any of my neighbours by coming here, Eagleton," he said accusingly.

The marquess laid a hand on his arm. "Lay your bristles, man. That lady is Miss Wynn, a friend of my wife's. She has come to bear her company until the baby is born, but we did not expect her until the morrow. She will wish to meet you as little as you wish to meet her, but it cannot now be helped. I would ask, however, that you forget that you ever met her. It should not be difficult, for you will not again."

Oliver's shoulders relaxed and his resentment was replaced by curiosity. He could hardly voice it, however, when he had been so reticent about revealing anything of himself. As he glanced back towards the temple, he saw her rush off towards the house. Whilst Eagleton went to greet his wife, she ran up the steps and flew across the lawn before ascending the next flight without checking her pace. Oliver frowned. It seemed she really was reluctant to meet him, but surely there was no need for her to flee as if her life depended on it?

As she reached the last of the stone steps, she tumbled to the ground. He stood uncertainly for a moment, his instinct to go to her aid warring with his reluctance to meet her. He glanced at his hosts, but they had not seemed to notice. The shrill scream that cut through the air moments later decided the matter. He sprinted across the stretch of grass, took the first flight of steps two at a time, and did the same with the second, before dropping to his knees beside the prone form.

He bade her remain still and reached for her ankle as he was fairly certain that she had tripped on the last step and thought she might have wrenched it. He felt her stiffen under his touch, before gasping out where the injury lay. He gently turned her over and looked into eyes that seemed almost black in her pale face. He saw shock momentarily break through the pain in them as she registered who had come to her rescue. His eyes fell to her wrist, but it was obscured by the long sleeve of her gown. He could see her hand was beginning to swell and there was also a bump on her forehead. He worked quickly and efficiently to secure her wrist so he could move her.

When he lifted her into his arms, he did not glance at her. The last time he had treated a female, it had caused him nothing but humiliation, and he would ensure that she knew his interest was merely professional. However, when she adamantly refused the suggestion of a sedative, he did look, and saw fierce determination blazing in her eyes. She meant it. He could not help but wonder why, and when, after carrying her inside, he finally pushed up the sleeve of her dress and regarded her wrist, a host of other questions crowded into his mind. He glanced up at her, but her gaze was averted. Her delicate jaw was rigid as if she were clenching her teeth, and two flags of colour stood out against the pallor of her cheeks.

"You are quite right not to look at it," Lady Eagleton said, coming to sit beside her and taking her uninjured hand.

The Adonis of a footman entered the room carrying a bucket of ice and several cloths. Oliver wrapped some slivers in one of them and placed it around his patient's wrist, before replacing it in the sling.

"I will leave you for a few minutes, ma'am," he said, rising to his feet and going in search of Eagleton.

The marquess entered the room as he approached the door. He went to him and murmured softly, "Miss Wynn is adamant that she will take no sedative, but I would be grateful if you would send for some brandy for it is entirely possible that she will need it."

"You do know what you are doing, don't you?" the marquess said, frowning.

"I have treated such cases before. In India, both my inclination and necessity demanded I turn my hand to any number of things." His lip curled. "I did not only pander to the whims of English ladies who professed that the climate had caused them to suffer a host of maladies, many of them imaginary."

A hint of a smile touched the marquess's lips. "I know it is not an unusual occurrence in ladies of a certain age who wish to make themselves interesting, but I have heard that the climate in India *can* be injurious to the health. You are an example of it, are you not?"

"Disease is everywhere," Oliver said. "And although it is true that the climate in India does not suit everyone, in my opinion, being so far from home with little to do can be just as injurious. However it was, I can assure you that I am quite capable of dealing with Miss Wynn's injury."

The marquess nodded. "There is some brandy on the table over there. You only need signal and I will fetch it."

Oliver returned to his patient, his mouth set in a grim line. So much for keeping his past a closed chapter he had not intended to reopen.

"Allow me to tend to your temple, Miss Wynn. Does your head ache?"

"Yes, a little," she murmured.

He dipped a bandage in the ice bucket, wrung it out and wrapped it about her head.

He gazed into her eyes. "And do you feel at all nauseous?"

"No," she mumbled. "I did when the pain shot through my wrist, but it has gone now."

"Very good. You have a bump, but I do not think it is anything to worry about." He took her arm out of the sling and moved her wrist gently this way and that, pausing when she winced or gasped. "It is not as bad as it could have been," he said, "and it is dislocated rather than broken. If you will not take laudanum, will you at least take a little brandy?"

"No. Just please be as quick as you can."

"Very well, but if at any time you wish me to stop whilst you take some brandy, I will do so."

He worked as quickly as he could, pressing and pushing until he felt things move into alignment. It took no more than a minute, but he was sure it had felt much longer to Miss Wynn. When he looked up, there was a sheen of perspiration on her brow, and her eyes were squeezed tightly shut. Admiration sparked in his breast. She had courage and an unusual tolerance for pain.

"The worst is over," he said. "I will bind it up tightly and fashion another sling. You must not try to use your arm in any way and be careful not to knock your wrist. I am afraid it will take two, perhaps three months before it is fully healed."

She opened her eyes and drew in a deep breath. "Thank you, Mr Carne."

"I recommend some hot, sweet tea and then bed. You have suffered a shock and must be kept warm and still."

"I shall see to it immediately," Nell said. "Timothy will carry you upstairs, Emma, and I will bring the tea myself."

Angelica had been looking on in some concern, but she now rose to her feet. "You have been very brave, my child. What you need is sleep. Speaking of which, I shall retire for my afternoon rest." She smiled at Oliver as he put Emma's arm in a more profes-sional-looking sling. "You are very efficient and competent, Mr Carne." Her eyes went to her grand-son. "Escort me to the door, if you please, Alexander."

Oliver busied himself collecting and folding the unused cloths and bandages as the room emptied. He placed them neatly on a table.

"I think it is you who needs a brandy, Carne. Although your hands were quite steady when you tended to Miss Wynn, I could swear I saw them tremble just now."

Oliver looked up with a wry smile and accepted

the glass offered him. "Thank you. I do not like inflicting pain on anyone, especially a female."

Lord Eagleton raised an eyebrow. "I am pleased to hear it, although I had the oddest notion that you did not like the fairer sex overmuch."

Oliver's lips twisted into something between a smile and a grimace. "I have no reason to love them, but I hope my prejudice does not extend to the whole sex."

The fact that he had frequently wished them all to perdition over the last year, now seemed a moot point. He had not been himself, was still not himself, but today he had found himself feeling more like the Oliver Carne he had once been than he had for a long time.

"Your wife and grandmother have been nothing but kind, and Miss Wynn showed great fortitude."

"And as she is under my protection, I am in your debt, Carne."

"Nonsense," Oliver said quickly. "I may no longer practise medicine, but it would have been the act of a brutish monster to leave her suffering any longer than was necessary."

"Why don't you practise medicine anymore?" the marquess asked.

Oliver sipped his drink, considering how best to answer. "I am now part of the landed gentry," he said. "We do not get our hands dirty."

How often had he heard his father utter those words?

"You were always part of the gentry," the marquess said gently. "And there were other, perhaps more acceptable professions open to you than that of physician, and yet you became one."

A queer grin touched Oliver's lips. "That my father might have borne," he said, "but my ambitions were not so lofty. I went to Edinburgh instead of Oxford or Cambridge and received a far more comprehensive training in medicine than I would have at either of those institutions. When I completed my studies, I took a post as an assistant surgeon with the East India Company."

"And so you chose to step out of the world you had been born into," the marquess said sighing.

"I did that the moment I chose medicine," Oliver said dryly. "I may have stepped another rung down the ladder of respectability, but that worried me not at all, and the opportunity to practice in India held no little allure."

The marquess looked at him pensively for a few moments. "In some ways, Carne, you remind me of my younger self. You are a better man than I was for you chose to do something useful with your life, but you are nonetheless stubborn, rebellious, and have your fair share of pride, I suspect. The trouble with pride is that it is a fragile thing that can strip you bare when it is taken from you." He frowned, his eyes growing distant. "It can also ensure that you allow old wounds to fester." He shook his head slightly as if trying to clear it. "Things sometimes happen to us that are not our fault, and yet they can make us feel shame as if they had been."

The hint of a smile touched the marquess's lips as Oliver sucked in a surprised breath.

"I will not pry into what does not concern me, but

in my experience, speaking of whatever it is that has wounded us, robs it of some of its power." He suddenly laughed dryly. "Good God! If that sounded trite, I apologise. I am unused to the role of friend. Suffice it to say, that if you ever wish to talk, you may be sure I will listen and help you if I can."

"Thank you," Oliver murmured, a little stunned that the man before him had divined so much on so short an acquaintance. Was he that transparent?

"I am afraid, however, that I must ask something more of you."

Oliver eyed him warily. "Go on."

"My grandmother is an extremely wise woman, and she has just pointed out that it might be unwise of me to allow Doctor Ramsey to attend Miss Wynn as she makes her recovery." He smiled dryly. "Just as you do not wish to cast aspersions on the whole of the female sex, so I hesitate to do so on those of your profession. A doctor, however, by the very nature of his work, travels frequently and attends a wide variety of patients. It would be very easy for such a one to let slip information about one of them."

"A doctor does not discuss his patients," Oliver said curtly. "Unless it is in the interests of medical science, of course."

"I wonder if you really believe that?" the marquess said.

Oliver at least believed it should be the case, but he had known colleagues who had done so. Perhaps he had been naive. If he had discussed one particular patient with his colleagues, it might have saved him much heartache and humiliation.

"I, however, do not believe it," the marquess

continued. "You profess that you do not enjoy inflicting pain on a female, but you must be aware that there are others who do not hesitate to do so."

Oliver nodded curtly.

"Do you think these ladies should be protected?"

"That should be the role of their fathers, husbands or brothers," he said, the words sounding hollow in his ears. Not all men were good men, after all. Just as not all women were good women.

"Undoubtedly," the marquess agreed. "In an ideal world, but we do not live in an ideal world."

Oliver knew that only too well.

"I cannot inform you of the particulars of Miss Wynn's case, for I do not know them. She has been under the care of a very respectable woman who does, however, and she has assured me that in the interests of Miss Wynn's safety, the fewer people who meet her the better. My grandmother suggested that you should continue to treat her rather than Doctor Ramsey, and I agree with her. It need not take up much of your time, after all."

That was true enough. Miss Wynn would need to be checked on the following day to ensure the head injury was as benign as he had suggested and there was no unusual inflammation in her arm, wrist, or hand, but after that, he need do very little.

"Very well. I will call in the morning."

"Thank you," Lord Eagleton said. "I feel certain I can rely on your discretion, and if the weather allows, you may enjoy your second sailing lesson after you have seen Miss Wynn."

Oliver took the long way home, mulling over all that had happened that day. He had known, of course, that he could not remain hidden away indefinitely, but his world had been turned upside down and the role he had carved out in it, taken from him. Although he had physically recovered from his illness, his mind had stubbornly refused to move on. He knew that he should be taking more of an interest in his estate, visiting his tenants with his steward, and learning all the things he had never thought he would need to know. Instead, he had been distracting himself with physical exercise and books. He had never wanted Carne Castle, had had no expectation of inheriting it, but he had, and to his surprise, he had discovered he liked it.

Whatever rumours were circulating in London could not touch him here. Besides, another scandal would soon eclipse it, he felt sure. His lips curled. How ironic that he had long ago distanced himself from a class of people whose morals and hypocrisy he despised, and yet now found himself once again part of their ranks and accused of such laxity himself. The only thing he had been lax in, was in taking responsibility as owner of his estate. He straightened in the saddle, determined that he would make a new beginning.

"Good day, Mr Carne."

He came out of his reverie and saw a man standing in front of a thatched farmhouse doffing his hat to him.

"Good day, Mr…"

"Mr Rowe, sir," the man said, seemingly gratified at being acknowledged. "I had heard as you were mortal ill a while back and am glad to see you out and about at last."

"Thank you, Mr Rowe. I am very well."

The man looked at him ruminatively. "You're still looking a mite thin."

"Joshua! If you don't come in, I'll feed your pie to the dog."

Mr Rowe grinned. "That's my Betty calling me in. We've more apples than we know what to do with this year. Why don't you come in and try her apple pie and take a glass of cider? You needn't be afeared; her bark's worse than her bite."

Oliver swung down from the saddle. "Thank you, Mr Rowe. I will."

# CHAPTER 7

Emma refused to stay in bed the following morning.

"I am quite well, Nell," she said when her friend entered her chamber to find Lizzy still helping her dress, a process which had taken rather longer than usual due to her injured wrist. "I came to bear you company, and that is what I shall do."

"Is this my sensible Emma?" Nell said. "If the roles were reversed, I am sure you would urge me to stay in bed."

"And I am equally sure you would not take my advice. When you were ill at the hall, you left your bed the moment your legs would hold you."

They looked at each other for a moment and then laughed.

"You are right, of course," Nell conceded, turning her eyes towards Lizzie, who was now busily tidying away her mistress's night things.

"It is nice to see you again, Lizzie," she said. "I

hope you have fully recovered from your travel sickness."

Lizzie attempted to curtsy, Emma's nightgown still clasped in her hands. Her foot became entangled in it, and she staggered sideways.

"I'm quite recovered, thank you, Miss Mars… Lady Eagleton."

Nell smiled. "I am pleased to hear it. Maria has agreed to help teach you how to dress a lady's hair elegantly. She will come to you shortly with Rachel, one of our maids, who will be your subject."

The girl's eyes brightened. "'Tis very kind of her, ma'am, and of you to permit her to do so."

"Not at all," Nell said. "Maria will enjoy it vastly, I assure you. She will teach you one style a day, and each evening you may practise what you learn on your mistress."

"Thank you," Emma murmured dryly as they left the room arm-in-arm. "If I come down to dinner looking as if I have a bird's nest on my head, I will have you to thank for it."

Nell chuckled. "I envisage no such catastrophe."

"No," Emma agreed, "neither do I. Lizzie is skilled with her hands and is an excellent needle-woman. If she becomes half as adept with hair, I shall be very pleased. What she primarily needs is a little confidence."

"Maria has that in abundance. Let us hope some of it rubs off on Lizzie."

They found Lord Eagleton awaiting them in the breakfast parlour. He rose to his feet and bowed.

"Good morning, Miss Wynn. Nell mentioned that she might take breakfast with you in your room, but I see you like being confined to your chamber no more than she."

"Good morning, Lord Eagleton," she said. "Apart from a sore wrist, I am perfectly well. I did, however, forgo the walk I usually take before breakfast."

"I am glad to hear you are feeling better, and as my grandmother always has a tray sent up to her room, I am also glad of the company. As for not taking your walk, I am sure Mr Carne will approve of your good sense, ma'am, when he pays you a visit this morning."

A flutter of butterflies seemed to take flight in Emma's stomach. "Is that necessary? I am very grateful for what Mr Carne did for me, but what more can he do?"

Lord Eagleton kissed his wife's hand and pulled out her chair. "He merely wishes to reassure himself that everything is as it should be."

Emma nodded her thanks to Timothy who pulled out her chair, her smile a little strained. "Very well."

"I have faith in Mr Carne's discretion," Lord Eagleton added, as if sensing her need for reassurance. "A man who values his own privacy is unlikely to violate another's."

Emma digested this. No doubt Mr Carne had thought her behaviour of the previous day very odd. First, she had fled his presence, and then she had refused to be sedated. He had not, however, asked for any explanation. Her stomach settled and she reached for a bread roll. She was sure he had wondered about her, as she had mused about why such a young, attractive man had become a recluse, but Lord Eagleton was right; he was as unlikely to pry into her circumstances as she would be to pry into his, at least openly.

She smiled ruefully. "Thank you for your reassurance, Lord Eagleton, and your understanding. I do not mean to be an awkward guest."

"You are not," Nell interjected. "And please call my husband Alexander. We are not formal here."

Emma sent the marquess a questioning glance, but his eyes rested on Nell, the soft glow in their depths belying his next words.

"My wife has no respect for my dignity, Emma, but she is such a termagant that I dare not gainsay her."

Nell laughed, her hand smoothing her mauve muslin gown over her rounded stomach. "You may resume your dignity when I no longer resemble a huge plum pudding."

"I have a particular fondness for plum pudding," Alexander murmured.

"Oh!" Nell gasped. "You beast! You should have told me that I resemble no such thing!"

He looked bewildered. "But, my dear, I meant only to reassure you."

"What a bouncer! You meant to enrage me!"

He suddenly grinned. "No, merely to tease you a little. The impulse was irresistible! You rise so easily to the fly, and you look enchanting when your feathers are ruffled."

Nell sent Emma a look of mock indignation. "You see what I have to endure, Emma?"

She saw very well and felt a twinge of envy. She also felt a little relieved. This marquess bore little resemblance to the man she had briefly seen at

Ashwick Hall. Marriage to Nell had softened him it seemed and made him more approachable.

"I do indeed," she said smiling. "But you must know that you are quite radiant, Nell, and do not resemble any sort of pudding in the least."

"Thank you," Nell said. "I knew I might rely on you for support."

"Of course," Emma agreed. "It is why I came."

"It is not the only reason I invited you, however. It is so peaceful here, and you may walk for miles without meeting anyone of any significance. I knew you would enjoy it. It is such a shame that you should have injured your wrist."

"It is certainly unfortunate," Emma said. "But I would rather it was my wrist than my ankle. I can still enjoy walking, at least, and bear you company."

Nell looked a little wistful. "I wish I could walk with you, but I am afraid that I cannot go very far without tiring."

Emma saw anxiety come into the marquess's eyes.

"I am not surprised," she said calmly. "There are two of you, after all, and I would not ask it of you. Once Mr Carne has satisfied himself that I am perfectly well, I shall walk before breakfast as is my habit, but I will not wander too far."

"If you wish to explore, Nell," Alexander said. "I will take you for a drive."

Sudden tears sprang to Nell's eyes. "I know." She hastily wiped at a drop that had fallen on her cheek. "Ignore me. It is just that I am so happy, so fortunate…"

The marquess looked nonplussed. "Then why are you crying?"

Nell gave a watery chuckle. "I have no idea. It is quite nonsensical, but I assure you I am perfectly well."

Manton came into the room and informed them that Mr Carne had called to see Miss Wynn.

"Thank you, Manton," Alexander said, swiftly rising to his feet. "I will greet our visitor whilst the ladies finish their breakfast."

As he left the room, Nell smiled wryly. "He will no doubt ask him about my odd behaviour. I try not to worry him, but as happened just now, I do sometimes suffer from spontaneous bursts of feeling that I cannot control."

"I am sure it is perfectly natural," Emma said.

"Angelica has assured us both that it is. Let us hope that Mr Carne will also reassure Alexander."

Emma sipped her tea. "Lady Westcliffe informed me that there are reasons why his anxiety is perhaps to be expected."

"Did she tell you what they were?" Nell said, surprised.

"Yes. She thought carefully before telling me of the death of his first wife and mother but concluded that it would be helpful for me to know so that I might understand Lord Eag… Alexander's anxiety."

Nell sighed. "It is understandable, but also quite wearing. To him as much as to me, I am sure. It is my hope that now you are here, he will not feel he must watch me quite so closely. It will do him good to go sailing with Mr Carne."

Mr Carne's laughing visage as he came up from the river came into Emma's mind, and again she felt a fluttering in her stomach. "It will also do him good, I am sure."

"That is precisely what I thought," Nell said. "I pretended to be irked when Alexander went with Mr Carne yesterday, but I was only teasing him."

A reminiscent smile touched Emma's lips. "I like the way you tease each other. My father used to tease me, and I, in turn, teased my br—"

She broke off abruptly.

"I understand," Nell said quietly. "And I would not wish you to speak of your circumstances if you would rather not, but I do not think Lady Westcliffe would have allowed you to come to me if she had not believed that both I and Alexander were to be trusted."

The temptation was great, but Mr Carne was waiting for her, and she thought Nell had enough to contend with. As she was so easily moved to tears in her current interesting condition, Emma's history was likely to overset her completely. She would be a poor friend to reduce her to such a state.

"Thank you. Perhaps another time. I really should not keep Mr Carne waiting."

"I will come with you and play propriety," Nell said, rising to her feet. "Although I am sure you have nothing to fear from Mr Carne."

"No," Emma said thoughtfully. "Indeed, if I am not much mistaken, it is rather Mr Carne who feels he needs protection. It was not until I was falling asleep last night that I recalled how adamantly he insisted that he treat me in the drawing room and that you should not leave my side."

"You are right," Nell said slowly. "Whatever

happened to Mr Carne, I think there must be a woman in the case."

"A woman patient, I presume," Emma murmured. "Mr Carne must have been accused of something, perhaps injuring her in some way. I wonder if that is why he became a recluse?"

"He must have been accused of something quite heinous for it to have such a dramatic effect on him." Nell smiled ruefully. "But perhaps we are making far too much out of nothing at all. Judging by the way he dealt with your injury, Emma, he is a very competent doctor. I cannot imagine him capable of intentionally injuring a patient."

"No, not intentionally," Emma said. "Or even at all." Her lips thinned and her voice hardened. "An accusation need not be true for it to be believed, it need only have the appearance of truth and an audience willing to believe it." She felt her friend's intent gaze upon her and forced a smile to her lips. "But you are right. We should not speculate on such flimsy evidence."

She should not speculate at all. She knew it, but for some reason, Mr Carne intrigued her. Perhaps it was because dwelling on his troubles prevented her dwelling on her own.

As they crossed the hall, she began to feel anxious. Yesterday, Mr Carne had seen something she had taken pains to keep hidden, and he would see it again today. Nell might also have observed it but had probably attributed it to her accident. A doctor was unlikely to make that error.

When they entered the drawing room, both

gentlemen rose to their feet. Mr Carne offered them a bow and a slight smile.

"Good morning, ladies."

"Good morning, Mr Carne," Nell said brightly. "I hope you have assured my husband that I have not run mad."

His smile widened. "The thought never crossed my mind. Uneven spirits and an occasional excess of emotion are only to be expected in a lady in your condition."

Emma glanced at Alexander and saw his colour was a little heightened as if he were embarrassed. Nell went to him, laughing softly.

"Did you think I was ignorant of your purpose? I must have lost my wits indeed if I had not divined your intention."

He drew Nell across the room and they began a hushed conversation. Emma felt Mr Carne's eyes on her and met them. His smile had faded, and his gaze was intent.

"You are a little pale, Miss Wynn. Please, sit down."

She went to the chair he indicated. "Am I? I feel perfectly well, I assure you."

He knelt in front of her and gazed into her eyes, no, not into them but at them. She found she could not be quite so clinical but could gauge nothing from his expression, her glance reflecting off his as if a film of ice covered their blue depths. She thought it just as well. If he allowed it, she thought it entirely possible that one might be able to drown in those eyes.

"Does your head still ache, Miss Wynn?"

"No," she murmured.

"Very good."

He stood and walked around her so that he might undo the knot of her sling. She shivered as his fingers brushed against her neck.

"There is no need to be afraid," he said gently. "I will take care not to hurt you."

A denial rose to her lips, but she closed them firmly. She was a little afraid and better he think that than that she was attracted to him. The thought was ludicrous, she was merely unused to such close physical contact. He knelt in front of her again, removed the sling, and began to unwind the bandages that bound her wrist and lower hand. His movements were assured, swift, and impersonal. When he had laid her wrist bare, she averted her gaze.

"Can you move your fingers?"

She wiggled them slightly.

"Good. I see only the swelling and bruising to be expected."

She let out a low sigh but then stiffened and gasped, her head turning sharply towards him as she felt his fingertip lightly trace the faint pink mark that circled her wrist. Her instinct was to pull it from his grasp, but she dared not lest she injure it further.

"I am sorry," he murmured.

His head was bent, but he raised his eyes for a brief moment. Long enough, however, for her to register the regret and compassion in them. She sat immobile, feeling exposed, vulnerable, and confused as he bound up her wrist, his manner once more businesslike and impersonal.

Was he apologising for touching her old injury or for

what she had suffered? Had he divined that the mark on her wrist had been caused by a shackle? What must he think? She drew in a long, silent breath. It did not matter. More important was the fact that his eyes had held no hint of suspicion or accusation. He had not automatically assumed that she was to blame. Whatever had happened to Mr Carne had not robbed him of his humanity.

"Thank you," she said brusquely when he had replaced her sling. "I enjoy walking. I assume there is no reason why I should not resume the habit?"

He looked down at her, a slight frown between his eyes. "If you fall again, you might injure yourself further."

She rose. "I have never fallen before. It will not happen again. I was tired after my journey and was careless."

"In your haste to avoid me."

She was surprised at his frankness but decided to repay it in kind. She raised her chin a little. "Yes. You clearly did not wish for the introduction."

His mouth tightened. "In effect, ma'am, I was responsible for your accident."

She could not miss the bitter edge to his softly spoken words and regretted her impulsive honesty. "Not at all," she said calmly. "The fault was entirely my own. There is no reason you should have wished to meet me, after all. I was merely embarrassed to have caused any awkwardness. If I had known that Nell was entertaining, I would not have come into the garden. Far from blaming you, sir, I have reason to be grateful to you, and I am, I assure you."

His jaw relaxed. "I will accept that I am partially

to blame, thus removing the need for you to feel any sense of obligation or gratitude."

Emma blinked at this volte-face.

"Is everything as it should be?"

Emma had not heard Nell approach. She turned her head. "Mr Carne has assured me that it is."

"Then let us away, Carne," Alexander said. "We may even make it into Plymouth Sound this time."

Mr Carne bowed and left the room in the marquess's wake. Emma's eyes followed him and remained on the closed door for several moments.

Nell laid a hand on her arm. "Is something wrong?"

Emma smiled ruefully. "Forgive me, I was wool-gathering, or rather reflecting on the enigmatic Mr Carne."

"And what have you concluded?" Nell asked.

Emma laughed softly. "Very little, other than he unsettles me."

Nell's eyebrows rose and a teasing light came into her eyes.

"Could it be that you are developing a fondness for our neighbour, Emma? He has rather arresting cobalt eyes, does he not?"

"I would not do anything so foolish," she said dryly. "Besides, it is impossible to develop a fondness for a person on so short and awkward an acquaintance. Or for one who is so prickly and changeable."

# CHAPTER 8

The weather turned, howling wind and driving rain persuading Oliver to remain indoors closeted with his steward, Mr Grant, for several days. By the time he emerged into a sodden landscape, he knew he owed the man a great deal, and he even felt a grudging respect for his uncle.

When he had, several months ago, received an account of his uncle's investments from his man of business in London, he had discovered that most of them were profitable and had realised that there might have been more to his uncle than met the eye. He had not wanted to consider the possibility; he had not wished to consider him at all. But whether or not he had any hand in choosing those investments, Oliver was now forced to acknowledge that Mr Cedric Carne had chosen those who served him carefully. The fact that Oliver's land was in such good heart was due to Mr Grant's good management and financial acuity.

His income did not merely depend on rents from the several farms he leased to sensible, hardworking tenants, or the more traditional crops grown on his own large farm. He apparently produced a healthy crop of lavender each year and had a lucrative contract with a well-known company that produced lavender water and perfume. Although he had not yet stumbled across them on his walks, he learnt that he also possessed many skeps that housed honeybees and that Crawford Honey and beeswax were much in demand. That had made his eyebrows almost disappear into his hairline. Crawford had been his mother's name. He had been unable to decide if his uncle's intention was an ironic reminder of the stinging tongue she possessed – although Oliver had only heard her use it when in the presence of her husband, and on occasion when berating Richmond, his eldest brother – or a sign that he had been genuinely fond of her as bees were of honey. Either way, it left a sour taste in his mouth.

His time with his steward had, however, sparked an enthusiasm for a world he never thought to inhabit; it had also overwhelmed him a little. He had so much to learn. That was no bad thing, he realised. He did not intend to sit idly by and let his steward do all the work. He wished to understand everything from crop rotation to animal management to beekeeping. He would start by riding out in the direction of the apple orchards that held the skeps.

He rode down the avenue, weak sunshine vying with scudding clouds above him, before turning onto the track that Mr Grant had informed him would take him to the apple orchards. He dropped to an easy trot, trying to view his surroundings with new eyes.

As he made his way between fields, past cottages,

and through woodland, he realised he was wending his way towards Eagleton's land. This no longer irritated him as it had a week since.

He sighed, acknowledging that so much had changed in that short time. He had changed so much in that time. Eagleton had been the catalyst that had wrought it. He had seen what Oliver had been unable to acknowledge. Rather than confront the anger and bitterness that had so long consumed him, he had wallowed in it. He had felt shame for something that had not been his fault.

He had worked hard and earned the reputation of being an excellent if somewhat unorthodox surgeon. Unlike some of his fellows, he had been fascinated by the arts acquired over centuries by both the Vaidyas and the Hakims, who practised what the English referred to disparagingly as country medicine. It had not always been so. Although they had not benefited from the knowledge of anatomy the European doctors possessed, it had been recognised that their methods had often been effective and that they had an intimate knowledge of the illnesses suffered by the indigenous population, as well as the medicinal value of the plants of their country.

Gradually, however, the inevitable feeling of supe-riority had overcome those governing the medical practitioners in India, and Oliver had begun to be frowned upon for his continuing observance of them. In one particularly unpleasant encounter with his superiors, he had even been accused of going native. It had been nonsense, of course, but when Sir Laurence Granger had made the precariousness of his position clear, he had been forced to reconsider his position. He had had no desire to lose the reputation he had worked so hard to acquire.

"You are young, impressionable, and idealistic," he had said. "You are also an able surgeon, but that will not save your career if you are seen to take the advice of the country doctors over that of your colleagues. If you take on a patient of mine, Mrs Thruxton, and treat her in the traditional manner, I may be able to dispel the unfavourable murmurings about you."

His insistence that he did not take the advice of the traditional practitioners over that of his colleagues but merely considered all the possibilities when treating a patient, had fallen on deaf ears, and the interview had ended with him agreeing to take on Mrs Thruxton. The result had proved disastrous anyway. Or at least, he had thought it had.

In truth, his pride as well as his reputation had suffered a severe blow, and the thought of stepping into his uncle's shoes had been anathema to him. Now, however, he was forced to admit that he was fortunate and that his stubborn adherence to old prejudices had coloured his perception.

He turned his head, his eyes sweeping over the vista surrounding him. All this was his as was the responsibility that came with it. It did not matter who had owned the land before or who would own it after him; people came and went but the land endured. What mattered was that it remained healthy, providing jobs and produce for the people as well as the markets farther afield.

The road now skirted a high wall, and although it was barely half past eight, beyond it he could hear voices and laughter. As he approached an opening, a cart laden with apples emerged and turned in the opposite direction. He rode into the orchard, coming to a halt just inside the wall. Trees stretched in neat lines, some so squat that children could gather the apples on the lowest branches, whilst others scampered between the trees collecting those that had fallen to the ground. Older children and adults could be seen in the higher branches filling burlap sacks with the fruit before lowering them to the ground. They worked in cheerful unison, their movements swift and assured as if they had done this many times before.

A man emerged from the trees, his wrinkled, weathered visage at variance with his upright posture and easy stride. He wore a wide-brimmed black hat which he raised as he came up to Oliver.

"Good morning, sir."

Oliver searched his mind for the name of the man who oversaw the apple harvest.

"Good morning, Mr Lanson."

The man smiled. "Fancy you a'knowing my name. It's more than I looked for. I was born and bred on this estate, and I swear you're the first Carne ever to do so."

Oliver was not surprised. His uncle's interests had lain otherwise, and he had inherited the estate from a cousin, who by all accounts, had been a curmudgeonly old man. He smiled wryly, even more determined to take a hand in his affairs.

"Then I am grateful that you work so steadfastly on my behalf." He waved his arm towards the hive of activity before him. "As do those under your supervision."

The man chortled. "Oh, that's not down to me but

my son, Richard. I take care of the bees, as did my father before me, and as will my younger son Thomas after I am gone. I've come today to make sure they're not disturbed by any of the little varmints swarming over the orchard."

Oliver dismounted. "I see. And where are the bees kept?"

"On the other side of the orchard. If you've a mind to come, I'm happy to show you."

Leaving his mount to graze, Oliver walked beside the man, nodding and smiling as curious eyes turned upon him. The orchard was longer than it was wide, and as they passed between the last row of trees, he came to a stop as he beheld the south-facing wall. Stones had been removed at regular intervals to form niches with overhanging lintels, and inside each one was a coiled straw basket with a woven lid atop it. The skeps.

"I presume they are situated like this to keep the worst of the weather off them?"

"That's it," Mr Lanson said. "We'll wrap the baskets in bracken presently to keep the bees warm for the winter." He shook his head. "Time was when they would be killed so that the honey could be got at. Now we've a lid on the skep, and wooden frames for them to build the honeycomb on, there's no need."

"I'm glad to hear it," Oliver said. "It seems rather unfair to take the results of their industry and then kill them for their efforts if it is unnecessary."

"Aye," Mr Lanson said, nodding his agreement. "'Twas a mortal shame. Mind you, there's plenty who don't hold with what they call new-fangled ideas and stick with the old ways."

"Oh?" Oliver said. "How new is this type of skep?"

"Thomas Wildman first came up with the idea almost fifty years ago according to Mr Grant, although we only adopted it ten years ago."

A satirical smile edged Oliver's lips. "Then the design is hardly new."

Mr Lanson chortled. "Things sometimes take a while to catch on. If you're interested, I believe there's a book in your library on the subject. I'm not one for reading, but Mr Grant showed me the diagrams and I understood well enough."

They had been walking along the wall as they spoke and had come to a wide opening that led into a second orchard. The trees had already been denuded of their fruit and beyond them he could see the wall held more skeps and a door partially concealed by ivy.

"Now, if you'll excuse me, I'll go and keep an eye on the children. The bees have turned quiet this past week, and they won't be happy if one of the little varmints decides to take a peek inside the skep."

Oliver's lips twitched. "Neither would the child be happy for long, I suspect."

Mr Lanson laughed. "That's true enough."

As he watched him go with his unhurried stride, Oliver saw his neglected mount coming towards him. He went to meet it, patted the horse's neck, took the reins, and led him across the second orchard. There was something slightly mysterious and appealing about a hidden door. It was stiff, and he had to exert some strength to open it. He disturbed a few bees who had been foraging amongst the small clusters of yellowish-green flowers that nestled in the ivy. He remained still as they buzzed about him for a moment, and then led his horse through the door, pushing it closed behind him.

A path led into a stretch of woodland. He mounted his horse and rode into it, surprising a squirrel who abandoned its task of burying an acorn at the base of a tree and darted up it. The amber carpet beneath him softened the sound of the horse's hooves, but not enough for him to escape detection by other woodland creatures. He heard a rustle and caught a glimpse of doe brown eyes before a deer disappeared into a bush, followed swiftly by the white bobbing tail of a rabbit. Other sounds of scurrying came from the undergrowth and then all was still, only intermittent birdsong and the babble of a brook disturbing the silence.

The sun slanted at an oblique angle through luminescent leaves of gold, orange, and yellow that shifted in the breeze like dancing flames. A slow grin curled Oliver's lips. The door had not disappointed but had led to a place of enchantment. When a pure, melodic voice rose above the whispering murmur of the stream, he laughed softly. It seemed only fitting that a water sprite should inhabit the woods. He could no more ignore it than the sailors in the myths had been able to withstand the lure of a siren's call.

He followed the line of the stream and when he came to a place where the land sloped gently down to it, he rode to the water's edge, and let his horse drink. He could now hear the rather melancholy words clearly and realised he knew the song. *The Child in the Wood* was a well-known ballad in Yorkshire, describing an uncle's greed. He abandons the young niece left in his care in the hollowed bole of a tree so that he might claim her wealth. His plan is foiled when she is saved, however, and the uncle confesses his crime.

He crossed the stream and saw a figure walking slowly away from him. It was not a water sprite but a wood nymph. Her cloak was moss green, and her hair with its tints of brown, gold, and red, in perfect harmony with the autumnal setting.

As the song came to an end, he dismounted. He was half afraid to call out in case she disappeared. His horse was not afflicted by so ridiculous a whim and whinnied softly. The figure stopped and then slowly turned towards him. She was not a mythical creature but flesh and blood, and yet there was something otherworldly about Miss Wynn today. Her large, dark brown eyes seemed to look through him rather than at him, and her pale skin had a luminescent quality.

"Miss Wynn?" he said, approaching her.

She blinked as if coming out of a trance. "Good morning, Mr Carne. If I have inadvertently strayed onto your land, I apologise."

"You have not," he said. "The stream marks the boundary. It is I who have trespassed. I wished to see the lady who possessed so beautiful a voice."

Good God! Where had that come from? It might be true, but he sounded like a dashed flirt. The hint of colour rising in her cheeks suggested she was as embarrassed as he.

"How disappointed you must be that it was only I."

He was not, and he wondered why she might think it.

"Not at all. I am pleased to see you looking so well,

and it was a privilege to hear you sing. Why did you choose so melancholy a song?"

"It is certainly a sad story," she said. "But at least it ends well."

He heard the note of wistfulness in her voice. "Yes. Justice is served in the end."

"It is only fitting that it should be."

He had the oddest notion that she was not referring to the song. They turned onto a wider path that led away from the stream.

"How do you like Cornwall?" he asked.

"I like it very well," she said. "Perhaps it is the season or my own fancy, but there is a magical quality to this landscape."

He smiled wryly. "I agree with you. I keep half expecting to see a sprite or goblin."

She looked at him curiously. "Although I understand precisely what you mean, Mr Carne, I am surprised that a man of science should be so affected."

"Are you suggesting, Miss Wynn, that men of science have little sensibility or imagination?"

He had spoken lightly, and yet he felt her withdrawal as her eyes fell from his.

"I should not generalise, of course."

They walked in silence for some moments, its awkwardness growing with each step. How difficult it was to converse with someone about whom one knew nothing. Miss Wynn was an enigma. She somehow possessed both a strength and fragility that fascinated him. He searched for a safe topic that was not completely asinine.

"Do you know anything of bees, Miss Wynn?"

She glanced up, and he saw amusement in her eyes.

"Nell mentioned that you did not enjoy small talk, but bees, Mr Carne?"

The teasing note in her voice drew a rueful smile from him.

"Now you understand why I avoid small talk. I am no hand at it. But my choice of subject is not as random as it must appear. I have come from my apple orchards which are situated beyond the trees on the other side of the stream. The walls house many bee skeps, and as I intend to learn about everything my estate and its people depend on..." He broke off. "Forgive me, I am rambling."

"There is nothing to forgive," she said, a smile he thought rather sweet curling her lips. "It is an admirable purpose. My father used to say that a man should understand every aspect of his business, and when he sold his and set up as a gentleman, he transferred that interest to the estate he acquired."

So, she was the daughter of a wealthy tradesman. He would never have guessed it.

"He sounds like a sensible fellow."

Emma sighed. "In most things, he was, but he should never have moved out of his natural milieu. He did it for me and my... well, never mind."

"He wished you to marry into the gentry," Oliver said gently. "It is an understandable aspiration."

"It was a foolish one. You underestimate his ambition, however. My father believed that if something was worth doing, it ought to be done well. He hoped for nothing less than a member of the aristocracy."

He heard disapproval in her voice. "A sentiment you did not share, it seems."

"The general reason members of the aristocracy marry the daughters of those who have been in trade is because they need money and think the acquisition of a title a fair exchange. It is a business arrangement and a hypocritical one, for whilst they are prepared to accept the wealth acquired through trade, they despise those who generated it."

"That may be true in certain cases," Oliver said, "but you should not underestimate yourself, Miss Wynn. You have more to offer than a dowry."

She smiled wanly. "That is what my father said, and it is true I have all the accomplishments required in a young lady of quality, but although I have met, on occasion, a gentleman who seemed to like me for myself, I never met one who could accept my father quite so readily. Knowing that he could never carry them off, he did not attempt to put on the airs and graces of the aristocracy. He said he was content to leave that to his children."

Oliver could imagine how his father would react to such a man. To his face he would have been coolly polite, behind his back he would have derided him.

"You were right to honour your father. I take it he did not try and force you—"

"No," she said quickly. "He would never have forced me to do anything. That is not why I—" She broke off abruptly, her eyes widening. "Mr Carne, I have said too much. I do not know what came over me."

She began to hurry away but two long strides brought him to her.

"Miss Wynn, the last time you fled my presence you suffered an injury. Please, calm yourself. You have told me a little of your past but have mentioned no names or places, and as far as I am aware, you have told me nothing material to your current circumstances. Even if you had, I would not betray you."

Her eyes searched his and seemingly satisfied with what she saw, she nodded.

"As for why you told me, we might put it down to the enchantment of this place, or perhaps to the loneliness that creeps up on you when you cannot share secrets that become ever more burdensome."

Her lips parted on a faint gasp. "You understand," she said slowly. "As Nell, would, I suspect, and yet I have said nothing to her."

His lips twisted. "It is sometimes easier to unburden yourself to a stranger. If it is any comfort to you, I came from the world your father wished you to inhabit, but I purposefully distanced myself from it. You have no need to persuade me that the people who move in that world can be hypocritical, cold, and calculating."

"Those qualities are not reserved for the aristocracy alone," she said softly.

"No," he agreed dryly. "I also have discovered that much."

They had come to the edge of the wood. A little way in front of them their way was blocked by a high hedge that sheltered the gardens of Pengelly Manor. The path led down a slight incline to a door set in the hedge. The shadow of a smile touched his lips.

"Is that the way you came, Miss Wynn?"

"Yes," she said. "It is partially concealed by ivy on

the other side, and I could not resist discovering what lay beyond it."

"There is another such door in my orchard, and I was overcome by the same impulse. If I were a fanciful man, I could almost imagine that we were destined to meet today."

She laughed softly. "By the whim of a mischievous sprite or goblin? Perhaps, although I am more inclined to put it down to coincidence. The likelihood of two neighbours meeting is hardly a startling event."

He grinned ruefully. "Spoken like a sensible woman, Miss Wynn. You relieve my mind to such an extent I will give you leave to explore my lands as much as you wish."

"Thank you," she said, "for your permission and your company." A glimmer of humour sparked in her eyes. "And for not asking me how my wrist is today; it becomes tedious."

She turned, went to the door, and disappeared through it without a backward glance. Oliver stared at it for several moments realising that she was right. He had referred to but not enquired about her injured wrist. Today, he had not seen her as a patient, but merely as Miss Wynn. A woman he felt strangely drawn to. But it would not do. He had kept a woman's secrets before and it had not ended well. He grimaced. Miss Wynn was nothing like that other woman, he felt sure, but he was in no position to help her other than as a doctor, and in truth, he should not even be doing that.

He mounted his horse and made his way back into the wood, determined not to invite any more confidences from the intriguing Miss Wynn.

# CHAPTER 9

Emma closed the door behind her and leant against it. Her heart was beating uncomfortably fast, and she closed her eyes, drawing in long, slow breaths. What had just happened? What had she been thinking? She gave a ragged laugh. She had not been thinking at all. Mr Carne had appeared out of nowhere and taken her by surprise. He had looked at her so strangely and then offered her a compliment she had not known what to do with. He was the last person she had expected to offer her outrageous flattery, and judging by the shocked look that had followed it, he had been as surprised as her.

She gave a low chuckle. He had attempted to make a recover, and just when things had been most awkward between them, had brought up the subject of bees. Her sense of the ridiculous had been tickled. He was quite adorable when flustered. She groaned. That train of thought would never do. It had seemed so natural to exchange confidences, but it had not been wise. If only he had not been so understanding, so sympathetic, so gentle.

*Are you suggesting, Miss Wynn, that men of science have little sensibility or imagination?*

She could certainly not level such an accusation at him, but there had been others she had known that fitted the description. She began to walk slowly towards the house. She would do well to give Mr Carne a wide berth. She felt as if she could trust him, but that did not mean she should.

He had called her sensible, but if he knew what she had been accused of, he might reconsider his opinion. Even if he did not, now was not the time to fall under the spell of a tall, handsome gentleman of whom she knew nothing apart from the fact that he also carried secrets that were burdensome, secrets that had caused him to spurn the world he had grown up in and others that had caused him to return to it.

She quickened her pace and resolved not to dwell on what those secrets might be. It was none of her business, and she had enough difficulties of her own to resolve.

Over the next week, she established a routine as unexciting as it was comfortable. After her early morning walk, she would breakfast with Nell and Alexander before retiring with her friend to the drawing room, where they would read, sew, and chat idly until Angelica joined them. Invariably, Lady Francesca's nurse, Mrs Jane Farley, would then bring her charge down to her stepmother, and they would take a turn about the garden. After a light luncheon, Alexander would often take Nell for a drive, leaving Emma to keep Angelica company until she took her afternoon nap. This was no hardship, for Angelica needed little encouragement to talk about her life in Italy, and as her long wished for meeting with her grandson and subsequent return to England was inextricably linked with Nell, it was from her that she learnt her friend's story.

"I know she won't mind me sharing it with you," she had said. "It would be painful for her to do so, but there is nothing that can hurt her now, and it might help you to know that however bleak things may seem, they often turn out better than expected."

Although Emma was saddened to hear of her friend's treatment by a husband who had married her only for her fortune and then squandered it, of her flight from Verona aided by Lady Westcliffe, and of the malicious rumours that she might have had a hand in her husband's death, in a way it did help her. Like Emma, Nell had kept her secrets, and when the time had come to share them, she had cleared her name and also found happiness. Her story had been almost as fantastic as Emma's, and yet she had been believed. This gave Emma hope that when the time came, she too might be believed.

If she was not entirely successful in putting Mr Carne from her thoughts, it was only when she retired for the evening and was between waking and sleeping that her discipline deserted her, and a pair of ocean-dark blue eyes set in a hollow-cheeked, serious face, swam into her mind. She could not help but wonder then what he had borne. She and Nell had been fortunate to be aided by Lady Westcliffe, but who would help Mr Carne recover from whatever disappointment he had suffered? Would he confide in Lord Eagleton?

She hoped so, for she suspected that if he put his mind to it, that gentleman could move mountains. He had already coaxed Mr Carne from a year of self-imposed isolation, after all. Perhaps that was enough.

The budding friendship between the marquess and his neighbour was impeded, however, by Mr Carne's sudden and apparently all-consuming interest in his estate, and then midway through the following week, whilst still at the breakfast table, Lord Eagleton received two letters, the first of which, judging from his lowering brow, seemed to exasperate him.

"Alexander?" Nell said. "Is something amiss?"

He sighed, dropped the letter, and ran his hand through his hair. "Why is it, when I pay my steward a generous salary, he need bother me with my tenants' petty nonsense?"

Nell's eyebrows rose quizzically. "I am assuming the tenants concerned are Mr Bantham and Mr Kelly?"

"Who else?" he said scathingly. "If it's not one thing it's another."

"What is it this time?" she asked with a wry smile.

"Sheep are disappearing from their farms, or so they say, and they are accusing each other of the theft. My steward's attempts to calm things down have failed and he thinks things are likely to escalate."

"Oh dear," Nell said. "This time it sounds serious. Perhaps you should go to the priory for a few days."

"They can go to the devil for all I care," he growled.

"You don't mean that," Nell said gently.

"Are you trying to get rid of me, Nell?" he said querulously. "You won't do it."

His mood was no better after he had read the second missive.

"More bad news?" Emma enquired, observing the deep furrow between his eyes.

"Yes," he said curtly. "Mr Winters, my man of business, is at the priory. He should have retired a few months since, and I have told him more than once that he should send his son if he deems it necessary to pay me a visit. He had intended to come on to Pengelly but has fallen ill."

"Then you must go to him," Nell said insistently.

"I will take very good care of Nell," Emma said gently.

"I am perfectly well," Nell added. "And as the baby is not due for some weeks yet, there is nothing for you to worry about."

He frowned at her for a moment and then nodded. "Very well. I will pay Carne a visit and then be on my way."

"And why will you pay Mr Carne a visit?" Nell asked, a slight edge to her voice.

"Because," Alexander replied, rising to his feet, "Mr Winters illness complicates things. Whilst I am sure I can knock some sense into my block-headed tenants within a day, I cannot in all good conscience abandon Mr Winters if his condition is serious. He is more than a mere man of business; he is one of the few people I consider a friend, and I owe him a great deal. That being so, I may be away for a little longer than I would wish, and I shall ask Carne to keep an eye on you."

Nell bristled. "You speak as if we are not sensible women entirely capable of looking after ourselves."

Alexander's lips twisted, and he dropped a kiss on her head. "Humour me."

She glanced up and touched his cheek, her expression softening. "Very well. If it will prevent you from worrying."

"It will help," he said.

Mr Carne paid his first visit two days later, and not quite in the traditional manner. They took their daily turn about the garden, and whilst Angelica and Nell rested for a moment in the temple, which had the twin merits of being a favourite haunt of Lady Francesca and offering shelter from the chill breeze, Emma carried on to the shingle beach by the river.

Ripples raced across the surface of the water before whispering against the pebbles at her feet. Two elegant swans glided by, seemingly unperturbed by either wind or current, and on the opposite bank, a heron stood on a fallen branch. It was so still that she could almost believe it to be a sculpture, but then its small head tilted on its elongated neck revealing a long, yellow beak, its spindly legs bent, and it sprang into the air. The bird looked ungainly, but then its legs straightened behind it, its neck curved, and it glided silently over the water with strong, deliberate beats of its majestic wings.

As it disappeared, another note was added to the melody of the softly lapping water. Turning her head, Emma saw it was the gurgling of oars cutting through water, their strong, deliberate beats as powerful as the heron's wings. Mr Carne had his back to her, and she could not help observing how the cloth of his coat strained against his broad shoulders each time he pulled, or how his mahogany hair curled against its collar. He turned towards the beach, glancing over his shoulder as he did so, and as their eyes met, an involuntary smile trembled on Emma's lips, the sight of him sending a small thrill of anticipation through her veins.

She watched silently as he timed his last pull of the oars with the surge of the rippling waves so that the boat's stern was carried onto the shingle. Twisting himself on the seat, he rose and sprang swiftly over it, pulling the boat ashore before the water could wet his boots. The sturdy wooden craft looked heavy, and she moved forward to offer what aid she could.

"That is unnecessary, Miss Wynn," he said as she put out her hand.

She let it drop and smiled wryly as he pulled it another foot up the beach. "So I see. I doubt I would have been much use anyway."

He straightened, smiling ruefully. "At the risk of being tedious, may I enquire how your wrist fares?"

They began to walk towards the garden, the pebbles crunching beneath their feet.

"It remains sore, but the pain has lessened to a dull ache. That is not so troublesome as being forced to rely on my maid for the simplest of tasks. I cannot even don my cloak without aid." She sighed. "I must not complain, however. If it had been my right wrist that had taken the brunt of my fall, I would have been in a worse case."

He sent her a slanting, enigmatic glance. "I have the impression, Miss Wynn, that you are not one to complain."

"It is a pointless exercise. It makes your situation

no better whilst making that of your companions worse."

His expression turned wry. "How I wish some of my patients had shared your wisdom."

She accepted the arm he offered to aid her up the gently sloping bank to the lawn. "Some allowance must surely be made for those who are truly sick?"

"I was not referring to those patients," he said dryly. "If you are far from home and unutterably bored or perhaps lonely, a fictitious illness might gain you sympathy, ensure compassionate or inquisitive visitors, and give you something to talk about other than the heat." A sardonic note crept into his voice. "If, that is, your doctor is prepared to maintain the fiction."

"Oh dear," Emma said, amused. "I have the strangest feeling you were not of their ilk."

"No," he said, his jaw tightening. "Only once did I fall into that error."

She heard the bitterness in his voice, but her instincts warned her not to enquire further. Glancing ahead, she saw that Nell, Angelica, and Lady Francesca had come out of the temple, and the awkward moment passed. Nell cried out as her step-daughter suddenly surged forwards, taking her unawares and causing the blue ribbons she held to slide through her fingers. Free of her leading strings, the child tottered towards Emma and Mr Carne. He went to meet her, swung her up into his arms, and threw her into the air, smiling as she laughed.

"You know that game," Emma said faintly, her surprise that he should know just what would please

Francesca most as nothing compared to the effect his unrestrained smile wrought on her fluttering pulse.

"We have met before," he said, returning her to the ground, taking the ribbons in a loose grip, and leading her back to Nell.

"Thank you, Mr Carne."

Nell's voice was a little breathless, and rather than take the leading strings, her hand went to her stomach. Emma glanced at her friend in some concern.

"I am sorry, Nell. I should have stayed with you and helped entertain Francesca; you are exhausted."

Angelica took the ribbons. "I was there, Emma, and you were not brought here to be nursemaid."

"No, but..." Her eyes widened as Nell sucked in a deep breath.

"Nell! Surely you are not... not..."

"No," she said. "It is just that my stomach sometimes tightens which causes me a little discomfort, and I think this babe is likely to be as lively as Francesca; he or she has just kicked me in the ribs, or at least that is what it feels like."

Emma glanced questioningly at Mr Carne.

"It is perfectly normal. If the babe had decided to make an early entrance, Lady Eagleton would be far more uncomfortable. I do suggest, however, that it might be best if Lady Eagleton returns to the house and rests."

"I quite agree," Nell said. "And I will rest after I have offered you some refreshment, Mr Carne."

He offered Nell his arm. "Very well."

They had taken no more than a few steps when Francesca strained against her leading strings, a tearing sound was heard as the ribbons parted company with her dress, and she raced forward pulling at the tails of Mr Carne's coat. Emma put out a hand to steady Angelica who had stumbled backwards as the girl had gained her freedom.

Mr Carne released Nell, turned around, and observing the ribbons dangling in Angelica's hand, said dryly, "It might be best if Lady Francesca's nurse accompanies her on these excursions. It is entirely possible that she might pull any of you off balance, and a fall would be unwise for ladies in your... well, it would be unfortunate."

Angelica chuckled. "What you mean, Mr Carne, is that an old woman, a heavily pregnant lady, and another with an injured wrist are incapable of looking after one small child."

An answering gleam of amusement brightened his eyes. "I took pains not to say any such thing, and it is not quite what I meant."

Nell sighed. "I see your point, however. Mrs Farley has said as much herself, but I do enjoy having her to myself in the mornings."

Oliver picked up the child, offered his arm again to Nell, and they began to meander towards the house.

"You need only wait until Eagleton is home."

Emma and Angelica followed in their wake, a pang of something she could not quite identify leaving Emma a little confused. Offering Nell his arm had been the right thing to do, the gentlemanly thing to do, and she respected him for it. It was certainly not jealousy she felt, it was more like longing. This realisation brought with it a certain measure of relief. It was not Mr Carne that had wrought it, but the image he had created. She had felt it before when in the presence of Nell, Alexander, and Francesca, although she had not allowed herself to acknowledge it for what it was; the desire to be part of a family that was happy and whole. She had been once, but that seemed a long time ago now.

"You can tell a lot about a gentleman who likes children even though he has none of his own."

"Yes," Emma said absently. "I suppose you can."

Angelica stopped walking. "Let us pause for a moment so that I may catch my breath."

Emma looked down, her eyes bright with concern. She was about to apologise for not noticing her fatigue when she realised that Angelica's eyes were regarding her acutely and she did not appear at all breathless.

"You are right, of course," the old woman said as if reading her mind. "I wished to speak with you. Although I have told you some of Nell's story, I have told you very little of my grandson's. I will not do so, but I can assure you that what he endured – and I am not merely speaking of the death of his mother and wife, but what he endured as a child – was unfathomable, despicable, and heartbreaking. He does not trust easily and if he has decided that Mr Carne is worthy of his friendship, you may be sure that he is worthy of yours."

"I am sure he is," Emma said, taken aback. "But I do not know why you feel the need to inform me of it."

Wise green eyes met her bemused gaze. "Because it needed to be said. I understand that you might be reluctant to share your pain with Nell at this time, but it is there, nonetheless. Nell and Alexander felt a connection because of their suffering, and it was instrumental in bringing about their happiness. If you feel such a connection with Mr Carne, you would be foolish to ignore it."

Emma did not know how to answer. There was something between them, the beginnings of a friendship, perhaps, but she could not simply ignore what had been drummed into her for the past year.

"I do not know why you should think so. Lady Westcliffe would—"

"Lady Westcliffe is a wonderful woman, but she is not here. I believe that people are sometimes brought together for a reason, Emma."

This was going too far for Emma's liking. "I mean no disrespect, Angelica, but my circumstances are very different from Nell's. Even if she did not know it, her husband was no longer a threat. If I am discovered before I am ready, I believe I will be in danger of losing my liberty."

Angelica regarded her for a long moment and then took her arm. "I am sorry, my dear. Forgive the sentimental ramblings of an old woman. You are right. I cannot and should not advise you when I know nothing of your circumstances."

Angelica had unwittingly echoed Emma's words to Lucy. Was it her imagination or had she heard a gentle note of reproof in them?

"I know you mean well, Angelica, but my circumstances are secondary at the moment. Nell must come first. I came to bear her company and support her as and when I can, to ease the worries in this house, not to add to them."

"And you have, my dear. You have. Alexander

would never have gone to Eagleton Priory if you had not been here, I am sure."

When they joined Nell and Mr Carne in the drawing room, Emma could not help but feel stiff and awkward. Nothing seemed to escape Angelica's acute gaze, and she did not wish to give her any further reason to suppose that she felt anything more than polite interest for their visitor. With this goal in mind, she chose a seat a little apart from the others, only occasionally adding her mite to the conversation. It seemed she had overplayed her hand, however, for Mr Carne was on the point of taking his leave when he glanced at her, a frown in his eyes.

"Are you sure your wrist is not paining you, Miss Wynn?"

"Perfectly sure," she said coolly.

"Then perhaps your sling is not quite comfortable. Allow me to adjust it for you."

Before she could deny it, he had crossed to her side, and his fingers began adjusting the knot at her shoulder. He bent down as if to observe it more closely, and she sucked in a breath, colour rushing into her cheeks as his warm breath tickled her ear.

"Have I offended you in some way, Miss Wynn?"

"No," she murmured, groaning inwardly as she met Angelica's interested gaze.

He drew back and began rearranging the angle of the sling, his eyes slipping to hers.

"Good. My words concerning Lady Francesca were not meant to wound you, but you admitted earlier that you can do little for yourself, after all. You can hardly be expected to care for a lively child."

"You did not wound me, Mr Carne, I assure you. I

am merely tired. I am a restless sleeper and in the normal course of events, I change my position several times during the night." A wry smile touched her lips. "Since my accident, I have had to sleep on my back, and it has proved difficult to learn a new habit, but at least my nightgown does not constantly become entangled in my legs."

Something shifted in his eyes, and she suddenly felt breathless, but it was gone before she could define it. He reared back and rose swiftly.

"There, that should be a little more comfortable," he said curtly.

He turned, bowed, and took a rather abrupt leave through the doors that led into the garden.

"Well," Nell said, laughter in her eyes, "you were quite right, Emma. Mr Carne is prickly and changeable. Whatever did you say to him?"

"Nothing," she said, bemused. "I meant only to reassure him that he had not offended me."

Nell and Angelica exchanged an amused glance.

"Well, never mind," Angelica said. "You can try again when he next visits."

# CHAPTER 10

Oliver crossed the lawn in long, loping strides. He had worked tirelessly for over a week, and when he had not been with his steward, he had set his hand to anything, the more physical the work, the better. He had helped collect the last of the apples, aided one of his tenants in mending a fence, and even helped Thomas Lanson strip brambles so the stems could be used to stitch the coils of straw used to make the skeps. This had enabled him to banish Miss Emma Wynn from his thoughts, at least during the day. The image of her turning towards him in the wood robed in her moss green cloak, her dark, otherworldly eyes huge in her delicately boned face had haunted his dreams, however.

Damn Eagleton! How dare he impose on him! The marquess had strode into Oliver's breakfast parlour, his caped coat flaring about his booted legs, held out his hand, and shook Oliver's, his catlike green eyes intense with urgency and purpose.

"Forgive me for disturbing you, Carne. I am called

away on important business and do not know how long it will take. No more than a week, I hope. I do not do this lightly, but you are the only man I know or trust enough to ask to drop in now and then to check all is well at Pengelly Manor." He had taken his shoulder in a firm grip. "I know I can depend on you."

Oliver had found himself agreeing, and with a brief nod, the marquess was gone.

Having reached the beach, Oliver pushed the boat into the river, jumped aboard, and slotted the oars into the rowlocks. Pulling savagely on the levers, he propelled the craft rapidly forward.

He had all but convinced himself that his dreams had been just that, dreams. That when he saw Miss Wynn again, it would be as a patient, and whatever spell had been cast in the woods would be broken. And then Eagleton had made his request, if such it could be called. Even so, he had told himself that when he met her in a drawing room setting, and in the presence of the far more beautiful Lady Eagleton, he would see her for what she was; a passably pretty woman, rather too thin for his liking, and possessed of a nose a little too long for classical tastes.

But he had seen her alone, standing wraith like on the beach, strands of hair blowing against rosy cheeks, and that sweet, sweet smile trembling upon her lips. Her soft, dark eyes had shone with welcome, and his determination to be distantly polite had crumbled.

He pulled harder, knowing that his rough, uneven strokes were making his task more difficult than it need be. If only talking to Miss Wynn was difficult, but in truth, he had never found it so easy to converse with a female. Before he had known it, he had been talking of his patients, and it was only when he had been reminded of his last one, that he had realised the danger he was in. He wanted no part of that history to reach Cornwall. He had put it behind him and started anew.

He rested the oars on his legs for a moment, drawing in long, slow breaths. He had transferred his attention to the safer waters of Lady Francesca and Lady Eagleton but had been constantly aware of Miss Wynn. He should have been pleased when she distanced herself from the party, and yet he had found her withdrawal a constant distraction. He had wondered if he had offended her in some way, and the thought that that might be no bad thing had no more crossed his mind than he found himself making an excuse to draw close to her. He groaned. That had been a mistake. As he bent to whisper in her ear, the fragrance of rose water and something else he could not identify had made him close his eyes and inhale deeply. He had dropped to his knees, supposedly to adjust her sling, but in reality, to alleviate the faint light-headedness he had been experiencing. And then she had mentioned her sleeping habits, how her night-gown became entangled in her legs, and he had fled before he embarrassed himself.

He once more picked up the oars and rowed as if his life depended on it. He was in no position to pursue a relationship with Miss Wynn, and if he understood matters at all, neither was she. His reputation was shot to pieces, and, if Eagleton were to be believed, some unknown danger lurked at the edges of Miss Wynn's life.

*You could make an effort to clear your name, and it is not beyond the realms of possibility that you might be able to help Miss Wynn.*

He grimaced, banishing the thought that had been hovering at the edges of his mind for some days. He had denied the accusations levelled at him, but he had not been believed and had found himself on a ship back to England before he had time to try and prove his innocence, his reputation in tatters, and the requested promise that he give up medicine, given. With hindsight, he had realised that there was no way to clear his name, and the chances of Mrs Thruxton exonerating him of the crime she had accused him of, less than none. So, as matters stood, he would be more of a hindrance than a help to Miss Wynn.

The thought persisted, however, and that evening he spent a restless night fruitlessly attempting to devise a way to prove his innocence. He awoke tired and dispirited but determined not to fall back into the lethargy that had so recently consumed him, consulted with Mr Grant, and then rode towards the village of Trehan to introduce himself to Mr Harris, the tenant who leased one of his outlying farms.

He found him in the yard of a long, rambling farmhouse, loading sacks onto a cart. He was of medium height, with a barrel of a chest, and tightly curling brown hair. He dusted his hands as he saw Oliver and nodded affably.

"Good day to you, Mr Carne. I heard as you were doin' the rounds." His nut-brown eyes twinkled as his visitor dismounted. "And as how you're not above a bit o'work."

Oliver grinned at the man's audacity, dismounted,

and held out his hand. "Good day, Mr Harris. Are you hoping I'll help you finish loading those…" He glanced at the unattractive, mud-flecked, brown objects, protruding from the sacks.

Mr Harris gave a crack of laughter. "They be potatoes, Mr Carne. Surely you've eaten 'em 'afore?"

"I have, Mr Harris, but I have never before seen them when they have just come out of the ground." He removed his coat, hung it carelessly on the gatepost, removed his hat, and began to roll up his sleeves. "I believe, however, that I am about to become intimately acquainted with them."

"They be heavy," the farmer warned him.

Oliver strode over to a sack, hoisted it up, and deposited it in the cart. "I believe I am up to the task."

"I'd been told you were a good sort," Mr Harris said approvingly, "and I can see I wasn't misled. By rights, it's my son Jago as should be helping me. I sent him down to the barn to bring me some fresh hay for the 'osses, and he should have been back by now. It's not like my Jago to be tardy."

Oliver reached for another sack. "Don't let it trouble you, Mr Harris. I'll enjoy the exercise."

They had just finished when a young man, presumably Jago, judging by his tightly curling hair and stocky build, drove a cart loaded with hay into the yard.

"You took your time," Mr Harris said. "And if it weren't for Mr Carne helping me, you might well have found me dead on the floor from a heart attack."

As the farmer was not even out of breath from his exertions, Oliver took leave to doubt this, but it appeared Jago overlooked this small detail. He gulped and reddened.

"I'm sorry, Father, but I really couldn't help it."

Mr Harris folded his arms. "Now don't you give me any excuses, Jago, and say hello to Mr Carne. He'll take you for a regular looby."

The boy raised his cap, bowed his head, and mumbled a greeting, the redness spreading to his neck.

"I'm pleased to meet you, Jago." Oliver nodded at Mr Harris. "Now, if there's nothing else I can do for you, I must be on my way."

"You're not a'going without so much as a mug of ale to whet your whistle," Mr Harris protested. "I won't hear of it. Come in and meet Mrs Harris or you'll put her nose out of joint."

"Father," Jago hissed. "There's summat I've got to tell you."

"When you've laid down the hay in the stable, Jago, then you may come and join us, and not a moment 'afore."

"But Father—"

"Jago Harris. Since when do you answer back?"

Not wishing to add to the young man's embarrassment, Oliver went to the gate to retrieve his coat and hat, but ignoring them, he stepped onto the road, the unmistakable sound of thundering hooves claiming his attention. This way only led to Eagleton's property and his, and even as he told himself that perhaps Eagleton had resolved his business more quickly than anticipated, he knew that he could hardly have travelled the forty miles from Okehampton unless he had driven through the night.

As the curricle hove into view, he scanned its occupants. There was a marked similarity between them; both possessed a beak of a nose and narrow-set eyes he knew to be of a cool grey. His stomach sank, and his chest tightened. He swore softly.

"Unwelcome visitors?"

He had not realised Mr Harris and Jago had come to see for themselves who was travelling at so reckless a pace down the generally quiet lane. He thought the young man's posture rather strange. He stood with his legs a little apart, his fists clenched by his sides, and his chin thrust slightly forward. If it hadn't been so preposterous, Oliver could almost imagine he was spoiling for a fight.

"Stand down, Jago," he said quietly. "I may not be overjoyed to see my visitors, but they were expected."

"You know 'em?" he said, regarding him with some suspicion.

"I do," he said, frowning. What was wrong with the boy? He had thought his behaviour the result of embarrassment, but could he be mentally deficient in some way?

The curricle drew up in a flurry of dust. Oliver met his brother's satirical gaze before his eyes moved on to meet his father's fulminating one.

"Good God!" Lord Painswick said. "Can't you even assume a veneer of respectability? Put on your hat and coat."

His companion, Viscount Crosby, allowed his eyes to rest for a pained moment on Oliver's soiled shirt. His lips twisted into a sneer, and he said in a soft, contemptuous voice, "It seems neither birth nor the acquisition of property can make my brother a gentleman. If I'm not much mistaken, he has been hiring himself out as a common labourer."

Oliver reached for his coat. "Not quite, merely offering a helping hand to a neighbour."

The earl growled, but before he could unleash the no doubt biting comment hovering on his tongue, Mr Harris stepped forward to stand on one side of Oliver. Jago, taking his cue from his sire, moved to his other side.

"And I'm right grateful to him," Mr Harris said.

The farmer, clearly being beneath his notice, Lord Painswick ignored him, but his eyes widened as they settled on Jago. "By Gad! Here's the gapeseed who left his cart in the middle of the road, nearly getting us all killed, and then sent us down a set of lanes that lead nowhere. It'd serve him right if I took a whip to him."

"True," Viscount Crosby drawled, "but as he is clearly dim-witted, I doubt very much he could help it."

"Now, look here—"

Oliver silenced Mr Harris with a gentle nudge.

"Comfort yourself with the knowledge that you are now on the right road," Oliver said. "If you follow it for a couple of miles, you'll see a turning for Carne Castle on your left. As that road is both long, narrow, and winding, I suggest you slacken your pace somewhat. I'll meet you there presently."

"You'll do no such thing," Lord Painswick barked. "You'll show us the way."

"Certainly," Oliver said softly. "If you don't mind waiting whilst I finish my business here. It shouldn't take more than half an hour."

Lord Painswick's already heightened colour, deepened to the hue of a ripe plum. "I've wasted enough time this day you… you…"

"Save your breath, Father," his companion drawled. "However much my brother deserves your thunder, I think we have entertained the rustics long enough."

Viscount Crosby flicked his whip and the curricle swept off. Oliver let out a long, slow breath.

As they turned and walked into the yard, he said quietly, "I'm sorry you had to witness that, and for any insult offered you. If the offer of ale still stands, I admit I could do with a drop."

"They be your family?" Jago said, looking at him intently.

"Unfortunately," Oliver said, sighing.

"But you don't like 'em?"

"Not overmuch," he admitted. "And until today, I hadn't seen them for over ten years."

"Good," Jago said firmly.

Oliver smiled wryly. "I beg you won't repeat that, however."

"I will keep my mummer shut if you will."

"Jago," Mr Harris said. "If you don't mind your manners, *I'll* take a whip to you."

"I don't care if you do," he said truculently, "as long as the young lady is safe."

A look of comprehension crossed Mr Harris's face. "Well, if they were offering some slight to a maid, there's some excuse for you, I suppose." He glanced at Oliver. "He's always rescuing something or other; a bird with a broken wing, a fox that's been caught in a trap, or an abandoned kitten, but 'afore today, he's never rescued a female." He chuckled. "He normally becomes tongue-tied in the presence of a pretty girl." He looked enquiringly at his son. "I assume she was pretty?"

Jago flushed. "It's not my place to say."

Mr Harris grinned. "Lord love you, son, you don't have to. I can't imagine you turning into a regular Galahad otherwise. Who was she? Not Maggie Bligh I hope; that girl's trouble and I won't have you courting her."

"It weren't her," he said. "I was trying to tell you 'afore, but you wouldn't listen."

Jago went to the cart and knocked on the side. "You can come out now, miss."

Mr Harris and Oliver exchanged a surprised glance, but their eyes swiftly returned to the cart as the hay began to tremble and a hooded figure sat up, wisps of straw clinging to the fine wool of her moss-green cloak. Oliver's mouth dried, and he strode to the side of the cart.

"Miss Wynn! Whatever are you doing in there?"

She pushed back the hood, saying wanly, "Hiding from your father and brother, it would appear."

Oliver frowned. She was pale and clearly shaken. "They have faults enough, but as far as I am aware, preying on innocent ladies of genteel birth isn't quite in their line. Do not tell me they offered you some insult?"

"They didn't get the chance," Jago said. "I'd just turned the cart onto the road when that fancy curricle swept around the bend. I thought it was going to crash smack into it, but it managed to stop just in time."

"Ah," Oliver said. "My brother thinks himself something of a Corinthian and prides himself on his skill. I expect he had a few harsh words for you. Again, I apologise."

"I weren't paying no heed; I had to calm old Samuel."

Oliver looked bemused.

Mr Harris enlightened him. "That's the pony he's got hitched to the cart."

"That's it," Jago said. "He was spooked and when I went to his head, I saw something move in the ditch. As it didn't run off, I thought it might be an injured animal, but when I glanced down, I saw it was a person. I could hardly believe my eyes when this lady looked up at me, put her finger to her lips, and begged me not to give her away."

"And being the upstanding, young man you are, you didn't," Oliver said smiling.

Jago puffed out his chest a little. "I did not. I may not be the sharpest tack in the box, but I'd have had to be a moonling not to realise she was scared stiff of the fine gentlemen. I led the cart halfway onto the verge so there weren't no chance of them seeing her. That's when they asked me the way to Carne Castle. They didn't ask me very nicely, mind you, so I sent 'em the wrong way."

"Thus giving Miss Wynn the chance to make her escape."

Jago grinned. "That too."

Mr Harris scratched his head. "It was very clever of you, Jago, but why was it necessary to put her in your cart?"

"She'd hurt her ankle when she jumped in the ditch, and when I told her it wouldn't take them long to fathom they'd been sent the wrong way, she insisted on it."

Oliver pinned Emma with a stare. "And your wrist?"

"It is fine," she said, colouring. "And I only twisted my ankle a little."

Mr Harris shook his head. "What I want to know, Miss Wynn, is why you jumped in the ditch in the first place. But you've been in that dirty cart long enough. Lift her down, Jago, and we'll discuss it over a brew."

"I'll do it," Oliver said, leaning over the edge and lifting Emma into his arms. Jago scowled at him.

Oliver offered him a sympathetic smile. "We are old friends, and it would not be proper for a stranger to carry her."

Emma smiled at the young man. "You were marvellous," she said. "Thank you."

Mrs Harris was rolling pastry as they entered the kitchen. She glanced over her shoulder and let out an indignant squawk.

"Josiah Harris, it would serve you right if I took this rolling pin to you. You should have taken our guests into the parlour."

She dropped the threatened weapon and wiped her hands on her apron.

"Don't get in a pet," Mr Harris said, grinning. "As Mr Carne has been helping me load the tiddies onto the cart, I don't think he's one for ceremony."

"I'm not," Oliver said. "And I'm very pleased to meet you, Mrs Harris. Allow me to introduce you to Miss Wynn, who is currently a guest of Lady Eagleton."

The woman executed an awkward curtsy.

"There's no need for that," Oliver said. "But I'd be grateful if you'd show me where I can set Miss Wynn down. She has injured her ankle."

"Oh, the poor thing. Josiah, take them into the parlour, and I'll fetch some salve for the swelling and some bandages. Jago, fetch me a tub of cold water."

He set Emma gently down on a sofa and glanced at Mr Harris.

"I take it your wife knows what she's about?"

The farmer chuckled. "None better. Who do you think mends all the injured creatures Jago brings home? And it's not just animals, it's her as folk come to first to get their salves and potions, and she's delivered more babies than I can count."

Mrs Harris entered the room armed with the promised items, Jago following close behind her.

"Josiah, if Mr Carne isn't standing upon ceremony, you can take him into the kitchen and give him something to drink whilst I see to Miss Wynn. The young lady will want some privacy."

Oliver looked at Emma intently. "How bad is it?"

"It is only a slight sprain, I am sure."

He nodded and left the room.

# CHAPTER 11

E mma winced as Mrs Harris removed her boot and stocking, gently prodded her ankle, and then nodded.

"You were right, miss, it's none too bad. Sit forward, if you will, and put your foot in the tub."

Emma sighed as the cool water calmed the hot ache in her ankle. "Thank you. Would you mind helping me remove my cloak, Mrs Harris? I think some hay has become caught in the neckline of my dress and it is itching."

The woman undid the clasp and pushed the cloak off her shoulders.

"You've hurt your arm n'all," she said.

Emma smiled ruefully. "Yes, I fell and hurt my wrist."

Mrs Harris tutted. "You ought to be more careful, miss." She leant forwards and plucked the offending wisps from her neckline. "Now, how on earth did these get there?"

"Your son gave me a ride in his cart."

The woman lifted Emma's foot onto her lap and dried it with her apron. "So he would. He's a good boy."

"Yes," Emma agreed. "He is."

Mrs Harris applied the salve to her ankle, smoothing it with gentle fingers before binding it and rolling Emma's stocking back into place.

"There, if you keep your weight off it for a day or two, all will be well. I'll not put your boot back on, as it'll be too tight." She brought a footstool and placed Emma's foot upon it, arranging her dress so that most of her stockinged foot was covered. "Now, you just rest here awhile, and I'll bring you a glass of my parsnip wine."

Emma groaned and leant back against the cushions as she left the room. Her stomach was churning with anxiety, and the effort of politely interacting with these good people was exhausting. It had been a close call, and only Lady Westcliffe's constant instruction to not allow herself to be seen had saved her.

She glanced up as the door opened and gasped softly as Mr Carne came into the room. He looked at her frowningly, two strides bringing him to her side. He lifted her dress and glanced at Mrs Harris's work. Seemingly satisfied, he let the garment drop back over her foot. Emma had wondered why he hadn't taken charge himself, but a moment's reflection had given her the answer. He didn't want the knowledge that he had once been a doctor generally known. She understood. It could only lead to awkward questions. She braced herself, fully expecting to face some herself.

Mrs Harris returned at that moment, however, a glass of slightly cloudy wine in her hand.

"This'll perk you up, Miss Wynn."

She accepted it, and not wishing to offend the woman, took a cautious sip, not expecting to like it. She discovered that it had a sweet, delicate flavour, and took another.

"Thank you, Mrs Harris. You are very kind."

"If you have quite finished, Miss Wynn, I'll see you home."

Mrs Harris nodded approvingly. "If the young lady's so nervous of strange gentlemen, it's the only thing to do." She smiled kindly at Emma. "Mr Carne told us as how you had a bad experience once when a gentleman tried to accost you in broad daylight, and that's why you jumped in the ditch when you heard a vehicle coming." She shook her head. "I dare say you are of a nervous disposition, which circumstance caused you to overreact a tad, but I can't say as I blame you. There's some who call themselves gentlemen who have no right to do so."

"Very true," Oliver said, removing the glass from Emma's fingers and handing it to Mrs Harris. He bent, pulled her cloak over her shoulders, fastened the clasp, and lifted her into his arms.

Mrs Harris picked up Emma's discarded boot and gave it to her. "Now, remember, keep that foot up for a day or two."

The family came into the yard to see them off. When Oliver lifted her into the saddle, she turned to them, smiling ruefully, a blush infusing her cheeks.

"I am sorry to have been so much trouble and am very grateful for all your help. May I ask one more favour of you?"

"Anything," Jago said promptly.

Mr Harris was more cautious. "We'll help if we can."

"What is it, my dear?" his good wife said in a motherly fashion.

"It is only a small thing," Emma said. "It is just that you were right, Mrs Harris, when you said I may have overreacted a little…"

"I don't think you did," Jago said gruffly. "Those gents looked like ugly customers." His eyes darted to Oliver. "I meant no disrespect, Mr Carne."

"None taken," Oliver said. "But I'd rather you didn't repeat that to anyone else. They are my family, after all."

He nodded. "I knows how to keep my tongue between my teeth."

"Yes, well," Emma said. "That brings me to what I wished to say. Not many people know me, and I wouldn't wish them to get the wrong impression. So, if you wouldn't mind…"

"We won't say a word," Mrs Harris assured her. "Aside from the fact that you're as pretty behaved a young lady as ever I met, you're a friend of Mr Carne's, and we wouldn't wish to cause you any embarrassment." She bent a stern glance upon her son. "So, Jago Harris, no bragging about how you rescued a fine lady from a ditch."

Jago flushed beet red, more in annoyance than embarrassment. "I wouldn't."

"I know you won't," Emma said, smiling gently at him. "Goodbye and thank you, again."

A tense silence stretched between them as Mr Carne led her down the road. Emma wanted to thank him for manufacturing a story that explained her odd behaviour, but that might lead to awkward questions she didn't know how to answer. She did not wish to lie to him, but the arrival of his brother and father had complicated everything.

"Is this what you consider being careful, Miss Wynn?"

She winced. His words were carefully enunciated and biting.

"Nell assured me that I might walk for miles and not see anyone of consequence."

He laughed dryly. "If you had kept to the woods and fields, perhaps."

She flushed. She had already berated herself for her stupidity and did not need him to also do so.

"I did not know you were expecting visitors, sir," she said coolly. "And as you have until very recently shunned them, I can hardly be blamed for not foreseeing the possibility."

He frowned but did not immediately answer. They turned onto the steep lane that led to Pengelly Manor, but the relief engendered by the knowledge that they would soon arrive was short lived. He led the horse onto a track that led into a copse.

"Where are we going?"

"We need to talk," he said, his voice flat and controlled.

"Nell will be wondering where I have got to," she said breathlessly. "I do not wish her to worry."

"A few more minutes will make little difference."

His uncompromising tone dissuaded her from making further argument she sensed would be futile.

A bench was set in a break in the trees to take advantage of the view of the river cutting through the valley below. Emma's breath caught in her throat as he lifted her down and set her on it, his gentleness at variance with the hard set of his jaw.

"You are angry." Her words were a statement not a question. His frown seemed permanently etched into his brow.

"Yes, but not necessarily with you."

"With your father and brother?" she asked, not quite able to keep the quiver from her voice.

His frown deepened. "Why did you jump into that ditch?"

She drew a deep breath and answered carefully, feeling as if she were groping in the dark. Her fingers curled about the edge of her cloak. "I do not know what, if anything, Lord Eagleton has confided in you."

"Very little, other than your safety may depend on as few people as possible knowing of your presence here. It is why he wished for me to see to your care rather than Doctor Ramsey."

"It is true," she said. "It is why I jumped in the ditch. I heard several horses and realised it must be a carriage or curricle coming down the road. My reaction was automatic; the lady who has cared for me this past year is very cautious and has made me so."

His blue eyes bored into hers. "That is not the full truth, is it?"

Her mouth dried and she paled. Why was he being so difficult? "Perhaps not, but it is better that you do not know the whole truth."

He sighed and pushed a hand through his mahogany locks. "I had already come to that conclusion myself, but circumstances have changed. If I am not much mistaken, although you did not know who the occupants of the curricle were when you jumped in the ditch, I am certain your ignorance was soon enlightened."

Emma's stomach knotted.

"I believe that you are acquainted with my father and brother. That being so, I wish to know how and what the nature of that relationship is."

Emma had heard enough to understand his relationship with his father and brother was not a close or even a friendly one. She doubted he would encourage them to make a prolonged stay, and that being so, she only had to remain within the grounds of Pengelly Manor to avoid them. As she would be unable to walk any distance for a few days, that would be no hardship.

This comforting thought was swiftly superseded by another less so. As it was common for members of the *ton* to gather in London when parliament was sitting, it was highly likely Lord Painswick and Viscount Crosby were acquainted with Lord Eagleton. Therefore, it was entirely possible that when they learnt of his presence in the neighbourhood, they might call on him. That must not happen.

Uncertain of how much to confide in Mr Carne, she stalled for time.

"What makes you think I am acquainted with your family?"

His lips twisted. "You are prevaricating, Miss Wynn, but I will humour you. That day in the wood you gave me a clue, although I did not realise it."

"I was not myself when you met me by the beck," she said quickly. "But I am certain I never said anything that might give you reason to suppose—"

"But you did. *The Child in the Wood* is a song well-known in Yorkshire."

"As it most likely is in a dozen places."

"Variants of it, perhaps, but you have just used the term beck, a term also commonly used in Yorkshire. My father's seat also happens to be situated in Yorkshire, not far from Northallerton, although I feel sure you already know that." He raised his brows. "Are you going to deny it?"

She shook her head.

"Good, because I have a strong dislike of lies. I am also far from stupid. Whilst your desire to hide yourself when you heard a vehicle approaching is perhaps understandable, if you had realised that its occupants were unknown to you, and therefore you unknown to them, I hardly think you would have chosen to stow yourself amongst a pile of mouldering hay, unless, that is, you did know them and were afraid of them. Now, I will ask you for the second time this day, has my father or brother ever offered you any insult?"

She licked her lips, her hand flying to her cheek in a nervous gesture that had not afflicted her since she was a child.

He muttered something under his breath and squatted before her, his eyes gentling.

"Forgive me, Miss Wynn. I do not wish to distress you. Seeing my father after all this time was enough to unsettle me and set my teeth on edge, but for others to witness his arrogant rudeness, appalled me, as does the thought that you might ever have been subjected to it. I should not, however, take it out on you. I had no intention of tangling myself in your affairs, but if my relatives' presence here has put you in some sort of danger, I would know of it. I wish only to help you."

Emma looked into eyes that were no longer guarded or angry, but earnest, and found herself sinking into their cool, blue depths. Tears sprang to her eyes, and her throat ached with the effort of not allowing them to fall.

"They must not see me," she croaked. "Or all might be lost."

The fear and dismay she had thus far held in check suddenly overwhelmed her, and she began to tremble, her escaping tears blinding her. There was a blur of movement, the bench gave a little as he sat next to her, and then she felt the soft, tentative dabs of a handkerchief on her cheeks.

"What, how and why?" he said softly.

She took the handkerchief and mopped her face. She somehow knew that she had nothing to fear from him, and the churning anxiety retreated, a quiet determination replacing it. She had been brave for so long; she must not weaken now.

"It is a long story, and there is no time to explain it all. I will admit, however, that I am acquainted with Lord Painswick and Viscount Crosby. My home was… is on the edge of the moors not far from Painswick Hall. Your father did mine the honour of paying him a visit."

She gave a watery chuckle at his stunned expression.

"Perhaps I should explain that my father was very wealthy, and I have a large dowry."

Comprehension, shock, and something else she

could not quite identify chased through his expressive eyes.

"Good God!" he said. "Have things come to such a pass that he would stoop to an arranged marriage with the daughter of a cit for his beloved eldest son?" He closed his eyes and sighed. "That was clumsy, and I hope you know, Miss Wynn, that I was expressing my father's views, not my own."

"You have no need to tell me that," she said softly.

"And your father agreed to it?"

She shook her head. "I told you he would not force me to do anything against my will. He merely agreed to our meeting at an assembly."

Grim amusement flickered in Oliver's eyes. "I'd warrant it was the first provincial assembly my brother had attended since he was a callow youth practising his dance steps."

"I do not know. He danced very well, however, and possessed a great deal of practised charm."

He looked intently at her. "You weren't taken in by it?"

"Not at all. I sensed the coolness behind it, and my opinion of the viscount did not change on our subsequent meetings. To give him his due, your brother did not pretend to be in love with me, merely promised to do his best to make me happy." She smiled wryly. "I did not believe him capable of making me happy."

"You were right," Oliver said with feeling. "He loves himself so much, he has precious little to spare for anyone else." A crack of sardonic amusement escaped him. "Good Lord! You dealt his pride a severe blow when you refused him."

"I was left in no doubt of it," she said quietly. "His

charming façade dropped, and he said some rather cutting things I have no intention of repeating."

"There is no need for you to do so," Oliver said, sobering instantly. "I can imagine your inferior birth, the undeserving honour he had bestowed upon you, and your father's failings were mentioned."

He clearly knew his brother well, and Emma found it difficult to comprehend how they had turned out so differently. "All of the above."

Her eyes dropped, her fingers working against the crumpled handkerchief in her hand. "My father became ill not long afterwards and he wrote to his brother, who had for many years been living in India, and fearing that he would not recover, pleaded with him to come home." She took a deep breath and glanced sideways at him. "Perhaps you knew him. His name is Mr Alfred Emmit."

Oliver's eyes grew distant as he searched his memory. "No, I don't think I ever met anyone of that name, although I cannot be certain." His blue orbs regained their clarity, and a faint grin twitched his lips. "One thing I am fairly certain of, however, is that your name can't possibly be Emma."

Her brow furrowed for a moment, and then a faint smile touched her lips as she found the source of his amusement. "I see what you mean. I would have been teased mercilessly if my father had named me Emma Emmit."

"Undoubtedly. If you felt it necessary to change your name, I can understand your choice, however. It is very close to your surname, and therefore you were unlikely to betray yourself by not responding when someone addressed you thus. I wonder if you applied the same logic when you chose Wynn?"

"Oh dear," she said, sighing. "How unimaginative I am. You have found me out, Mr Carne."

"But you do not intend to share it with me. It is proper that you should not on so short an acquaintance, and so I will not press you. But I interrupt. You were speaking of your uncle."

Her voice dulled. "There is no time to talk of him now. I really must get back or Nell will send a search party to look for me. I will say only this; my uncle thinks I am dead. He must continue to think so until I choose to confront him. If he learns otherwise and should discover my whereabouts, I, and perhaps my brother will be in danger. That is why I was so afraid when I realised who was in the curricle." She dropped the handkerchief, turned towards him, and laid her hand on his sleeve. "I believe you my friend, Mr Carne, and would ask that you prevent your relations from visiting Lord Eagleton when he returns, or even better, find a way to be rid of them before that day arrives."

He smiled grimly. "It will be my pleasure, Miss Wynn."

# CHAPTER 12

Oliver would have liked to know more about Miss Emmit's uncle. The more she revealed, the more questions he had. But she was right. Now was not the time. His tardiness in following Lord Painswick to Carne Castle would have enraged him more than he had intended. Besides, he had no desire to upset her further that day.

He carried her to his horse, and after lifting her into the saddle, swung up behind her, his arm encircling her waist.

"For the sake of speed, you understand," he murmured in her ear.

"Of course," she said, a slight tremor in her voice.

He liked the feel of her pressed so closely to him but was glad the journey took only a few minutes. Each time he was in her presence, the more drawn to her he became, and the desire to protect her grew ever stronger. But surely that was Eagleton's job. His rank and connections must weigh more heavily than his, and as far as he knew, any scandal attached to that gentleman's name was in the far distant past.

As he carried her to the door, he said, "Miss Emm… Wynn. When Lord Eagleton returns, it might be better if you let him into your confidence. He is in a far better position to help you than I."

"You are helping me," she said softly. "And I am very grateful. Thank you. As for the future, I have others to support me, and Lord Eagleton has worries enough. I will not add to them."

He smiled wryly. "And neither will you risk upsetting Lady Eagleton at this delicate time."

"No," she said, returning his smile. "I am glad you understand. But you may be sure that after Nell is delivered safely of her child, I will confide in them if it becomes necessary."

He raised an enquiring eyebrow. "And how will you explain your current condition?"

A glimmer of humour sparked in her eyes. "I merely turned my foot in a rabbit hole. A story not as inventive as your own, but then we have already established that I lack imagination."

He laughed softly. "I do not believe it, Miss Emm… Wynn."

She smiled ruefully. "Although I have given you my true name, it would be better if you still thought and referred to me as Miss Wynn."

The door opened and Timothy stepped out. Oliver deposited Emma in his arms.

"Thank you, Timothy. See Miss Wynn comfortably bestowed, will you?"

He turned, mounted his horse, and directed it to the gate he knew would lead into the woods. He came to a halt midway across the stream, for a moment imagining he could hear Miss Wynn's melancholy song echoing amongst the trees. He shook his head wryly, telling himself he was a fool. He gained the opposite bank and stopped once more.

"You are a fool twice over," he murmured, as the words of the song came back to him. She had not chosen that particular ballad at random, he realised. The song opened with a dying father sending for his brother! His mind jumped to two later verses, and he recited them under his breath.

*The father being dead and gone,*
*The unkle then contrived*
*To make the child's estate his own,*
*And of its life deprive it.*
*A wicked thought came in his head,*
*And thus concludes to serve it;*
*He takes it up out of the bed*
*And then resolves to starve it.*


*With wicked mind, into a wood*
*He then the infant carries;*
*And tho' he would not shed her blood,*
*Yet there alive he buries*
*Within a hollow oaken tree;*
*He stop'd the mouth from crying,*
*That none might hear and come to see*
*How the poor child was dying.*


The circumstances were not quite the same; she was not an infant, and the estate must belong to her brother, but he would lay odds her uncle did not wish to part with her dowry. His mouth thinned as he remembered those faint marks on her wrist. He had not, of course, put her in a tree, but if his surmise was correct, he had certainly put her somewhere where no one would hear her cries, or if they did, were unlikely to take notice of them. A red mist descended, and he kicked his heels, suddenly eager to meet his relatives. He hoped to God he was wrong, but if he was not, they would be sure to know it.

He had known anger before, a cold, bitter, hard anger that had consumed him. This was different; it scorched him, breathed reckless retribution in his ears, and instilled a desire in him to shake the truth out of his brother. It was fortunate, therefore, that it took him some twenty minutes to reach his stables. By then, reason had asserted itself once more, and he had recalled that discretion was all important if Miss Wynn's interests were to be served.

He found his way to the house dogged by the undersized terrier he had found struggling in the river the first time he had taken the rowing boat out. He had been disgusted to see two young boys on the opposite bank, eagerly watching in anticipation of his demise. He had hauled the pitiful creature into the boat. Observing the bones jutting through his matted coat, the thought that it might have been kinder to let him drown had flashed through his mind. The puppy was malnourished and near death. Yet it had observed him with hopeful, brown eyes, and it was not in his nature to let anything die if he could prevent it. He had brought it home and given it to Jem, who had charge of the stables. The head groom had shaken his head dourly.

"It's a lost cause, Mr Carne."

"Be that as it may, Jem, you will do everything in your power to aid him."

He had, and against all expectations, the dog had thrived. He could not be called an attractive creature. He had a flying ear, a black patch about one eye, and a shaggy white topcoat, through which peeked other black spots. He also had an imperfect understanding of whom he had to thank for his existence. Whilst Oliver may have plucked him from the water, it was Jem who had nursed him back to health, and yet it was Oliver's presence that sent him into a state of ecstatic fervour. Jem had to shut the terrier in a stable to prevent him from chasing after Oliver's horse each time he went riding.

As Oliver reached the side door closest to the stables, the dog jumped up, his paws scrabbling against his breeches.

"Down, Beau!"

The dog obeyed, observing him with worshipful, hopeful eyes, both his tail and body wagging furiously. As always, he whined when instead of being invited to accompany him into the house, he found the door shut firmly upon him.

Hurley was hovering on the other side.

"At last!" he said.

Oliver's interaction with the dog had cooled his anger further, and Hurley's rare lack of composure allowed a shaft of amusement to break through his ire.

"I hope you have afforded my father and brother all the courtesy they deserve."

Hurley snorted. "You may be sure of that! But nothing is good enough for them, and if they've asked me one question, they've asked me a dozen."

"And how did you answer them?"

Hurley's eyes twinkled. "I was as ignorant as you could wish."

Oliver grasped him by the shoulder. "Good man. Where have you put them? Not in the library, I hope."

His uncle had inherited a house that according to his valet, had not had a penny spent upon it for many a year. Mr Cedric Carne had, over the next several years, renovated it in a flamboyant and sumptuous style singularly his own. Oliver had no taste for spindly gilt-legged chairs, oriental silk wallpaper, or elaborate drapery, and had made the library his domain. It was the one room that had escaped such opulence, excluding the towers, his uncle having died before he could turn his attention to them.

"No, sir. I put them in the drawing room."

"Very good. And which chambers did you allot them?"

The butler chuckled. "I chose the west tower, seeing as it is as far from your room as I could manage."

The west tower was not derelict, but its rooms were spartan when compared with the silk-tented beds and crocodile-legged chaise longues in the guest chambers of the main house.

"That was either brave or foolish," he said dryly. "Did they not protest?"

"Not when I showed 'em the rats in the first-floor chambers of the house."

Oliver's brows rose in surprise. "It is the first I have heard of rats in the house."

Hurley winked. "That's because there wasn't any, until I put that mongrel cur you saved to good use. He caught two in one of the barns, and I brought them up to the house."

Oliver choked back a laugh. "You are an unconscionable rogue, Hurley."

The manservant grinned. "I'm merely looking after your interests, sir."

Oliver handed him his hat and twitched his cravat. "Well, I best put off the moment no longer." He strolled away, but then paused, looking over his shoulder, a light of unholy amusement in his eyes. "Oh, and Hurley, I think Beau deserves a reward, don't you?"

"He's already had a bone from the kitchen."

"Paltry," Oliver said. "He has a strong desire to enter the house. Give him the run of it."

The butler's eyes widened. It seemed that whilst he was prepared to use the dog for his master's ends, the prospect of having him in his domain did not delight him.

"But, sir, you can't let that flea-ridden terror into the house. He'll chew the furniture, get under everyone's feet, and make a nuisance of himself. What's more, he's a nipper."

Oliver grinned wickedly. "I'm counting on it."

A slow smile spread across the butler's face. "I've not seen you so on point for many a day, and so although it goes against the grain, sir, I'll do it."

"Yes, but first give Beau a bath. I do not believe him to be flea-ridden, but he rolled in something no doubt unsavoury in the yard. When he's clean, you may let him loose."

In the normal course of events, Oliver would have changed before greeting visitors, but as his purpose was to rid himself of his father and brother as soon as possible, he decided against it. The moment he set foot in his drawing room, his irate parent rose to his feet, bending a fulminating eye on him.

"I see your timekeeping is as tardy as your dress."

Oliver offered Lord Painswick a brief bow. "My business took a little longer than expected, sir, and I did not wish to leave you waiting any longer than necessary, but I will certainly go and change my raiment if you prefer."

Lord Painswick's brow lowered. "I do not prefer. You have kept me waiting long enough."

At his brother's entrance, Viscount Crosby had not risen from the window seat he occupied, but merely turned his head and set one booted foot idly swinging. His gaze lingered on Oliver a moment before sweeping over the sumptuously decorated room. A disdainful smile curled his lips.

"Whilst I understand my father's reluctance to wait any longer, I must say, brother, that you look rather out of place in such luxurious surroundings. I find it quite shocking, not to mention wasteful, that what I imagine to be a small fortune has been squandered to create such a vulgar result." He gave a soft laugh. "But that was clumsy. It has just occurred to me that you might approve it, as those who have come from trade and think to improve themselves by aping their betters, so often seem to. I do hope, however, that my uncle did not squander quite all his fortune, for of what use is a house, if one cannot maintain it?"

Lord Painswick did not seem overly enamoured by these barbed shafts.

"I would remind you, Richmond, that however estranged were my brother and I, and however much I deplore his tasteless extravagance, he was raised a gentleman, as was Oliver."

"Just so," Richmond drawled. "I can't think how I came to forget it."

"Too many late nights addling your brain, as well as lightening your pockets, I imagine," Oliver said dryly.

The viscount's eyes grew sharp. "Oho! How is this? Does my little brother still preach propriety when he is accused of raping the wife of an official of the East India Company and getting her with child? A little hypocritical, don't you think?"

The gloves had come off in earnest, and Oliver did not fight shy.

"And denigrating a class of honest, hardworking people when you would marry one to restore your own squandered fortunes is not hypocritical?"

He had the satisfaction of seeing a dull flush rise in his brother's cheeks and decided to test his theory.

"And one who was quite mad by all reports. I hear she was put in an asylum, a fate I am not convinced she deserved as she had the good sense to turn you down."

"And just how do you know all this?" Lord Crosby said through gritted teeth.

Oliver noted that he denied none of it. "I still have a few friends who occasionally write to me."

He turned and went to a sideboard as a thought struck him. He poured himself a glass of wine as he sifted it. It was true that two boyhood friends had written to him in India, and a few missives had been sent to Carne Castle. At first, he had been too ill to read them, and then too downcast. He had shoved them in a drawer and eventually, they had stopped coming. It was, he now realised, entirely possible that they had written of the events surrounding Miss Emmit.

"If you do not find a way to put a stop to the rumours surrounding you, I doubt you will have any friends left," Lord Painswick said irritably.

Oliver's hand shook a little, and he took a sip of wine before turning around.

"You don't believe the rumours?"

"Of course, I don't! I had an earful of your damned morality when last I saw you before you went to Edinburgh, and I thought it a great impertinence."

An old bitterness welled up, and Oliver was powerless to quench it.

"You must admit, sir, that to discover that both my parents had taken lovers and that my uncle was not my uncle but my father, may have given me some cause."

"It should have given you reason to be grateful!" Lord Painswick snapped. "I brought you up as my own, didn't I?"

"If you mean you allowed me to reside under your roof, then yes. But we both know that you could hardly bear the sight of me."

"Can you blame me?" Lord Painswick barked. "By the time you turned eight, you were the spit of my brother. Your mother and I married for convenience, not for love, and it was always agreed that after she had presented me with two sons, she might follow her own desires if she was discreet. That she should have relations with my brother was an atrocious betrayal, however, on both their parts! It is not you who was the injured party, Oliver, but I!"

On some level, Oliver knew this to be true, although he found it incomprehensible that any husband should allow his wife to share another man's bed. He might have felt more sympathy for his father if not for the inequalities of his upbringing. He had had to watch as Richmond and Francis had gone fishing, shooting, or riding with their father whilst he was left behind. He had never had a kind word for him, and on the rare occasions he had been in his father's presence, he had felt his scorn. Richmond had been quick to emulate him and had tried to make his life a misery.

Even so, Oliver had studied hard at school, determined to prove himself and perhaps gain his father's approval at last. But when he had finished his studies at Eton and come home with glowing reports, he had learnt the truth, and realised that all his efforts had been utterly pointless.

"But it is fruitless going over old ground," Lord Painswick said gruffly. "The world thinks you my son and will continue to do so, therefore any scandal attached to you, touches all of us. Something must be done about it."

Oliver sat down, his expression bleak. "Who brought the tale to England? The company was very eager to have it hushed up, and as Mrs Thruxton's accusation could not be proved, agreed that if I returned to England and never practised medicine again, no more would be said of the incident."

"I have no idea," the old gentleman said irritably. "All I know is that I was enjoying a glass of wine and reading the newspaper at my club when I was approached by a stranger who begged a quiet word with me. His name was Sir Laurence Granger. He said that you were a fine surgeon and it had distressed him greatly when you were accused of forcing yourself on a lady, a Mrs Thruxton, I believe, and getting her with child. He said he wished he had spoken up for you as he did not believe it in the least."

"Did he?" Oliver said bitterly. "It is a pity he did not speak up for me at the time."

"Yes, he said that also, but apparently there were circumstances that made that rather awkward, particularly the fact that the lady's husband had been away from home on company business for some three months and had returned to find his wife clasped in your arms. Sir Laurence came to warn me that he had heard whispers circulating in Town and thought, quite rightly, that I would wish to know. It was very decent of him, as he was far from well. The poor man was coughing up blood into his handkerchief."

That did not sound promising for Sir Laurence, but Oliver put his medical interest aside and concentrated on the point in hand. "But you have not heard those rumours?"

"I have not," Lord Painswick said. "Although I doubt anyone would say anything to my face. I believe they have not yet reached the higher echelons of society, but it can only be a matter of time. This Mrs

Thruxton has apparently returned to England, her husband having acquired a position in the London offices of the company. Perhaps it is she who started the rumours. As London is now all but deserted of any company that matters, we have a small window of opportunity to quash them. It must be done before parliament resumes in the new year."

Oliver's eyes slipped to his brother. "Who is the lucky lady you hope to make your own?"

Viscount Crosby's eyes narrowed. "Sarcasm is a blunt tool, brother, unless wielded with subtlety."

"You must forgive me," Oliver said softly, "I haven't had near as much practise as you."

"Will you two stop bickering like overgrown schoolboys!" Lord Painswick snapped. "Both of your futures depend on us finding a solution to this problem."

Oliver closed his eyes. He was right. They were both right. He was responding to his brother in kind, but that was not his way. He had prided himself on not being anything like his family, and he must not let those standards slip. As well as old grievances affecting his reactions, they were coloured by the knowledge that Richmond had paid court to and then insulted Miss Emmit. The thought that if he cleared his name, he might be able to help her, again crept into his mind. Another swiftly followed it. *Eagleton will be too busy fussing over his wife and child to be of any material use to Miss Emmit, and although there are others who have offered her their help, you know you will not feel comfortable sitting idly by.*

He sighed. "You must forgive me; I am finding this family reunion a little overwhelming. I concede that my brother and I wrangling will solve nothing, however." He regarded Richmond with a cool gaze. "I have no reason to love you, brother, but I will give quarter if you will."

Viscount Crosby held his gaze for a searching moment, but then his eyes dropped, and Oliver was surprised to see a hint of colour tinge his cheeks.

"Very well. Let us call a truce."

"This is better," Lord Painswick said. "Whatever your parentage, Oliver, we are still bound by blood." He cleared his throat. "I will admit you have some reason to resent us, but I had hoped that with age you would also acquire wisdom and learn that nothing is as simple as it often appears to an idealistic youth. We must pull together and make a plan of some sort. Someone is the father of that child. Have you no idea who might be the culprit?"

Oliver leant back in his chair and ran a hand through his hair. "I have asked myself that time and time again, but I have found no answer."

"Well, think again! The crisis we faced has passed; your brother has curbed his more excessive habits, and we have sold Farnham. Those circumstances combined with some fortunate investments, have made us once more solvent. But just when our fortunes are restored, this latest trouble falls upon us."

A spasm of pain chased swiftly across Oliver's face. Farnham had been meant for Francis. He had been the only member of his family he had maintained a correspondence with. He had been a lively hey-go-mad creature and had acted as a buffer between him and Richmond.

"Do not take everything he says to heart," he had said. "Richmond sharpens his tongue on me too, you know, and does not mean the half of it. Now come, halfling, put down those books and I will take you for a turn in my curricle."

Those rides had been exhilarating and terrifying at the same time. Francis had been as reckless as he had been carefree, and it had led to his demise in a curricle race. By the time the news had reached Oliver, his brother had been six months in the ground and he about to board a ship back to England. It had only added to his despondency. It was no wonder he had succumbed to illness on the journey.

"Ah, I see that grieves you as it does us all," Lord Painswick said on a heavy sigh. "Farnham was always meant for my second son, but Francis can have no need of it now, and neither can you."

What was not said but lay heavy in the air between them, was that it was to Farnham, a tidy estate just over the border in Scotland that his mother had been banished shortly after Oliver had been sent to Eton, and there she had died not long afterwards from a bout of influenza, alone and estranged from her family. Oliver wondered if some small sliver of guilt over that circumstance as well as his financial straits had prompted his supposed father to sell it.

Lord Painswick cleared his throat. "You must see, Oliver, that Richmond's marriage has become a matter of some importance."

Oliver's lips twisted. "I do. Indeed, I see that it is a matter of some urgency. An heir becomes imperative. The thought that there is the remotest possibility that I might step into your shoes must keep you awake at night."

"I think we are wasting our time," Richmond said.

Oliver glanced at him, hearing the note of weary resignation in his voice. Did he also detect a hint of anxiety? Could it be that it was not a marriage of convenience he contemplated, but a love match?

"Not necessarily," he said. "Who is she?"

For a moment he thought his brother would not answer, but then he shrugged.

"The widowed daughter of the Earl of Tetbury, Lady Amabel Kingston."

His voice softened as he spoke her name, confirming Oliver's suspicions.

"Does she return your regard?"

"I have reason to hope so," he admitted. "But if our family's name is slandered…" He broke off as if unwilling to voice the thought. He regarded Oliver intently, for once no hint of disdain in his eyes.

"Well, brother? Will you make a push to clear your name?"

Oliver sighed and crossed his legs, suddenly weary of both his current situation and the antipathy between him and his family.

"I might, if there was a way to do it."

Lord Painswick frowned thoughtfully. "Could this Mrs Thruxton be persuaded to rescind her accusation if given an incentive?"

"A bribe?" Oliver said. "I doubt it. Any admission that she lied about so heinous a thing would spell her ruin. Besides, if anyone got wind of such a transaction, I would appear as guilty as before."

"Why did she accuse you?" Richmond pondered. "Who was she protecting?"

"As to the first of your questions, I fear I was in the wrong place at the wrong time. She asked me to get rid of the baby, and she became quite hysterical when I refused. She threw herself in my arms, and moments later, her husband walked in. Perhaps her accusation was her way of punishing me for refusing to help her. As for the second, as I have already intimated, I haven't a clue."

"You must try to find out," Lord Painswick insisted.

"And how do you suggest I do that, sir?" Oliver said, exasperated. "If there had been any rumours of a lover, I hope someone would already have informed me of them. Perhaps you think I should seek an interview with her, and plead with her to lay the blame in the right quarter, in the hope that her conscience has been troubling her?"

"That's it," Richmond said slowly. "Ask Mrs Thruxton to explain her actions. If she believes you to be quite alone, there is every chance she will do so. Only you won't be alone; her husband and one other, preferably a lady of the *ton*, will be somewhere concealed so that they might overhear the conversation."

Oliver pondered this, a faint hope stirring briefly in his breast, before reality once more set in.

"I doubt she will see me willingly or that her husband is likely to agree to such a plan."

"Some subtlety will certainly be required," Richmond said. "Therefore, you had best leave everything to me." He rose to his feet, the languidness he customarily assumed quite absent. A faintly malicious grin twitched his lips.

"Yes," he murmured. "I think it might be contrived."

"How?" Oliver asked.

His brother laughed softly. "My plan is not yet fully formed, and as you are unlikely to approve of my methods, it is perhaps better that you remain in ignorance. Leave it to me. I will write to you when it is time for you to play your part. We, however, must away in the morning. There is no time to lose."

A frantic scratching against the door made Lord Painswick raise his brows.

"We will certainly be away in the morning. Good God, Oliver! You really ought to do something about your rat infestation."

"I have it well in hand," Oliver murmured going to the door.

Beau charged into the room, ran in rapid circles about Richmond, sniffed at Lord Painswick's boots, and collapsed panting at Oliver's feet, his tongue lolling disgracefully from the side of his gaping mouth. Oliver bent and patted him.

"Good boy, Beau. But I have a feeling your services will prove unnecessary."

"I don't see that," Lord Painswick said testily. "Set him to work in the upstairs chambers."

As he straightened, Oliver met his brother's gaze. Richmond's grey gaze was as sharp as ever, and Oliver suspected he had guessed some part of his plan. That did not surprise him, the look of amused respect in them did, however.

# CHAPTER 13

Emma discovered herself capable of hobbling down to breakfast the following morning. Lizzie insisted on aiding her.

"Mrs Primly always says that when there's two instances of bad luck following one after another, a third is sure to follow. It wouldn't do for you to go tumbling down the stairs, Miss Wynn."

Emma found it ironic that Lizzie, who was generally accident prone, had suffered no embarrassing incidents worth mentioning since arriving at Pengelly Manor, whilst she had suffered two. She sincerely hoped that Mrs Primly's gloomy pronouncement would not be borne out. She accepted the maid's arm.

"Thank you, Lizzie. I shall take extra care, you may be sure."

When they entered the breakfast parlour, she was surprised to discover it empty. Interpreting her expression correctly, Lizzie said, "I saw Maria take a tray into Lady Eagleton's room. She's feeling a little tired as she couldn't get comfortable last night."

"Oh, I see. Well, that is only to be expected, I suppose. Thank you, Lizzie. That will be all."

She had barely seated herself at the table, when Timothy came into the room, carrying a plate of toast and a pot of tea. She watched in appreciation as he made her tea just the way she liked, with a spoon of sugar and a dash of hot milk. He then swiftly buttered her toast and spread a thin layer of marmalade upon it.

Emma smiled wryly. "Thank you, Timothy. I look forward to the day I can butter my own toast again."

He placed a small, silver bell by her elbow. "Think nothing of it, Miss Wynn. If there is anything else you require, just ring."

Left alone, Emma's thoughts turned to Mr Carne as they did all too frequently. She had also spent a rather restless night, her mind, then as now, seemingly set on going over the events of the previous morning. She could not help but wonder what had happened to create such a rift in Mr Carne's family. She could not doubt that something momentous had occurred; he had admitted his dislike of them, and they had never spoken a word of him. It was fruitless to ponder that question, however, as there was no way of her divining the answer.

She took a bite of toast and chewed contempla-tively. She had an inkling that it would have taken something equally momentous to bring them back together, and she imagined that it must be something to do with whatever had brought Mr Carne back to England. If there were some scandal attached to him, it would, of course, reflect badly on his family. She put down her toast, a twinge of guilt robbing her of her appetite.

Poor Mr Carne. His reunion with his family could not have been easy, and she had added to his burdens by asking him to get rid of them with all possible haste. To be alienated from one's family was a terrible thing, and perhaps she should rather have encouraged him to attempt a rapprochement with his father and brother.

She sighed and pushed back her chair. She had been able to think only of her own predicament, and in truth, so had he. He had had no thought for himself but had only wished to help her. A delicate flush of colour crept into her cheeks as she remembered him mounting his horse behind her and slipping his arm about her waist. She should have felt alarmed at being in such close proximity to a man, and yet she had not. She had, for a moment, felt startled and breathless as was only natural, but as the minutes passed, her racing heart had calmed, and she had felt only safe and protected. When they had drawn up in front of the house, she had been aware of the desire to remain cradled in his arms a little longer.

She stumbled and laid a hand on the back of a chair, her fingers trembling a little. She believed Mr Carne her friend, sensed that he was a good man, an honourable man, but she must not consider the possibility of him ever being anything more whilst her circumstances were so precarious, and his, whatever they were, unresolved. If she were to have any chance of succeeding in her aims, she must be seen to have led a blameless existence these past twelve months. If any hint of scandal was attached to Mr Carne, however undeservedly, she must not become embroiled in it.

"Miss Wynn?"

She saw that Timothy had come again into the room.

"Do you need me to carry you, ma'am?"

She released her grip on the chair. "No, thank you, Timothy. I can walk; I was merely wool-gathering. I wonder if there might be a walking cane that I can use, however, to help with my balance?"

"Certainly, ma'am. If you wait there a moment, I will be back directly."

True to his word, he returned holding a Malacca cane with an ivory handle. He followed Emma into the hall as if to satisfy himself that she was capable of using it. Wishing to see if there was anything she could do for Nell, she mounted the stairs slowly, one hand on the banister and the other firmly clasping the cane, aware all the time that Timothy was following in her wake.

She turned her head, saying dryly, "If I do fall, Timothy, I am likely to send you tumbling down the stairs also."

His lips twitched. "I don't see that, ma'am. It'd take more than—"

"Timothy! Timothy! Come quickly."

Emma looked up to see Maria appear at the top of the stairs, her eyes alive with a mixture of anxiety, excitement, and exasperation.

"There you are! Why is it that a man is never where he is wanted? First, Lord Eagleton sees fit to go off at a time of the most inconvenient, and then I have to waste time finding you."

"But, Maria," he protested. "I have been attending Miss Wynn."

Maria's eyes rested on Emma for a moment. She sighed. "Why do you insist on climbing the stairs like a snail, Miss Wynn, when my Timothy could carry you in a fraction of the time?"

Emma's eyebrow's rose at her tone, and Maria threw up her hands.

"Forgive me, Miss Wynn. I meant no disrespect, but I am… how you say… up in the trees."

"Up in the boughs?" Emma suggested.

"Si," the maid said. "That is what I said."

Angelica's voice sounded on the landing. "Maria? What is all this to-do about?"

"It is my mistress," Maria said. "She has had a few pains and I fear the babe might be coming, and at such a time, with his lordship away and the accoucheur and monthly nurse not due for another few weeks. Timothy must go for Doctor Ramsey."

Emma attained the landing. "Are you sure, Maria? Nell has suffered the odd pain before, but it has proved to be nothing."

"I know," the maid said. "But me, I am not one to cause a grand fuss for nothing. She could not sleep last night, she has hardly touched her breakfast, and she has had three pains already this morning."

"Well," Angelica said, "let us see her first."

Maria again threw up her hands. "Yes, but, Signora Montovani—"

"And," Angelica continued calmly, "there is no need for any urgency. A woman's lot is not always a kind one, and unfortunately, these things take time."

They found Nell pacing her bedroom floor, her hand held to her back. She smiled wanly.

"I believe it was a false alarm. The pains have subsided, only my back aches horribly, and I feel a little nauseous."

"Ah," said Angelica. "I suggest you take a warm bath, my dear."

Emma noted her friend's pallor and the faint sheen on her brow. "Perhaps it would be better if you sent for Doctor Ramsey, however," she said. "Just to make sure."

"Si," Maria said. "It is what I have been saying."

Nell shook her head. "I do not want him. Besides, it is Friday, and he will be visiting his mother in Plymouth." Her tone turned plaintive. "I wish Mrs Lambton were here. Although she is officially to be my monthly nurse, she delivered most of the babies in my village."

"We can send her a letter today," Angelica said, soothingly. "As she lives only sixty miles distant, she might very well arrive within a week."

Nell sat on the edge of the bed and rested her forehead against the post.

"In the meantime," Emma said, "perhaps we might send for Mrs Harris. Just to confirm whether the baby is coming or not, you understand. She is the lady who bound up my ankle, and a good, honest woman, I believe. Her husband said she had delivered more babies than he could count."

"That is a very good idea," Angelica agreed. "A midwife delivered my children, and although I do not deny that improvements in medical knowledge are a good thing, experience is often equally important."

"Very well," Nell said. "I would be more comfortable with a woman. You may send a note and a carriage to bring her to me, Emma."

"I will arrange the water for the bath," Maria said, hurrying from the room.

"Would you also like me to write to Mrs Lambton on your behalf?" Emma asked.

Nell smiled. "Thank you. I cannot seem to concentrate on anything. But if you bring me the letter when you are finished, I will add a personal note and the direction."

Timothy was still on the landing awaiting instruction. Smiling ruefully, Emma requested that he carry her down to the drawing room and wait there whilst she wrote a letter. She had just handed it to him when she had a thought. Although she did not like to disturb Mr Carne just at present, she thought she ought to ask him to visit. Even if Nell's baby was not on the way, she had not looked well. She bade Timothy wait a moment longer, and then dashed off another missive. She handed them both to him.

"You are to take the carriage and deliver the letter addressed to Mrs Harris. Hopefully, she will return with you. The second letter is to go to Carne Castle. Ask one of the grooms to deliver it and await an answer."

"Right away, ma'am."

Timothy's actions did not match his words, however. He stood regarding her with a frown in his eyes.

"Is there a problem?" Emma asked.

"There's likely to be if no one makes a push to inform Lord Eagleton of what's going forward."

The thought that it might be best for all concerned if the marquess remained in blissful ignorance crossed Emma's mind. She recognised the truth of Timothy's words, however.

"I see. Perhaps that question can be addressed when we know for certain what is happening."

The footman bowed. "Very well, ma'am."

Emma returned her attention to the desk, drew forward a sheet of paper, and once more applied her pen, this time addressing her letter to Mrs Lambton. When she deemed that Nell had had enough time for her bath, she made her way upstairs once more. She found her friend in a shift and nightgown, sitting by the fire with Angelica in attendance.

"Feeling better, Nell?" she asked gently.

"Much better," she affirmed. "My back is not so painful."

"I am glad to hear it. Do you feel up to reading the letter I have written to Mrs Lambton?"

Using the arm of her chair to aid her, Nell stood, took the letter, and made her way to the desk set under her window.

"Whilst I look over this, sit down, Emma, and rest your foot on a stool. I am sure you had not intended to march up and down the stairs so much this morning."

Emma did not argue. It was true, and her ankle was throbbing a little. Angelica smiled at her.

"Now you are here to bear Nell company, I shall go to the nursery and inform Jane that she need not bring Francesca down today. I shall not be many minutes."

Nell looked up as if she would protest, but then

winced and seemed to change her mind. "Yes, perhaps that would be best."

She picked up her quill, a frown of concentration on her brow, and added a postscript to the letter. Emma could hear Maria arranging things in the dressing room, but as a light knock fell upon the door, she came out and flew across the room, throwing it open.

The barest hint of exasperation shaded Manton's wooden voice. "That is no way to answer the door, Maria. A lady's maid should act with moderation at all times."

The maid was unimpressed with the butler's pronouncement. "Bah! I do not care for your moderation. Me, I have blood in my veins, and I care only for my mistress, and it is to her I answer! Now, have you something to say or have you come to poke your nose where it is not wanted?"

"Maria!" Nell protested faintly.

Manton's tone became frigid. "There is a Mrs Harris downstairs. Apparently, she has come to see Lady Eagleton."

"Then why did you not bring her up immediately?"

Angelica's voice sounded outside the room. Emma had no idea what she said as she spoke in fluent Italian. The melodic words were said in a steely tone Emma had not heard Angelica use before. They had a profound effect on Maria. The maid took a step back, her cheeks colouring and her eyes dropping.

"I am sorry, Manton. Forgive me."

"Bring Mrs Harris up, if you will, Manton," Angelica said.

She came into the room, and Maria retreated once more to the dressing room.

"You have indulged that girl too much," Angelica said dryly.

"Perhaps," Nell admitted. "But I would not like to tame her natural liveliness too much, and as Manton cannot hide his disapproval of Maria, he provokes her."

She put down her quill as Mrs Harris appeared in the doorway.

"Come in, Mrs Harris," Emma said, reaching for her cane and rising to her feet.

She made the introductions, pleased that the woman did not seem overwhelmed.

"I'm honoured to meet you, Lady Eagleton, Signora Montovani, and it's nice to see you again, Miss Wynn. But I think it would be best if you sat down and put up that foot."

"Thank you for coming so promptly," Nell said, placing her hands palm down on the desk and levering herself up.

"Think nothing of it, my lady. How often are the pains coming?"

"Not very frequently," Nell said. "Over half an hour apart, I believe." She put her hand to her side and winced.

"Is that another one?" Mrs Harris asked, putting down the carpet bag she carried.

Nell shook her head. "No. The baby has frequently kicked me under the ribs, but now there is a constant pain there. And I think I can feel a hard lump."

Mrs Harris untied what Emma guessed to be her

best Sunday bonnet, laid it down, and unfastened her cloak, her movements swift and businesslike.

"But the babe is still moving?"

"Yes, only the kicks feel lower down in my stomach. Or perhaps they are not kicks but the darling's hands pushing."

"Perhaps," Mrs Harris said. "And have you had a sudden rush of water?"

Nell coloured. "Do you mean have I had need of the chamber pot?"

The woman chuckled. "Bless you, no, my lady. Has no one told you that there is a fluid-filled membrane surrounding the baby, and when the babe is set on coming, it bursts and the fluid leaks out?"

"I had intended to inform Nell what to expect," Angelica said. "However, I thought there was time enough. We thought it might be a Christmas baby."

"I see. Forgive me for asking, Lady Eagleton, but *have* you needed to use the chamber pot more often than usual?"

Nell nodded. "I thought my stomach was upset. I have felt nauseous, you see."

"Ah," Mrs Harris said, nodding her head. "That is interesting."

"Is it?" Nell asked, bemused. "Why?"

"A lady often has to relieve herself more often when the baby is about to come."

Nell gasped, her hand going protectively to her stomach. "But it is too soon."

"Perhaps, perhaps not," Mrs Harris said. "When last you had your courses, did you notice anything unusual?"

Nell frowned as she recalled the incident. "Yes,

now that you mention it. The bleeding was very light and only lasted a few days."

Mrs Harris smiled knowingly. "I have attended others who have thought their babe was coming early but experienced the same thing, and the babe was perfectly ready. It is my belief that it is not part of the usual cycle of monthly bleeding at all. But get you up on the bed, Lady Eagleton, and let me have a look at you."

Maria had clearly been eavesdropping, for she came out of the dressing room carrying a stool. She laid it by the bed and helped her mistress climb onto it.

"I am Maria," she said, assuming a cool dignity. "Lady Eagleton's maid, and I am pleased to meet you, Mrs Harris. You seem a sensible woman."

That lady chuckled. "I should hope I am."

"I will help you in any way I may be permitted."

Mrs Harris nodded. "You can arrange your mistress in such a way that I may examine her belly but her modesty remains preserved. There's no need for anything overly intrusive as yet."

"Si, certamente."

"Afterwards, if you have a lying-in bed, perhaps it could be brought?"

"Si, si."

"And if you are to help me," Mrs Harris added, "it would be better if you used the good Lord's English."

"But the lord knows all languages," Maria pointed out.

"He may well do," Mrs Harris agreed, going to the fire to warm her hands. "But I don't."

## CHAPTER 14

O liver found dinner with his family less difficult than he had expected. Lord Painswick, pleased with the fare offered him, and happy in the knowledge that some sort of plan had been set in place to clear Oliver's name, became more amenable. Richmond did not have a great deal to say, but due to the distant look in his eyes and twist of his lips, Oliver did not put this down to rudeness but to him cogitating on how best to achieve his aim. The only awkward moment came when Richmond shook off his abstraction and asked about Eagleton.

"We passed a sign for Pengelly Manor, and as I recall it belongs to Eagleton. I wonder if I should pay him a visit before we leave tomorrow. I've a mind to meet his wife. There were rumours that she might have had a hand in murdering her first husband, Flint, although that was disproved, I believe. As no one of ton has ever met her, speculation still abounds. When Flint did not bring her to Town, the consensus was that she must be plain if not downright ugly, and that he had only married the vicar's daughter for her money. Now Eagleton has made her his wife, it is agreed that she must be breathtakingly beautiful, and as he is keeping her to himself, it must be a love match."

Oliver's lip curled. "You wish to gather fodder for the gossips?"

His brother merely smiled. "Truth is not gossip. Besides, it is always so delicious when one possesses knowledge that everybody else desires."

"There is no time for courtesy calls, Richmond," Lord Painswick insisted. "We will rise early and be on our way."

"Very well," Richmond said, sighing.

"Console yourself with the knowledge that Eagleton is away at the moment, and if you must know, Lady Eagleton is a breathtakingly beautiful woman, she is also a thoroughly pleasant one."

"You are acquainted with the marquess and his wife, eh?" Lord Painswick said, a measure of approval in his voice.

Oliver shrugged. "He is my neighbour, after all."

"Well, perhaps there's hope for you yet, boy," he said gruffly. "I expect it is Eagleton who owns most of the land about here?" He shook his head. "There's no need to answer that. Of course he is. His family has always been rich as Croesus, and I can't see my brother playing the gentleman farmer." He snorted. "Cedric liked his comforts. I never understood how he maintained his lifestyle." A frown etched his brow. "He did not leave you under a mountain of debt, did he?"

Oliver did not correct his misapprehension, merely

171

saying, "No, he did not do that. Now, if you will excuse me, I have some work I must attend to."

He did not see them again until daybreak. After an early breakfast, they took their leave. To his surprise, Richmond shook his hand.

"I have not the half of your virtues, brother, and I am not proud of how I have behaved towards you." He smiled ruefully. "My resentment towards a younger sibling was perhaps unworthy of me. Francis often told me so. If you had remained in our sphere, and I had known you as an adult, we might have called a truce before now. Believe it or not, I am trying to eradicate the worst of my habits."

His words sounded sincere.

"In order to be worthy of Lady Amabel Kingston?" Oliver asked softly.

Richmond's grip on his hand tightened. "Yes. She is a remarkable woman, and if you help ensure our name is not smeared by these vile rumours, I will be forever in your debt."

A ghost of a smile touched Oliver's lips. "Then you had best make sure your plan bears fruit. I will come when you send for me."

He went to the library and was greeted by an ecstatic Beau. He patted the dog before sending him back to the rug in front of the fire. The terrier obeyed, but his eyes followed Oliver as he moved to his desk and pulled open a drawer. He sat frowning for a moment as something his brother had said finally registered. *My resentment towards a younger sibling*. Had his dislike been fuelled by resentment? Oliver had thought he had merely aped their father; Richmond had always wished to be first oars with him. His words suggested it had been more than that, however. It had been one of Richmond's carelessly flung insults that had alerted Oliver to the fact that Lord Painswick was not his father, but that did not explain why he had resented Oliver when they had been children. Richmond could not have known the circumstances of his birth then.

He sighed. He had never understood his eldest brother and he doubted he ever would. Despite Richmond's claim that he would be in Oliver's debt if he helped clear their name, he suspected that once the deed was done, he would revert to form.

He rifled through a few papers in the drawer and withdrew several letters. He dropped them on his desk, recognising the lazy script of his childhood friend, Mr Frederick Ashton, and the neater hand of Mr Robert Kirkby. He had wished to wait until his family had departed before testing his theory that they might have written to him of the events surrounding Miss Emmit. He silently corrected himself. Miss Wynn. She was right. If he became used to thinking of her as Miss Emmit, he might let the name slip. It was seeming ever more familiar to him.

He picked up a missive, his hand hovering over the wafer. Beau sat up and whined, his tail thumping on the carpet.

"Do you know, Beau, I think you may be right?" Oliver murmured.

He dropped the missive. It somehow felt like snooping. Miss Wynn had done him the honour of confiding some part of her story, and it would be dishonourable to attempt to discover anything more without her permission. He gathered up the letters, his hand pausing over the last one. His name was scribed in a flourishing hand. This had not been with his uncle's other papers but had been entrusted to his valet, Steen. He had given it to him when he had begun to regain his strength. He had never opened it and didn't know if he ever would. He placed it on the pile and dropped the letters back in the drawer. Rising, he crossed the room and sat by the fire. A crisp, cool November had arrived, and a chill hung in the air. Beau lay down, resting his head on Oliver's boot.

"I suppose you would think it an act of callous cruelty if I were to send you back to the stables?"

The dog's tail wagged once, and he closed his eyes.

"I understand. You are exhausted from hunting non-existent rats," Oliver said conversationally.

A brief knock sounded on the door and Hurley entered the room. His eyes rested on Beau for a moment. "Shall I take him back to the stables now your guests have departed, sir?"

Beau lifted his head and growled.

"He does not appear to like the idea," Oliver said.

"But, sir," Hurley protested, "he ripped the silk hangings in the red bedchamber."

Oliver's lips twitched. "His instincts are impeccable. They made the room look like a bordello. I take your point, however. He shall be confined to this room when he is not taking the air. That will be all, Hurley."

"There's rats in this house, all right," the butler muttered. "They're all in your garret. But it's not the dog I've come about, sir. I have a letter for you from Pengelly Manor and a groom is waiting for your answer."

Oliver rose swiftly to his feet. "Then why didn't you say so immediately?"

He took the missive and scanned its brief contents.

*Mr Carne,*

*Forgive me for disturbing you. I would not do so if I did not feel it to be necessary. Lady Eagleton is in some discomfort and does not look at all well. As Doctor Ramsey is not available, I have sent for Mrs Harris to help ascertain whether the birth of the babe is imminent. If it is, I would feel happier if you were present in case of any difficulties. If it is not, I would be grateful if you would determine what it is that ails Lady Eagleton.*

*Your friend,*

*Miss Wynn*

"Hurley, bring my medical bag and get some lavender oil from the still room."

Oliver rode with all haste to Pengelly Manor. Whether or not he liked it, Eagleton had entrusted him with the care of his wife. He sincerely hoped that Lady Eagleton was not about to give birth. He had been led to believe that the babe was not due until towards the end of December, and although it was difficult to predict precisely when a child was due, the disparity was much larger than he liked.

He was shown immediately upstairs and waited on the landing whilst the butler knocked on the door to announce his arrival. The blond Adonis of a footman waited beside it, his expression wooden and his jaw rigid. The door opened a crack and after a few soft murmurings, closed again.

"If you will just wait a moment, sir."

A few minutes passed and then Mrs Harris slipped out of the room.

"Mr Carne, I had no idea you used to be a surgeon."

"As I no longer practise, I do not advertise the fact. How is Lady Eagleton?"

"It is early days yet, but I believe the babe is coming. There is a problem, however."

"I know it is premature—"

"No, it's not that, sir."

Oliver glanced at Timothy and saw the footman quickly avert his gaze. He drew Mrs Harris a little way down the corridor.

"Why is that not the problem? Lady Eagleton did not expect to be brought to bed until the end of next month. That is almost two months away."

Mrs Harris quickly explained her theory as to why she thought the date had been miscalculated.

"It's my belief that the babe is no more than a few weeks early. You may disbelieve me if you choose, but the child is coming regardless."

Oliver searched the homely-looking woman's eyes. "Mrs Harris, I mean no offence, but how many births have you attended?"

She met his gaze squarely. "Oh, probably about eighty all told, although I have been in full control of the delivery for only sixty of them." She let that sink in for a moment before adding dryly, "How many have you attended, sir?"

An appreciative smile twitched his lips. "I am aware that there are some doctors who feel superior to a mere midwife, but I am not one of them. Theory and lectures are all very good, but they cannot trump experience. I will admit that I have attended not nearly as many births as you. Tell me what the problem is."

"The baby has turned. I felt the head under the ribs. In my experience, a breech birth is often long and difficult. I have a copy of *Domestic Midwife* by Margaret Stephen, and she has some good advice on how to deal with such difficult presentations. I have managed to deliver two babies feet first. It wasn't easy, and although both babe and mother survived, the mothers suffered some damage. One of them has not managed to bear another child. Lady Eagleton has narrow hips, and I fear for her and the child."

A chill ran down Oliver's spine. "Have her waters broken?"

"No, Mr Carne. As I said, it is early days yet."

He nodded and drew in a deep breath. "Then there is still a chance I might be able to turn the babe by massaging the stomach."

Mrs Harris looked sceptical. "I do not mean any offence, Mr Carne, but have you ever done it before?"

He smiled. "None taken. And yes. I had read of such a manoeuvre when I was a student, although I do not think there are many who practise it. I witnessed and participated in it whilst in India. I spent some time in remote villages in the mountains, and whilst there I worked with a particularly skilled Dai; that is the Indian term for a birth attendant. She showed me how it was done. If the waters have not broken, I believe there is some chance of success and little danger to the babe."

Mrs Harris chewed her bottom lip as she considered his proposal. After a moment or two, she gave a decided nod. "If there's little danger, there's nothing to be lost and much to be gained. If you can turn the babe, I believe I can do the rest. I suspect Lady Eagleton would be more comfortable with a female delivering the child. I have seen many a babe come scatheless into the world from a small woman if it is but the right way round."

"How much have you told Lady Eagleton?"

"I'm a straightforward woman, Mr Carne, and I don't hold with hiding the truth." She sighed. "Nor do I hold with scaring the mother senseless. I've told Lady Eagleton that the baby is in an awkward position and that might make the birth more difficult. Miss Wynn, Signora Montovani, and her ladyship's maid are with her, so they know too. I thought it was best they be prepared. That way, if something does go wrong, it won't be a complete shock."

Oliver squared his shoulders. "Very well, Mrs Harris, let us go in."

A hush descended on the room as he entered. He saw that a lying-in-bed had been brought into the room although it was as yet unoccupied. Angelica sat on the large four-poster, smoothing the hair from Nell's brow. She was the first to break the silence.

"We were not aware that Emma had sent for you, Mr Carne, but I am glad that she showed such foresight. It appears that things are not as straightforward as they might have been."

"So I have been told, but I may be able to rectify the problem."

His eyes turned to Lady Eagleton, who had the sheet pulled up to her chin. He offered what he hoped was a reassuring smile.

"'There is a chance I may be able to turn the baby by massaging your stomach, Lady Eagleton."

"Will it hurt?" she asked anxiously.

"It might be a little uncomfortable, but it should not be painful. It will not take long and will make things much easier for you."

"And it will not hurt the baby?"

"I do not think so. Delivering the baby in its current position is more likely to endanger both of you."

The little colour that remained, leeched from Nell's face.

"Am I to blame? Is it because I did not allow Doctor Ramsey to bleed me, or stay in my bed and eat only broth?"

Mrs Harris gave an undignified snort. "That's hogwash. How do you think the average good woman who already has a child or two and can't afford to lie abed manages? I'll tell you how. Unless they're ill, in which case their family or neighbours might step in to help, they carry on as normal until the time comes."

Nell's eyes went from her to Oliver. "Do you agree?"

"I do," he said unhesitatingly. "When last I saw you, you seemed in the best of good health and acted accordingly. Today, you clearly felt unwell and have kept to your room. There is no blame here, Lady Eagleton. But if I am to turn the child, it should be now, before your waters break and your pains quicken."

"Let him do it!"

Oliver regarded the plump young maid who hovered on Lady Eagleton's other side. Both her dark colouring and accent spoke of her Italian heritage. She took her mistress's hand, her vibrant, brown eyes boring into hers.

"This Mr Carne has a good face, and he took good care of Miss Wynn when she hurt her wrist. Let him try."

"Yes, do."

Oliver turned his head towards the fire. Miss Wynn sat there. She met his eyes and smiled.

"I trust Mr Carne to do what is right."

He ignored the slight contraction of his heart. There was no room for emotion at such a time.

"Very well," Nell said. "If you will give me a moment to arrange myself."

"Certainly," he said. "But it would be better if you moved to the other bed. As it is lower and narrower, it will make my task easier."

He glanced at Maria and spoke with quiet authority. "Do not place any pillows beneath your mistress's head, but place one under her knees."

He strolled to the fire and held his hands out to the blaze, sending Emma a sideways glance. "I appreciate your faith in me."

Again, her sweet smile dawned. "Think nothing of it."

He did not feel he deserved her approbation and only hoped he proved himself worthy of it. His outstretched hands trembled a little, and he knew a moment's self-doubt.

Miss Wynn's soft, brown eyes remained steady on his. "You must have faith in yourself, Mr Carne. I feel certain you were an excellent doctor."

He nodded, removed his coat, and rolled up his

shirtsleeves. "Perhaps someone might close the curtains and light some candles."

Mrs Harris regarded him sternly. "I'm not one of those who hold with keeping every breath of air from a birthing chamber, Mr Carne."

"Neither am I," he said, glancing at the grey sky outside the window. "But it is a gloomy prospect. I wish to create a peaceful atmosphere so that both mother and child will relax."

Having moved and arranged her mistress, Maria bustled to obey his instructions.

"He is right," the maid said. "The English weather is as moody and unpredictable as an old crone, and there is nothing so depressing as a grey sky."

Oliver hardly heard the voluble maid, his concentration all for the task ahead. He opened his bag and withdrew a phial of ointment. He poured a little on his hands and rubbed them together.

"What's that?" Mrs Harris said, interested.

"Lavender oil. It is what I had to hand. It will allow me to massage Lady Eagleton's stomach smoothly, and so cause her the minimum of discomfort. Please feel free to observe, Mrs Harris."

"You may be sure I will," she said, stepping up to the bed.

He glanced at Nell and smiled. "Breathe deeply, Lady Eagleton. Both you and the babe need to be calm."

Nell nodded and closed her eyes. He rubbed his hands gently over her rounded stomach until he saw the stress begin to leave her face. Her nostrils flared as she inhaled the pleasant aroma of the lavender, and she sighed. Only then did he allow his fingers to probe a little deeper.

He glanced at Mrs Harris. "I can do this alone, but it is easier with two pairs of hands. Would you like to help?"

Pleasure and anxiety mingled in her button-brown eyes. "If you think it's safe for me to do so."

He held her gaze steadily. "I do. My fingers are pressing beneath the babe's buttocks. I have lifted them out of the pelvis, and I want you to hold them there whilst I locate the head."

"Very well, sir."

When she had positioned her hands correctly, he slid his towards the top of Nell's swollen stomach and probed for a moment. "Ah, there you are." He smiled gently. "Take a long, slow breath, Lady Eagleton."

Using two hands he gently began to press and pull.

"Good Lord!" Mrs Harris murmured. "It's moving."

Oliver grinned "So it is. Keep a firm grip, Mrs Harris, but do not try and force things. Pull gently when I tell you."

She nodded, her brow furrowing in concentration.

Nell gasped. "It feels so strange."

"We are halfway there, Lady Eagleton, and you are doing very well." Oliver glanced at Mrs Harris and changed the position of his hands. "I shall now push gently down on the head, and when I stop you may push gently on the buttocks."

A few more minutes, and it was done.

Mrs Harris laughed softly. "You did it! In all my years, I've seen nothing like it."

"We did it," Oliver said, a satisfied smile on his lips. "Thank you for your help."

"No, sir, it is I who should thank you for opening my eyes as to what might be done."

"Thank you, both of you," Nell said, her voice strained. "Do you think I might get up and walk? It helps with the pain in my back."

They eased her into a sitting position, and she slipped from the bed. She had taken only a few steps before she stopped, a hissing gasp escaping her. Oliver and Mrs Harris each took an arm to steady her.

"That was the most painful yet," she murmured.

"Don't you worry, my dear," Mrs Harris said. "It will probably go more quickly now."

It appeared she was right. Oliver had no sooner washed the lavender oil from his hands when Nell gasped again.

"Oh," she said, looking down at the puddle at her feet.

"It's perfectly normal," Mrs Harris said. "Giving birth is a messy business."

"Thank heaven Eagleton isn't here," Nell murmured. "I doubt I could keep him from my side, and I would not like him to see me like this."

"That is understandable, my dear," Angelica said. "But I do think we should send someone to the priory to inform him."

Emma rose to her feet. "I will ask Timothy to go. He suggested it earlier, but I thought it best we wait until we were certain of how things stood."

"That's it," Mrs Harris said. "Off you go, Miss Wynn. There are altogether too many people in here. Her ladyship needs room to breathe, and she don't need to be worrying about anyone but her and the baby. She'll do better without an audience."

"Yes," Nell said. "Although I would like Maria and Angelica to stay with me."

"I shall leave Lady Eagleton in your capable hands," Oliver said. "But I will only be downstairs if you require any assistance."

"Very good, Mr Carne. Oh, and Miss Wynn, perhaps you can arrange for some broth to be sent up."

"Oh," Nell said, gasping. "I don't think I could."

"You're mistaken, my lady," Mrs Harris said sternly. "You need to keep your strength up for what lies ahead."

# CHAPTER 15

E mma stepped out of the room to find her maid hovering on the landing.

"Lizzie, have you seen Timothy?"

"Yes, ma'am. He told me to wait here in case I was needed to fetch anything."

She frowned. "But why would he ask you to do his work?"

The maid clasped her hands together, her expression earnest. "I didn't mind, Miss Wynn, not when he told me how things were. He said his first duty was to inform Lord Eagleton that the babe was coming and there was some sort of problem." The maid gave a sob. "Oh, Miss Wynn, Mrs Primly was right, bad luck does come in threes, but I never suspected that it would strike Lady Eagleton."

"That is nonsense," Emma said firmly. "There is no bad luck here, nor is there any longer a problem. I asked Timothy to wait until we knew how things stood. I don't know why he felt it necessary to go before I had spoken with him."

"I think he may have overheard Mrs Harris and I speaking," Oliver said. "She mentioned there being a problem, and I drew her away as I thought Timothy was eavesdropping."

"It is a pity you did not do so immediately. The news that Nell has been brought to bed will be enough to send his anxiety soaring, but when Timothy informs him all is not well…" She sighed. "Well, it can't be helped now, and it will soon be forgotten when he arrives tomorrow to discover Nell has been safely delivered of a child."

"If she is," the maid said, apparently not quite ready to disbelieve the perspicacity of Mrs Primly.

"Lizzie," Emma said, exasperated. "If you are so enamoured of Mrs Primly's superstitions, you are free to return to Ashwick Hall."

The maid's eyes widened, tears starting to them. "Don't send me away, Miss Wynn. I've never felt so happy as I have since I started waiting on you. I didn't mean it."

Emma was touched, but she bit back the apology that hovered on her tongue. Lady Westcliffe had been right. Kindness should be administered with some discrimination.

"Very well," she said. "But if you repeat your forebodings to anyone—"

"I won't," Lizzie said quickly. "I promise."

"Then you may bring a chair and your sewing to occupy you."

The maid curtsied and hurried away, tripping over her feet as she did so. Only Oliver's quick reactions prevented her from falling. Emma sent him a grateful smile as the maid mumbled her thanks and carried on her way.

"Thank you. I was a trifle hard on her, I know. Poor Lizzie always becomes clumsy when she is distressed or worried."

"I do not think you were overly hard on her," Oliver said, swooping without warning and lifting her into his arms. "It would not do for her to repeat her superstitious nonsense to the other servants."

"I can walk," Emma protested, her words robbed of their efficacy by emerging in a squeak rather than her usual measured tone.

"You can, but you shouldn't. Certainly not on the stairs, and as Timothy is not here, I am merely acting in his stead. Besides, if you should happen to injure any other part of yourself, all your good work will be undone, and Lizzie will forever more believe in whatever other nonsense Mrs Primly may have uttered."

It seemed that his success in turning Nell's child had raised Mr Carne's spirits. Emma had never heard him use such a lively, bantering tone, nor had she ever seen such exhilaration in his eyes. It was infectious. Her heartbeat quickened, and a smile danced in her eyes as she gave a spirited response.

"Very well, but if you act as a footman, then you must obey orders as one would. You will put me down the moment we are in the hall."

He grinned. "Yes, milady, of course, milady, anything you say, milady."

Manton awaited them at the bottom of the stairs, the butler's expression suggesting that he thought their levity out of place.

"May I enquire how Lady Eagleton fares? Timothy mentioned there was some difficulty."

Emma shook out her skirts as Oliver set her down. "Mr Carne has solved the problem, and all is going forward as it should. Mrs Harris would like some broth sent up to Lady Eagleton, and perhaps you might bring a tea tray to the drawing room. Mr Carne will remain here for the present, in case he is needed."

"Of course," the butler said, his eyes going to Oliver. His lip quivered, and his voice trembled with emotion. "And thank you, Mr Carne. We are all extremely fond of Lady Eagleton, and if anything untoward should happen…"

"There is no reason why it should," Oliver said gently.

The butler raised a hand to his eyes. "No, of course not."

At that moment, the front door burst open, and Lord Eagleton flung into the house. His raven locks were windblown, and his eyes held a wild glitter. Emma's heart sank. He must have already been on his way home and had clearly met Timothy. This was the man Emma had first seen at Ashwick Hall, his expression austere and his face alabaster. This was the man Lady Westcliffe had foretold she would have to support when Nell was brought to bed. Gathering her resolution, she walked forward to meet him, her cane tapping on the tiles of the entrance hall. He did not check his pace but brushed past her. She stumbled sideways and put out the walking stick to steady herself, but it touched the floor at an angle and slipped. She fell, the cane skittering away from her.

She had the presence of mind to twist herself so that she fell on her uninjured side.

The marquess did not seem to notice but carried on towards the stairs, his voice cracking like a whip through the air.

"Carne. How is my wife?"

Emma turned onto her back, and for the briefest of moments, her eyes met Mr Carne's. They were chips of ice and held a question. She shook her head, saw his jaw clench, and then he was moving. Two strides brought him to the marquess, his arm drew back, and he delivered a crushing blow to Lord Eagleton's jaw. Taken unawares, the marquess staggered backwards and crumpled to his knees.

"Your wife is in no danger that I am aware of," Oliver said through gritted teeth. "What you should rather ask, is how is Miss Wynn. You have just knocked an injured woman to the ground."

Emma struggled to sit up, her heart in her mouth, fearful of what dreadful retribution the marquess would wreak upon Mr Carne. He did not seem to comprehend the words just spoken to him.

"That," the marquess said softly, rising to his feet, "was a huge mistake."

Oliver put up his fists. "Let's see, shall we?"

Emma glanced at Manton, but he stood as if rooted to the spot. She turned, and putting down her hand, levered herself onto her knees. The men were circling around each other, each jabbing at the other but missing their spot. Then Eagleton closed, his feet dancing, and his fist pummelled Mr Carne's shoulder. He tried to follow up with an undercut to his jaw, but Oliver leant away, his back bending to avoid it.

Anger suddenly coursed through Emma's veins. How foolish men were. If Mr Carne thought she wished him to champion her in such a way, he was much mistaken, and the marquess had no right to attack the man who had done his best to make the delivery of his babe easier. She gasped as the men closed again, Mr Carne coming off worst from the encounter as he received a punishing blow to his stomach.

"Stop it!" she said imperatively.

Her words had no effect. She was determined to attract their attention before they did each other serious injury. Her eyes never leaving the fracas, she edged sideways, her hand grasping for the cane. When she felt the smooth ivory of the handle beneath her fingers, she rose to her feet, her eyes narrowed. She sent the walking stick spinning, hoping that all the years spent playing quoits with her younger brother might finally prove useful. As Lord Eagleton seemed to have the upper hand, she aimed for him.

She followed the arc of the cane's progress, its motion seeming uncommonly slow. She wondered if she had hit her head when she fell, for although she had not felt any hurt to her skull, she could not quite fathom what she was seeing. The ivory handle remained the same, but beneath it a thin, steel blade turned end over end, making its inexorable way towards the marquess. She moved forward and stumbled as her slippered toe connected with a cylindrical object. Glancing down she saw the Malacca husk of the cane.

Her eyes snapped up. She had not imagined it. Timothy had given her a sword stick! Cold sweat dampened her brow as she saw the marquess and Mr Carne locked together, now wrestling rather than boxing. Her aim had been all too accurate, and it seemed the blade must embed itself in Lord Eagleton's back, but even as she opened her lips to scream a warning, the combatants fell apart, each stumbling backwards. The blade fell between them, bounced off the marble tiles, and slid across the floor. They froze, exchanged a glance, and turned towards her, the marquess's nose bloodied, and Mr Carne's right eye half closed and swollen.

Emma subdued the impulse to shrink from their amazed gaze and hobbled forward.

"You will both stop this immediately." Her eyes raked over Lord Eagleton. "Lady Westcliffe warned me that you might become quite irrational when Nell was brought to bed, but I did not expect you would assault my person." She did not know if his winging eyebrow denoted offence or surprise, nor did she care. She turned to Oliver. "And you, Mr Carne, should know better. Not twenty minutes since, I saw you use your hands to protect two lives, and yet I have now been forced to witness them wielded violently."

The marquess shook his head as if to clear it. "Miss Wynn, I did not mean... I hardly saw you... please accept my apologies." His eyes went to Oliver who was cradling his right hand. "Carne, you had every right to knock me down. I don't know what happened..."

A wry smile tilted Oliver's lips. "I was overcome by a primeval instinct to punish you for endangering Miss Wynn, thereby furnishing you with an excuse to direct your fear and anxiety towards me." He turned apologetic eyes towards Emma. "I am sorry you had to witness that. I take it you have suffered no further injury?"

She shook her head.

"Carne," Lord Eagleton said. "What did Miss Wynn mean when she said you had used your hands to protect two lives?"

"I suggest you both retire to the drawing room and discuss it there," Emma said sharply. "I will arrange for some ice to be brought so you may tend your injuries."

"I will see to it," Manton said, recovering from his state of immobility.

"No," Alexander said. "I must go to Nell."

"You will not go to Nell," Emma said, her tone that of a governess addressing a recalcitrant child. "Your appearance would alarm her. Besides, she does not want you there; she said as much. Mrs Harris, who is attending her, quite rightly said that Nell should not have an audience, that she should be able to concentrate only on herself and the baby. Angelica and Maria are offering her support. You will only make her lot more difficult. I do not know if you are aware of it, but Nell constantly frets over you worrying about her."

"She is right," Oliver said. "If there is any reason for concern, Mrs Harris will send for me."

Alexander ran his hand through his hair. "Carne, Francesca came early, and my first wife died."

Oliver released his right hand, revealing swollen, bloody knuckles, and dropped his left on Alexander's shoulder. "We think there is a distinct possibility that the babe is not as early as you suppose. Come,

Eagleton, whilst we clean up, I will explain everything."

With one last, longing look at the stairs, the marquess capitulated. Emma retrieved the sword and returned it to the cane, reflecting on what strange creatures men were. One moment they had been pummelling each other as if they were bitter enemies, and now they were once more friends, neither of them seeming to harbour any resentment towards the other.

"Miss Wynn?"

She saw they had halted and were once more regarding her.

"Yes, Mr Carne?"

"I am intrigued to know just who you were intending to impale with that sword?"

Her rush of bravery and righteous indignation had passed, and she felt her cheeks flame. "I was not aware it was a sword stick." As she saw amusement light his eyes, she raised her chin, a flash of spirit returning. "But if it had hit one of you, it would have been no more than you deserved."

"Eagleton," Oliver said, shaking his head. "You have been harbouring a viper."

The shadow of a smile touched the marquess's lips, but his eyes remained darkened by worry.

"We undoubtedly deserved it, Emma. Again, I apologise. Timothy should be in soon. I would appreciate it if you would ask him to enquire as to how my wife fares."

She nodded and they disappeared into the drawing room. Emma had no intention of waiting for the footman, however; he had caused enough mischief that day. She glanced up the stairs, the ache in her ankle suggesting that she really should not attempt to mount them again just yet. There was a blur of movement and a flash of brown hair. She smiled wryly. She could hardly blame her maid for being drawn by the scuffle in the hall.

"Lizzie," she called.

The maid appeared shame-faced at the head of the stairs.

"You are not in trouble," Emma assured her. "Go to the kitchen and fetch the broth Mrs Harris ordered. When you deliver it, you will say that I wish to know how things are progressing, and then you may report back to me."

The maid ran down the stairs. "Yes, Miss Wynn."

Emma put her hand on her arm as she reached her. "And Lizzie, you did not hear or see anything, do you understand?"

The maid nodded, regarding her mistress with awe. "You were marvellous, ma'am. I don't know how you were brave enough to give the marquess such a dressing down."

On reflection, neither was she. She settled herself in a chair by the fire at one end of the hall. Lizzie soon returned, followed by Manton and Timothy, who carried ice and strips of cloth. The butler regarded her with new respect, and the footman came forward, his blue eyes penitent.

"I'm sorry, ma'am. I should have waited—"

"Yes," Emma interrupted him. "You should have. Do not compound your error by keeping Lord Eagleton and Mr Carne waiting."

A flush of colour stained the young man's cheeks.

He bowed, turned, and followed the butler to the drawing room.

Lizzie soon returned. "Maria took the broth from me, ma'am. She said that the pains are coming swift and strong, but her ladyship is bearing it well. Mrs Harris says all is as it should be, although the babe's in a hurry, and she doesn't think it will be long now."

Timothy came into the hall. "I'll relieve you now, Lizzie. I've to check how her ladyship fares."

"Lizzie has already done so," Emma said. "And I will pass the information on. You may certainly return to your post, however, and bring us news when the baby is born."

"Yes, Miss Wynn."

She gave the gentlemen another five minutes to tidy themselves up before going to the drawing room. Mr Carne held an ice-filled cloth to his cheek, the marquess one to his nose. They rose as soon as she entered the room.

"Please sit, gentleman. All is going as it should and there is no need for any alarm."

She decided not to mention that the babe's birth seemed imminent. It was possible that Mrs Harris might prove to be mistaken, although she hoped for all their sakes that she would not be. She sat down, set on turning the marquess's thoughts in another direction.

"How is your man of business, my lord?"

"I see I am still in disgrace," he said, lowering the cloth from his nose. "I seem to remember that we agreed you call me Alexander."

"Yes, but I have had little opportunity to do so, and am as yet unused to it."

"Mr Winters is much better, although he will rest a

few days longer at Eagleton Priory before returning to London."

"I am pleased to hear it. I had a very pleasant stay there. Your housekeeper was very kind."

She carried on in the same vein for some minutes, and if the worry did not completely leave his eyes, his posture relaxed somewhat. When her tongue began to run dry, Mr Carne began to question him about the history of the priory, its acreage, and what were the estate's main sources of income. They passed almost an hour in this way, but then Alexander's fingers began to drum against the arm of his chair. His head snapped round as the door opened, and Timothy came into the room. They rose to their feet in unison.

"Well?" Alexander snapped.

A broad smile crossed the footman's face. "You have a son, my lord, and her ladyship is doing well."

"Thank God!" he said, striding from the room.

Without quite realising what she did, Emma went to Oliver, her hand outstretched. He took it, and they stood thus for perhaps a minute, simply smiling at each other.

"It is a happy day," Emma finally murmured.

"Then I am forgiven?" he asked softly.

She reached up to his face, her fingers gently tracing the swelling beneath his eye. "Yes, you are forgiven, you ridiculous man."

He took her hand in his and held it against his chest. "It is nothing."

She was drowning in the deep waters of his eyes, and her breath hitched as they came ever closer. Her own fluttered shut as he brushed a gossamer kiss across her lips. She sighed and waited for another. It did not come. Her hand was released, and she opened her eyes to see him step away from her, frowning.

"Forgive me, Miss Wynn. I should not have taken such a liberty."

It was only then she remembered all the reasons she could not become involved with this man.

"And I should not have allowed it," she said. "We shall put it down to the exhilaration of the moment and forget all about it."

# CHAPTER 16

It was early, not yet nine o'clock, but Oliver had already taken Beau for a walk and rowed until his shoulders burned. He now sat at his desk, attempting but failing to apply himself to the account book his steward had left there. He pushed it away and leant back in his chair, closing his eyes.

Put it all behind them and forget all about it? Could she do so that easily? It was a question Oliver had asked himself every day for the past week, and he was no closer to the answer. After checking that Lady Eagleton was comfortable and the baby healthy, he had toasted the new arrival and taken his leave. He had returned to Pengelly Manor on two occasions since, ostensibly to check Lady Eagleton had suffered no adverse effects after the birth. As Mrs Harris visited her every day, and he had assured Eagleton that he might send for him if he was at all concerned, his excuse was flimsy at best.

The truth was, he could not forget. Emma's scent, her pleasing, upturned face, and the sweet, fleeting taste of her lips were branded into his consciousness and refused to be dislodged. Almost equally enchanting was the image of her as a furious virago dressing both him and Eagleton down. He was in love with her, and he wanted some confirmation that she felt the same way, or if not that, at least a sign that she was not indifferent to him.

He had not intended to declare himself; until he cleared his name he was in no position to. A look would have done, but he had not seen her on either occasion. He could only conclude that she was avoiding him. That brought him to his second question. Why?

Several answers occurred to him. It might be merely because she was embarrassed, but he did not think so. She was no schoolroom miss. Had his brother given her such a disgust of him that she wanted nothing to do with the Carne family? He would not believe her so unjust. She was far too sensible. Was she afraid that he might discover that she had once been in an asylum and feel less of her because of it? He sighed. That theory didn't hold water either. *I trust Mr Carne to do what is right.* She trusted him, and the remembrance of those words touched him as deeply as his first hearing them had. But then why must she avoid him? He frowned as something she had once said came back to him.

*My uncle thinks I am dead. He must continue to think so until I choose to confront him. If he learns otherwise and should discover my whereabouts, I, and perhaps my brother will be in danger.*

A shaft of daylight broke through the fog in his mind. He had told Emma nothing of his reasons for returning to England and then living the life of a hermit, and she had not asked. She must have wondered, however. If she thought any hint of scandal attached to him, she must keep her distance. Somehow her uncle had persuaded two doctors to commit her to an asylum, and it would be held against her. If she were to have any chance of re-establishing herself, of perhaps being granted custody of her brother, she must prove that her incarceration had been unlawful and unnecessary. She must also show that she had led a blameless life this past year, and if any whisper of scandal attached to her through him, it could ruin her chances.

Hurley came into the room, carrying a breakfast tray. Oliver felt a spurt of irritation at the interruption. He needed to think.

"Just leave me some coffee, Hurley. I am not hungry."

Beau, sensing his master's mood, left his place by the fire and rushed up to the butler, baring his teeth and nipping at his ankles.

"Desist!" Oliver snapped. "Or back to the stables you will go."

The dog immediately retreated.

"He's not fit to be in the house," the butler muttered.

"He senses your dislike," Oliver said. "And he is repaying it in kind. If you change your attitude, so might he."

Hurley put down the tray and brought the coffee to the desk, laying a letter beside it.

"Thank you," Oliver said absently.

As the butler retreated, he glanced at it. His eyebrows rose.

"That was quick work," he murmured, tearing it open.

*Half-Moon St, 6th November, 1817*

*Oliver,*

*Having arrived in London only two days since, I have not as yet managed to make Mrs Thruxton's acquaintance. I have, however, discovered her direction and shall not delay in manufacturing a way to do so.*

*I do not know if the fate of the hope of this country has yet reached you, but it is with a heavy heart I report that in the early hours of this morning, Princess Charlotte died after giving birth to a stillborn son some hours previously. It feels a little unseemly to be plotting at such a time, yet I fear our situation becomes ever more precarious. I doubt not that this double tragedy will persuade many to return to Town in order to attend the funeral. Whilst it is only right and proper that they should pay their respects to so virtuous and fair a lady, I am sure you will understand that we must move with some urgency.*

*I ask that as soon as you receive this letter, you make haste to Town. I shall arrange rooms for you at Grillon's Hotel on Albemarle Street. This is not meant as a slight. I cannot feel you would be comfortable under the same roof as Father and me, and to be frank, I do not blame you.*

*Richmond*

Oliver's lips twisted at his brother's description of the princess. He was reminded that Richmond was fiercely patriotic and with those he considered his own kind, gentlemanly. It was a pity he had no respect for those he considered beneath him. He did see the need for urgency, however. His brother's feelings aside, his own now made it a matter of the first importance that he clear his name. He would go, but not before he had seen Miss Wynn.

He went to his room, ordered Steen to pack his bags, and allowed Beau to follow him to the stables, knowing a twinge of guilt when he ordered Jem to take care of the dog once more.

"I shall be leaving today, perhaps for some weeks, and I fear that if I leave him to Hurley, he might be tempted to poison him," he said dryly.

Jem grinned. "Tempted he might be, but he'd never do it."

He rode away, Beau's accusatory barks following him. When he came to the turning that led to the orchard, he paused. Miss Wynn's ankle had had ample time to recover and there was every chance she would be taking her morning walk. Of course, she might have gone in any number of directions, but his instincts told him otherwise. He turned onto the track. It seemed fitting that they should meet in the woods, for it was there they had first exchanged confidences. He fully intended to exchange a few more. He would not leave with matters between them so uncertain.

He tied his horse to a tree in the orchard and opened the door to the woods. It had changed since his last visit. The leaves had a yellower hue, casting a warm, buttery light across the glades. Those beneath his feet were laced with a frosting of silver and crackled crisply as he walked. He followed the line of the stream until he came to a small wooden bridge, his eyes scanning the opposite bank. As he crossed it, he startled a pheasant. With a rustle of feathers, it took to the air. And then he saw her, sitting on a fallen log. She rose as he approached, her eyes widening, and he had his answer. In the few seconds it took her to regroup, he saw love and longing in their soft, brown depths.

"Mr Carne."

"Don't," he said softly, closing the few feet remaining between them. His hand cupped her cold cheek. "Don't pretend there is nothing between us, Emma." He bent his head and his lips whispered against hers. "I have respected you almost since the moment we met, but respect turned to enchantment when we met here in the woods. I have been haunted by you ever since. With every meeting, my feelings have grown and like a clinging vine have wound themselves around my heart and mind, and now they will not be denied. I love you, Emma, and the time for secrets is over."

Her lips opened on a protest, but he stopped it with another kiss, this one long, tender, and sweet. She melted against him, and he fought the desire to pull her closer, remembering her injured wrist. When he finally raised his head, his blood was thumping in his ears and his heart beating an erratic tattoo.

"Oliver," she murmured, "we can't… I can't… there are reasons…"

"I know," he said gently, sitting on the log and pulling her down beside him. "You are afraid that any association with me might reflect badly on you, and you are right."

She nodded. "Were you accused of doing something in India? Perhaps to a patient?"

He took her hand. "Yes. Something quite heinous. I was accused of forcing myself on a woman and getting her with child. But it was not true."

She squeezed his fingers. "You need not tell me that. I am fully aware that something need only appear to be true for it to be believed, however outrageous the claim or uncharacteristic the behaviour."

His fingers briefly touched the buttons of her glove. "You would, of course. Are both wrists marked?"

A touch of colour alleviated the pallor of her cheeks. "I thought you might have understood the significance of my scars. Only one wrist bears them. I was shackled when I tried to escape the asylum."

His chest tightened. "How, then, did you gain your freedom?"

Her expression turned bleak, and putting his arm about her waist, he pulled her against him, the scent of roses filling his nostrils as she laid her head on his shoulder. She began to speak in a low, expressionless voice.

"It was late, and I was woken by shouting and running feet. I could smell smoke and realised there must be a fire. When it began to seep under the door, I realised I had been forgotten. I began to pull frantically against the shackle, hoping that I might somehow pull my hand through it or perhaps detach it from the wall. Just when I was about to give up all hope, my door burst open. Doctor Ogilvy, one of the two doctors who owned the asylum, had not realised that Mrs Kirk, the warden who oversaw my floor, had punished me in such a way. When he saw I was not with the other patients, he questioned her and came back for me. He released me and told me to put on my boots.

"There was a stairway at each end of the landing,

but they were, by then, both ablaze. We were trapped. Doctor Ogilvy was overcome by the smoke and collapsed. I tried to rouse him but could not. I crawled to Mrs Kirk's room. I knew there was a tree outside her window; I had observed it whilst taking the weekly half hour of exercise we were allowed in the garden. I grabbed a dress and cloak from her wardrobe, opened the window, and threw them out. I somehow managed to climb down, grabbed the clothes, and fled."

"My poor, brave girl," Oliver murmured, stroking her hair. "And then?"

There was a pause, and Emma sat up. "I am afraid I did not just steal Mrs Kirk's clothes. In the pocket of the cloak, there was a purse. The asylum was situated a few miles from York. I walked there and purchased a ticket on the London stage. My first thought was to reach my brother, who was at Harrow, but I only had enough coins to take me as far as Grantham. It is there I met Lady Westcliffe. She heard me begging the landlord to give me work as a maid. It was the only way I could think of earning enough money to take me the rest of the way."

Oliver was appalled but drawing on the detachment he had learnt to adopt when treating his patients, managed to keep his tone calm. "You mentioned her once before. I assume she is the lady who has taken care of you, and who will help you going forward?"

"Yes," Emma confirmed. "She and her husband. Although Mrs Kirk's clothes were plain, as I was sent to a seminary for young ladies, my speech was not, and that drew her attention. She tended to my wrist and promised to help me if I told her why I was in my current predicament. She showed me that I could offer my brother no help until I reached my majority and then only if I could prove that I had been wrong-fully incarcerated. She made me see that until then, it would be safer if both my brother and uncle thought me dead."

Oliver frowned. He could not remember ever meeting a woman as level-headed and sensible as Emma. Rather than falling into hysterics, she had shown great presence of mind to escape the asylum, and again when she had concealed herself from his relatives, never mind that she had just related to him her painful history in the calmest of ways.

"Did your uncle bribe this Doctor Ogilvy and his colleague?"

She shook her head. "I don't think so. I had never met my uncle; he left England to make his fortune abroad before I was born. He fell in love with India and eventually became the owner of a tea plantation. He wrote regularly to my father, however, and he would read us his letters. I felt as if I knew him and was fond of the image of him I had created. When my uncle arrived, I greeted him with pleasure. My father had wished him to help us until we recovered from his loss, and I attained my majority. On that date, I would become my brother's guardian."

She stood, walked a few steps away, and then returned, looking down at him. "He seemed very personable and treated us well, but he was not quite as I had imagined. He overindulged my younger brother, granted his every wish, and told him he need not return to school until he was ready. At first, I allowed it. I thought it was his way of being kind, but after a while, I began to protest that my father would not have approved. He would merely smile and say I was being too hard on my brother, but the smile did not always reach his eyes. I knew he was annoyed. And then he began to belittle me in small ways in front of Adrian, although he passed it off as a joke."

"In effect, he was trying to drive a wedge between you," Oliver said.

She sat down, turning to him. "You understand. Yes, I think that was his intention, and he began to succeed. What thirteen-year-old boy would not be influenced by a male relative who granted his every wish? Eventually, I lost my temper, and I told him that I did not believe the uncle whose letters I had read, would behave in such a way." Her hand crept to her face in the nervous gesture he had seen once before. "I had several times had the strangest notion that he might not be our uncle. It seems incredible, I know. There is a portrait of him and my father when they were eighteen, and I would frequently find myself before it. There is some likeness between them, but no more than might be coincidence, and the more I studied it, the more I became convinced that he was not my uncle but an imposter." She turned away, her eyes lowering. "It sounds mad even to my ears."

Oliver reached out a hand and gently placed a finger under her chin, encouraging her to look at him. "I do not know Mr Emmit, but I know you, Emma. Your instincts are good. Did they not alert you to my brother's insincerity? Did they not lead you to trust in Lady Westcliffe?"

"Yes," she murmured, "and they have led me to put my faith in you, Oliver."

He wanted nothing more than to take her in his arms, but there was something else he very much wished to know.

"If your uncle did not bribe Doctor Ogilvy, how did he persuade him that you were unhinged?"

"Although I did not know it, he had written to Doctor Ogilvy about what he called my hysterical delusions. He invited him to visit us, saying that he was an acquaintance he had met at the York races. He was a perfectly pleasant man, and I treated him with respect. But at dinner that evening, I began to feel ill. I was overcome by a hot flush, my eyes blurred, and I began to feel anxious. I heard my uncle address me, but his voice was distorted and seemed to come from far away. When I looked at him, I saw a monster. His face seemed maniacal and his eyes red flames. I staggered to my feet, and when his hand reached for me, his fingernails appeared to be talons. I know not what I said, but I wrenched myself away and ran towards the door. I must have fainted, and when I came to, I was being encouraged to drink something. I lost consciousness again. The next thing I remember is waking up in a strange room with bars on the windows."

Oliver's stomach clenched. "What had you drunk that evening?"

"I was not inebriated," she said defensively.

He smiled gently. "I never imagined that you might have been."

"I had only one glass of wine."

"And was that your habit?" Oliver asked.

"No, I prefer lemonade, but my uncle said it would not do to appear so unsophisticated in company."

"And how did it taste?" he probed.

She shrugged. "I am no judge, but it had a spicy tinge. Lady Westcliffe believes that I may have been drugged."

Oliver also believed it. He could think of several plants in India with hallucinatory properties that might cause such an effect. A vision of purple and blue flowers climbing around a verandah came into his mind. The hairs on the back of his neck stirred. He felt sure the recollection was important and tried but failed to remember where he had seen it.

"Oliver? Do you doubt me?"

"Never!" He took her face in his hands and kissed her once more. "Emma, how can you think it?"

"I sometimes doubt myself," she murmured.

He saw it in her eyes, and he could not bear it. "Don't," he muttered fiercely. "You are as sane as I, and I will do everything in my power to help you prove it, but first I must clear my name."

A soft gasp escaped her. "Can you do it?"

"I must do it. My brother has devised a plan that I think may succeed. He awaits me in London. I leave today."

She pressed a light kiss to his cheek. "I am glad for you. It is a terrible thing to be estranged from your family. I miss my brother every day. I do not know what drove you away, but perhaps your time with him might help heal the rift."

He smiled wryly. "It is complicated. Are you sure you wish it? For if I am successful, I intend to ask you to marry me. Do you really want Richmond as a brother? He was not kind to you."

Her eyes shone with happiness. "If I am successful, I will marry you regardless of the outcome of your endeavour. As for Viscount Crosby, he was perfectly gentlemanly towards me apart from on that one occasion, and you must remember that I had severely wounded his pride."

"That does not excuse him," he said, his voice hard.

"Perhaps not, but I forgave him long ago."

He embraced her. "You are too good, too kind, and I am judgemental and stubborn. Are you sure you wish to tie yourself to such a man?"

"Oliver!" she squeaked.

He let her go. "I am sorry, Emma! I should not have held you so tightly. Did I hurt you?"

"No," she gasped. "It is just that I could not breathe."

# CHAPTER 17

E mma laughed softly, her heart soaring. "Oliver, have you any idea how wonderful it is to be able to share my burdens with someone who truly cares for me?"

"Does not Lady Westcliffe care for you?" he said, smiling.

"Oh, yes, in her way. But it is not at all the same. She cares for all her ladies, and I will forever be in her debt. However, her philanthropy is motivated by a desire to right the wrongs of an unequal society that allows women to be used as men see fit and children to be abandoned and left to scavenge in the street like rats. You do not offer me charity or pity but have come to love me despite my circumstances, and when you have your own battles to face and conquer." She raised her hand and traced her fingers over his face from his forehead to his chin. "And I love you. Not because you are an object of pity, but because you are a gentleman, because your instinct is to protect, and because however much you try to convince the world otherwise, you care about those around you. If you are stubborn, I am glad of it, for a stubborn love will not be dislodged by the first ill wind that blows; it will not believe malicious gossip but listen to the heart rather than the head."

He smiled ruefully, capturing her hand and kissing it. "You make my stubbornness a virtue, Emma."

She laughed. "I may have become a little carried away. It is just that here, in this moment, I feel so happy. I can, of course, see that your stubbornness might hinder you in other areas of your life. You mentioned that you are judgemental; were you refer-ring to your relationship with your family?"

He sighed. "As I said, our relationship is compli-cated, and I do not wish to go into it now. If I restore my honour, I will ask you to be my wife, and I will explain everything."

"But—"

He put a finger to her lips. "Shh. It is not always better to think with your heart. I am honoured that you have said that if you succeed in re-establishing yourself you will marry me regardless of how I fare, but you must see that unless I restore my honour, I cannot offer for you. You would forever be tainted by the association."

The bubble of happiness inside Emma began to deflate. "And if you succeed and I do not? Would you cast me off?"

He took her head in his hands and rested his fore-head against hers. "Of course I would not. But the cases are not the same. I am not the only person you love. You have your brother to consider. He too would be tainted by the association."

Emma's heart plummeted. He was right.

Oliver drew back, his eyes offering an apology. "I should not have spoken of my feelings so freely or raised your hopes when I cannot be certain that I can fulfil them, but you looked at me in such a way, I lost my head." He brushed tendrils of hair from her cheek. "Do not look so downcast, love. Just as you wished to turn one of my flaws into a virtue, so my brother will use his less desirable traits to advantage. He has a sharp tongue and sharper wits. I suspect intrigue comes as naturally to him as breathing, and as his interests will be served as much as mine if our venture succeeds, I have every confidence that it will."

"Yes, of course," she said, summoning a smile. "My wounding his pride would be nothing compared to how it would be crushed if his name was besmirched."

"That is motivation enough for him to do his utmost," Oliver agreed. "But it is not his most powerful incentive."

Emma's head tipped to one side, her glance questioning. "It is not?"

"I may have done my brother an injustice when I told you he loved himself so much he had precious little to spare for anyone else." A rueful grin twitched his lips. "And it appears we have more in common than I could have guessed. He too is in love with a woman he assures me is remarkable, and as she has apparently inspired him to attempt to eradicate the worst of his bad habits, I must believe him."

Emma's heart lightened. "I am happy for him, and I too begin to believe he will succeed. Love is a powerful motivating force, is it not?"

Oliver rose to his feet, bringing her with him. She shivered as he took one last, lingering kiss. "So much so that I will do whatever it takes to prove myself worthy of you. Now, although I would like to linger here with you, I must tear myself away. The sooner this business is over, the better. Promise to write to me if your situation changes. A letter sent to Grillon's Hotel in Albemarle Street should find me."

He did not wait for her assurance, but turned, retracing his steps across the bridge, his pace swift. Emma watched him until he disappeared from view, a blend of love, worry, and hope making her heart ache.

"Good luck," she murmured.

She was late back and hoped to find the breakfast parlour empty, wishing to revisit every touch given and received, every tender word spoken. Her wish was not destined to be granted, however. The marquess remained seated at the head of the table, jiggling Lady Francesca on his lap whilst attempting to keep his breakfast from her prying fingers. He glanced up, his acute gaze narrowing as he observed her. The nonsensical notion that he could read her thoughts crossed her mind.

She breathed a sigh of relief as his attention was reclaimed by his daughter. The child had plunged her hand into the pile of congealing scrambled egg on his plate and brought it to her mouth. This method of eating proved hopelessly inefficient, as when Lady Francesca dropped her hand, her cheeks were liberally smeared with it. Alexander pushed his plate away and grabbed a napkin, wiping the child's hand and face before she could transfer the egg to his immaculate blue coat.

"Good morning, Emma," he said, a wry smile touching his lips. "My daughter appears to be as greedy as my son. When I offered to take her for a short while, I was led to believe that she had already enjoyed her morning repast."

Emma seated herself at the table. "She is an inquisitive child. It is only natural that she should wish to sample whatever you are eating." She smiled. "Might I ask why you thought it necessary to bring her down to breakfast?"

"My son expressed the wish to be fed several times last night, and as Nell insists she will not have a wet nurse, both she and Mrs Farley were repeatedly disturbed. The babe is now asleep, and I thought him more likely to remain in that state of milk-drunk oblivion if I removed Francesca from his vicinity, thereby allowing both my wife and the nursemaid a chance to catch up on their sleep."

"It was very thoughtful of you."

"It was short-sighted, misguided, and idiotic of me," he said. "I should never have allowed Nell to persuade me that she no longer needed the monthly nurse as she had both Maria and Mrs Harris to look after her." He rose to his feet as Timothy came into the room carrying Emma's toast and tea. He waited only for the footman to arrange everything to her liking before he passed his daughter to him.

"Lady Francesca would like you to take her for a walk, Timothy."

"Of course, sir," the footman said, his voice wooden, but his lips twitching. He cleared his throat. "If I might be so bold as to mention it, my lord, I believe you have some egg in your hair." He raised his hand to his own blond locks. "About here."

Emma stifled a laugh as Francesca clapped her hands as if this was an achievement deserving of applause.

"I am going for a ride," Alexander said carefully. "Perhaps I can persuade Carne to come sailing."

"You won't," Emma said, feeling her cheeks warm as the marquess observed her.

"And how do you know that?"

"I saw him whilst walking in the woods."

He raised an eyebrow. "Clandestine meetings, Emma?"

"We met by chance, and he mentioned that he was going to London immediately."

A spark of interest lit the marquess's eyes. "That must have been an interesting exchange."

"Yes," she said. "It was."

He grinned. "No wonder you looked so dreamy when you entered the room. Has he ridden ventre à terre to Town to acquire a marriage licence?"

"No," she said quietly. "He has gone to prove a malicious rumour that is circulating about him a lie."

"So, he is finally facing his demons," Alexander said softly. "My compliments, Emma. Let us hope he succeeds so that I can wish you both happy." He laughed as her blush deepened. "I knew he was in love with you, of course, and hoped that might give him the impetus to set his house in order."

Her eyes widened. "He told you?"

Alexander smiled wryly. "In a way. Nell and I had our suspicions that there was something between you, but I knew for certain when he knocked me to the ground." He frowned. "Tell me, does Carne's situation complicate yours?"

She nodded. "Yes, I am afraid it does. Oliver knows how important it is that no hint of scandal attaches to me, and he will not ask me to marry him if he cannot repudiate the rumours."

He sighed. "And he is stubborn enough to stand by that assertion. Give me five minutes to clean myself up and then meet me in my study; we should not be interrupted there. I have thus far not pressed either of you for information, but the time has come for me to be enlightened. It may be that I can help in some way."

An instinctive refusal rose to her lips, but she did not utter it. Everything had changed; Alexander was no longer consumed with worry for Nell, and her and Oliver's fate had become inextricably entwined. "Very well."

After she had finished her long recital, Alexander did not speak for some minutes but sat staring down at his hands, his brow deeply furrowed.

"Good God!" he finally said. "It is a tangled web, indeed."

"I know," Emma murmured. "Can you help?"

He ran a hand through his hair. "Perhaps, perhaps not. I do not know what measures Lord and Lady Westcliffe have taken on your behalf, and it would be dangerous to meddle when I am in such ignorance. When do you reach your majority, Emma?"

"Next week," she said.

"What do you intend to do?"

"Lady Westcliffe did not wish to discuss the entirety of her plan until her husband had finished his enquiries. I know that she has two well-respected doctors in mind to testify to my sanity and intends to produce some character witnesses to show that my behaviour this past year has been above reproach."

A cynical smile touched his lips. "I will, of course, offer to be one of them, something I am sure Lady Westcliffe is depending on." A glint of amusement flashed in his eyes. He leant towards her and lowered his voice. "I will not, of course, mention the incident with the sword."

"Thank you," she murmured. "Lord Westcliffe is hoping to discover some information to substantiate my theory that Mr Emmit is not my uncle."

"That," Alexander said, "might be more difficult to prove. I am only slightly acquainted with Lord Westcliffe, but he is both well-connected and diligent in his duties to parliament. Having such a respectable gentleman champion your cause must increase your chance of success."

"And Oliver?" she said. "Can you aid him?"

He sighed. "I would like to; he is one of the few people I consider a friend, and I owe him a great deal. But as he is already on his way to London, and I do not feel inclined to leave Nell quite so soon, I fear we must trust his brother to bring the thing off."

Emma shifted in her chair. "Do you know Viscount Crosby?"

"He is a few years younger than I, but yes, I am acquainted with him. He has always appeared a little high in the instep and rather aloof, but who am I to criticise him for that? I can at least give him credit for never attempting to toad eat me."

"Do you think Oliver can trust him? Do you think the viscount capable of change?"

"If he is truly in love with Lady Amabel Kingston, certainly." Alexander's eyes grew distant, and a flicker of a smile touched his lips. "Before I met Nell, I was a selfish creature, haunted by demons and self-doubt. That all changed when I fell in love with her, and I would have done anything to earn her love."

Emma rose to her feet. "Thank you, Alexander, for everything."

Manton came into the room. "The post was late today, my lord. It brought the newspaper and a letter for your grandmother. I asked one of the maids to take it up as Timothy is otherwise engaged."

"And yet you have two others in your hand," Alexander said.

"Yes, my lord. One is for Miss Wynn and was delivered by a rather unprepossessing gentleman, and the other is for you. A groom from Carne Castle has just brought it."

"Oh?" Alexander said. "Does he expect a reply?"

"No, my lord." The butler glanced at Emma. "However, the person who brought your letter, ma'am, is taking some refreshment whilst he awaits your answer." He cleared his throat, his eyes returning to the marquess. "And he had the audacity to request a word with you, my lord."

Emma took her letter and sank back into the chair, her hands trembling. It must be from Lady Westcliffe, and she surmised that she had entrusted Finn to deliver it.

*Dear Emma,*

*I have reason to believe Mr E— will be in London on business the week after next. As he has little influence or acquaintance in Town, this would be the perfect opportunity for us to move against him. There are several things we must do before that happens, however, and so I ask that you come as soon as possible. Finn will escort you as before.*

*Lady W*

Emma's heart began to race, and her mouth dried. The moment she had been waiting for was almost upon her.

"Manton, bring Miss Wynn a glass of wine."

Alexander's imperious tone brought Emma's head up. "No, I do not want one, a glass of water would be most welcome, however."

"Very well, ma'am."

As the butler left the room, Alexander came to her and offered his missive. "It appears your letter was as brief as mine. Shall we save time and exchange them?"

She took his and offered up hers.

*Eagleton,*

*I am finally taking the advice you gave me and confronting my past. I am sure you can guess what has motivated me to do so. You asked me to watch over Lady Eagleton whilst you were away, and now I ask you to return the favour. Emma is not my wife, but I hope very much that she soon will be. If anything should happen whilst I am away regarding her future, I would ask that you offer her your assistance in any way you can.*

*Carne*

"Well," Emma said, a smile curving her lips. "That was brief."

"But to the point," Alexander said. "As was Lady Westcliffe's missive. It seems I will be going to Town, after all."

"But Nell and the baby—"

"Are both thriving," Alexander interrupted. "It

was inclination not necessity that made me reluctant to go, but I am quite surplus to requirements, and as this morning proved, I am no hand at playing nursemaid for any length of time. Angelica can keep Nell company, and Timothy is quite capable of watching over them all."

"There really is no need," Emma assured him. "Finn is perfectly able to protect me. When you see him, you will understand."

"A big, burly fellow, I presume, judging by Manton's description."

"Yes, he is," Emma confirmed.

"That's all well and good, but if you think he can ensure your comfort at the posting inns as well as I, you are much mistaken. Besides, you read Carne's letter. He has called in a favour, and as a gentleman, I am honour bound to repay it."

A chuckle came from the doorway.

"How long have you been there?" Alexander asked.

Angelica smiled. "Long enough. Emma, you need not feel at all guilty about my grandson accompanying you. Nell and Edward need only each other for the next few weeks, and the truth is, Alexander has very little to do. It will do him good to go."

"Thank you, Grandmother," he said dryly. "For emphasising my complete irrelevance."

She went to him and patted his cheek. "I am delighted that you feel you can go. I came to tell you I received a letter from Bernardo this morning."

"My Italian cousin," he elucidated for Emma's benefit. "Who fell in love with a girl who proved to be his half-sister."

Emma's hand flew to her mouth.

"Yes, it was a terrible shock for both Bernardo and Sofia," Angelica said. "The poor girl retreated to the nunnery where she had attended school and would see no one apart from Count Fringuello, the gentleman who put a stop to their elopement."

Emma wrinkled her brow thoughtfully. "Wasn't it one of his ships that brought Nell back to England?"

"Yes," Alexander said, his voice hardening.

Angelica slipped her arm through his. "You know he was only doing what Nell asked him to, Alexander. You like the count, really, and so you should be pleased by Bernardo's news. Sofia and the count have married."

His eyebrow flew up. "And how has Bernardo taken the news?"

"Philosophically. Now, when are you two leaving?"

"We will go tomorrow," Alexander said decisively. "If you will excuse me, Emma, I will go and meet Finn and leave Angelica to pry from you the exact nature of Carne's interest."

"I never pry," she said, smiling at Emma. "I merely enquire. Come, sit with me, my dear."

# CHAPTER 18

After Oliver had dashed his note off to Eagleton, he went to the library shelves. Several of them were occupied by a series of black notebooks in which he had recorded his experiences in India. The image of the blue and purple flowers creeping up a verandah still plagued him. They had been of the *Ipomoea* family and had been referred to as moonflowers. Their seeds were known to have hallucinatory properties if taken in large enough quantities. Emma's suggestion that she had been drugged had prompted the memory. He doubted it could have any relevance to her case, but it irritated him that he could not place where he had seen them. He was fairly certain it had not been in Calcutta.

"Your bags have been taken to the carriage, sir."

He looked over his shoulder and saw Hurley standing in the doorway.

"Hurley, do you remember the trip we took up into the hills?"

"I try not to, sir," the butler said, shuddering.

Oliver chuckled. "You did not have to accompany me to India. I believe I gave you a choice."

Hurley snorted. "And how would you have fared if I hadn't? You'd been raised as a gentleman and had no idea of how to look after yourself. You always had your head in a book, and would have forgotten to wash, eat, or change your clothes if I hadn't reminded you."

"I was never that bad," Oliver protested. "And neither was our trip into the hills. I will allow the villages were rather crude, but you must allow the scenery was beautiful."

"I was too busy swatting the insects to notice. The only decent place we stayed was that tea plantation."

"When was that?" Oliver asked.

"I don't remember the precise date, sir, but it was somewhere between March and May of 1814."

As Oliver began to rummage through some of the notebooks, Hurley cleared his throat.

"Are you certain you don't want to take me instead of Steen? Surely he's ready to be put out to grass?"

Oliver pulled a volume from the shelf, crossed to his desk, and retrieved several letters from the drawer. He knew Hurley was a little jealous of the valet, and had occasionally reflected that Steen, who had a quiet dignity Hurley lacked, would have been far more suited to the role of butler. However, he had not chosen Hurley for the role because of his manners, but rather because of his lack of them. He had known that no unwelcome visitors would get by him, and so it had proved until that fateful visit from Eagleton.

"I don't think he'd thank you for saying so, and he has the advantage of knowing London well."

"That I do, sir."

The valet had entered the room unobserved.

"I meant no disrespect, Steen," Hurley muttered.

As Oliver had never seen the valet discomposed, he was not surprised when he merely inclined his head a fraction. He came forwards and took the notebook and letters from Oliver. "Unless you wish to read in the carriage, I shall put these in one of the bags, sir."

"Thank you, Steen," Oliver said with a wry smile. "I wish I could read in a carriage; how much quicker the miles would fly, but it is the one place I cannot."

"It makes him sick," Hurley said. "As anyone who had known Mr Carne for more than five minutes would know."

The valet again inclined his head. "Thank you for the information, Hurley. You may be sure that if Mr Carne is afflicted by travel sickness, I will know just what to do for him."

"There will be no danger of that," Oliver said, "I am a seasoned traveller, after all."

He would come to rue those words over the next few days. It would have been more accurate to say that he *had* been a seasoned traveller; a year confined to his estate had lessened his tolerance for long hours in a carriage. By the time they stopped each evening, he only had enough energy to stretch his legs, eat his dinner, and fall into bed. He marvelled at Steen's resilience. When he mentioned this, the valet merely smiled.

"I travelled all over the country with your uncle, as far as Scotland on one occasion."

As Oliver had no wish to discuss Mr Cedric Carne, he changed the subject.

When they arrived in London, the mood was rather subdued. There was less traffic than he expected, many shops appeared to be closed, and the majority of the pedestrians were dressed in black; even the crossing sweepers wore black armbands. It seemed that Princess Charlotte had been universally popular and was mourned by all.

Grillon's Hotel had an air of quiet elegance and was everything a gentleman of the haut ton could wish for. Steen had reliably informed him that King Louis XVIII had been a former guest of the establishment. Oliver never had been, nor had he any desire to ever be, a member of that elite. He would have preferred to stay somewhere a little more informal and much less conspicuous.

Steen, however, was in his element. Assuming an alarmingly lofty attitude, he insisted Mr Carne be taken to a comfortable salon and provided with a glass of wine whilst he inspected the room and rendered all comfortable. Oliver then received a level of deference that made him acutely uncomfortable.

Within a few minutes, Steen returned bearing a note. He could not quite keep a hint of disapproval from his voice as he said, "Apparently, sir, your booking was cancelled. I believe this letter explains all."

Oliver scanned its few lines.

*Brother, plans have changed. On reflection, I had a notion that Grillon's might not suit you. You are instead to go to 21 Green Street. I feel sure you will find this new arrangement more to your liking. Richmond*

Whether his brother had decided his pocket could not stand the expense or that he would be out of place, he neither knew nor cared. He was both relieved and grateful for his insight. Lodgings would suit him, if not Steen, much better.

Ten minutes later, they drew up in front of a tall, narrow townhouse with a green door and a gleaming, golden knocker. He had no chance to ply it, as he had barely stepped down from the carriage when the door opened to reveal a man of short stature but regal bearing. He bowed as Oliver set his foot on the first of the steps that led up to it.

"Mr Carne, welcome."

His first thought was that perhaps he was a retired butler who rented out rooms, but this notion was dispelled as the darkly suited man stood aside, and two footmen ran down the steps.

"Marcus will show the coachman the way to the mews, and Anthony will see to your bags and show your valet to your room. I've orders to show you straight to the study the moment you arrive. If you'll follow me, sir, I'll show you the way."

A host of queries rose to Oliver's tongue, but as the butler had already turned and was walking away, he had no opportunity to utter them. He followed him into a dimly lit hall and down a corridor to a room towards the back of the house. Opening the door, the butler announced him and stood back to allow him to enter. Oliver sent him a questioning glance, but the man remained mute, although his lips twitched as if he were repressing a smile.

His brow slightly furrowed, Oliver strode into the room. Two gentlemen awaited him. Oliver froze as he observed them. One dark and powerfully built, with serious, grey eyes, the other fair, a little plump, and his blue orbs guileless. Oliver's frown faded, a wide smile swept across his face, and he moved forward his hand outstretched.

"Freddie! Robert! How is this?"

The two men ignored his hand, but each took an arm and began to clap him on the back. He started to laugh. "I am pleased to see you too, but I would appreciate it if you would stop pummelling me before I am black and blue."

They fell back, the darker gentleman going to the sideboard and pouring a glass of wine. "It would serve you right and perhaps act as a reminder not to ignore us in future."

"I say, Robert, that's a bit harsh," the fair gentleman protested.

"No, it's not, Freddie," Oliver said, sobering for an instant. "As usual, Robert is right. I will try to explain later, but for now, could you please inform me what is going on? Why are you both in London? How did you know I would be?"

Robert handed him the wine. "Sit down, Long-shanks, and all will be revealed."

Oliver grinned at his friend's use of his old nick-name. "Very well, Sobersides," he retaliated, dropping into a nearby chair.

"Enough of your impertinence," Robert said, the twinkle in his eyes suggesting the name was no longer quite so appropriate as it had once been. "That is no way to address a viscount."

"That's right," Freddie said. "He's Viscount Kirkby now, and although I don't have a title, I'd be grateful if you didn't refer to me as cherub."

"I won't," Oliver assured him. His grin faded. "I didn't know, Robert."

The viscount lifted an eyebrow. "So, not only have you not replied to our letters this past eighteen months, but neither have you read them."

Oliver winced. "I'm sorry, and about your father too. I was fond of him."

The viscount gave a lopsided smile. "You weren't overly fond of him when he threatened to box your ears for accidentally shooting one of his sheep. Only the fact that you were clearly more upset by the incident than he, saved you."

"By God! I had forgotten that incident," Freddie said. "You swore you'd never pick up a gun again, didn't you?"

Oliver smiled. "I did, and I never have."

"That's just as well," Robert said. "You couldn't hit a barn door at twenty paces. I only wish Freddie would follow your example. He managed to shoot one of my beaters when he came for my shooting party last year."

"It was only a graze," Mr Frederick Ashton protested.

"But we digress," Robert continued, ignoring this interpolation. "In answer to your questions, Oliver, we knew you were coming to Town because your brother informed us of it. That alone would have been enough to ensure our arrival; his suggestion that you might need our support guaranteed that we came post-haste. As I acquired this house with the title, both he and I agreed that it might be better if you stayed here."

Oliver took a sip of his wine, gathering his thoughts.

Richmond had surprised him. Perhaps he really was trying to change. He could certainly not remember him ever doing anything so thoughtful before. "Did he inform you why I needed your support?"

"By Jove, didn't he just?" Freddie answered, his eyes growing round. "We knew it was all a hum, of course."

"That goes without saying," Robert said quietly. "And we will, of course, do everything within our power to help extract you from this quagmire." He sighed. "I cannot help but wonder, however, why we had to hear of this perfidy from Crosby rather than you."

Oliver drained the remainder of his wine. "A mixture of illness and despondency are responsible for that. I have barely left my estate this past year. I didn't want to see or speak to anyone."

"Good Lord! What did you do with yourself?" Freddie asked.

"Read every last book in his library, I expect," Robert said dryly. "What dragged you from this deep hole of self-pity?"

Oliver ran a hand through his hair. "I see you're as insensitive as ever, Robert."

"Isn't he, though," Freddie said with feeling.

"And it appears, Oliver, you are as oversensitive as ever."

He gave a reluctant laugh. "Touché. It is not what, but who, but there will be time enough for that story when I have extracted myself from this mess."

"When *we* have extracted you from this mess," his friend corrected him.

A cynical smile touched Oliver's lips. Perhaps his

brother's actions had not been motived by altruism, after all. "He has parts for you to play, does he?"

"Indeed, he does," Robert confirmed. "Did you really think we would be content to merely hold your hand?"

Freddie looked startled. "Surely that's not necessary? I'm very fond of Oliver, but I can't see what help that would be."

Robert's pained expression set Oliver's shoulders shaking, and a strangled laugh escaped him. "F-Freddie. He meant it m-metaphorically."

He realised the futility of expressing himself in such a way to his childhood friend almost immediately and attempted another tack.

"Did your nurse never hold your hand as a child?"

"Not as far as I remember," he said.

"One can hardly blame her," murmured Robert, setting him off again.

Enlightenment dawned on Mr Frederick Ashton. "Oh, you mean we are not here to merely offer sympathy. I don't know why you didn't say so in the first place. You know I've no brains."

This was uttered with no hint of disgruntlement; Freddie had always been extremely good-natured. It was why, despite the obvious differences between them, Oliver and Robert had always let him tag along and ensured, when at school, that only they had the privilege of teasing him.

"That is not true," Oliver said, brushing a hand over his eyes. "It is just that your mind works in a different way."

Robert smiled. "No doubt it will be given up for scientific study."

"I don't like the sound of that," the much-maligned Freddie said.

"Then it shan't happen," Oliver assured him, his voice shaking. "Now, tell me, has Richmond managed to make the delightful Mrs Thruxton's acquaintance yet?"

"We've all met her," Freddie said. "Viscount Crosby thought it might look a bit conspicuous if he bumped into her alone. Only it wasn't he who bumped into her, but me. Not that I meant to, you understand. I would never be so disrespectful to a lady."

Robert sighed. "I keep telling you, Freddie, that she is no lady. She has done a very bad thing. An evil thing. To Oliver."

"Yes, yes, of course. But it is hard to believe. She is such a pretty little thing."

"Sometimes bad things are presented in deceptive packages."

Freddie did not look convinced. "Yes, well, if you say so."

"Did she not turn on you and berate you for a lumbering clodpole amongst other choice insults?"

"Yes," his friend admitted. "But she apologised very prettily afterwards."

"Only once Crosby had introduced himself, picked up her parcels, dropped several cliched compliments in her ear, and begged her to excuse you."

Freddie looked a little crestfallen. "Oh, do you think she didn't mean it?"

Becoming in equal parts exasperated and confused, Oliver said, "Could someone, preferably you, Robert, explain a little more lucidly how this meeting occurred and precisely what happened?"

"It would be my pleasure. Crosby set on someone to visit the taverns and coffee houses within a three-mile radius of the company offices, claiming he was trying to discover his old friend Mr Thruxton. It transpires the gentleman frequently visits a tavern in Holborn on his way home. He was followed, and once his direction was discovered, this person observed Mrs Thruxton's movements. When she made an excursion to the Pantheon Bazaar, word was sent to Crosby with a description of her and what she was wearing, and we all sallied forth. It was quite busy, and locating her might have taken some time, particularly as she is not overly tall." His tone became sombre. "It was the day after the announcement of Princess Charlotte's death, and many had flocked there to purchase black cloth. Freddie stepped sideways to allow two ladies to pass…"

"And cannoned into Mrs Thruxton. Yes, all becomes clear."

He nodded. "She was accompanied by a plump matron, a Mrs Ripley, who I gather is her mother. She was quite as incensed as her daughter, and I smoothed this rather formidable dame's ruffled feathers whilst Crosby went to work on Mrs Thruxton."

Oliver sighed. "Mrs Ripley brought her daughter to India to find a husband, and once she had achieved her aim, returned home. She disliked the climate. It is a pity. If she had stayed to keep an eye on her daughter, I might not be in this mess."

"It seems she is keeping an eye on her now," Robert said. "So much so, she is living with her."

"No wonder Mr Thruxton visits a tavern on the way home," Oliver murmured. "What do we do now?"

They both turned their heads as a gentle snore answered this query.

Oliver's lips twitched. "I see Freddie still falls asleep anywhere."

Robert observed him with a fond eye. "As you see." His gaze returned to Oliver. "The next part of the plan involves my wife."

"Your wife?"

"Something else you would have known if you had read my letters."

"Who is she?"

"Come and see. She is most anxious to meet you."

# CHAPTER 19

E mma lay on her bed, her eyes closed with weariness. She had that afternoon been interviewed by two eminent doctors, and although they had questioned her gently, they had been very thorough. They had gone away to write their reports but had indicated they would be favourable. They could not entirely rule out the possibility that she had suffered a bout of hysterical mania but could certainly attest to the fact that she seemed completely in her senses now. The behaviour Doctor Ogilvy had witnessed might have been attributed to a number of other things, which certainly included the possibility of being drugged, but might also be explained by an unfortunate reaction to the crab she had eaten that evening at dinner, the onset of a short but virulent fever, or her delicate nerves being temporarily overset by the death of her father and her uncle taking his place.

They had both examined her wrist and proclaimed their dissatisfaction that she should have been restrained in such a manner, suggesting that locking her door would have been more humane and just as effective if the warden had feared she would again attempt to escape. Her injury was so much improved, they opined that the sling was no longer necessary, and she might begin to use her hand although her wrist should remain bandaged.

This would, of course, make dressing much easier, but that had not been Emma's first thought. That had been reserved for Oliver. He would be pleased with her progress, and she would like to show her gratitude by wrapping both her arms tightly about him.

She had confided in Lady Westcliffe, and whilst that lady had professed her admiration for Mr Carne's very proper feeling, she had insisted that he had been correct, and until he had successfully dispelled the rumours, Emma must have no contact with him. For him to be so close and yet inaccessible was frustrating.

She sighed and sat up as Lizzie came into the room.

"Is it time to dress for dinner already?"

"Almost, ma'am. Her ladyship's maid informed me that she doesn't think full mourning for the princess is necessary for a dinner at home, and that the lavender silk and a black ribbon in your hair will be quite appropriate. I thought it best we start now because there are guests coming to dinner. I wouldn't want you to go down looking anything but your best."

"Guests?" Emma said, her heart sinking. She was not at all sure she was up to making polite conversation with strangers.

She went downstairs with a lagging step, pausing in the hall as she heard voices in the drawing room.

Taking a deep breath, she pasted a smile on her face and went in. Lady Westcliffe saw her immediately and brought the lady she was speaking with across the room to meet her. Emma judged her to be in her late twenties, and while she was attractive in her way, she was not nearly as beautiful as Lady Westcliffe, but then, few ladies were. Her best features were her flawless skin, glowing chestnut hair, and clear, turquoise eyes.

When she came forward, her hand held out and a friendly smile on her lips, Emma added charm and grace to the list.

"This is my good friend, Lady Amabel Kingston, my dear." She smiled as that lady took Emma's hand. "Amabel, this is Miss Winifred Emmit."

The thought that Lady Amabel's name sounded vaguely familiar was superseded by the surprise she felt at being thus introduced. A rush of emotion made her hand tremble as she lightly grasped Lady Amabel's fingers.

That lady gave her an understanding smile. "I am so very pleased to meet you, Miss Emmit. I imagine it is strange to hear yourself addressed by your real name after so long."

Winifred's eyes flew to Lady Westcliffe.

"It is time to be yourself again. Amabel knows everything, my dear. She often helps me in a variety of ways. You may put your complete trust in her, I assure you."

"I believe, Miss Emmit, that we have an acquaintance in common. It was you that Viscount Crosby proposed to, was it not?"

Emma's eyes widened as she remembered when

and in what context she had heard Lady Amabel's name.

"Yes," she said, "but he did not really wish to marry me. It was a question of duty, and he was never in love with me as he is with you, nor did he pretend to be."

Lady Amabel took her arm, a slightly mischievous smile tilting her lips. "You interest me greatly. Walk with me a moment, Miss Emmit. You may confide in me with the utmost confidence; there is a possibility, admittedly a remote one at present, that we might one day be sisters by marriage, after all."

When Winifred looked alarmed, she added quickly, "Forgive me, that was uncharacteristically clumsy of me. I was referring to me marrying Viscount Crosby, not you marrying his brother, who I admit, I have a great desire to meet. Tell me all about him."

Winifred was reluctant at first, but Lady Amabel did not ask her anything overly intrusive. By the time they had taken a few turns about the room, she appeared satisfied and led Winifred towards Lord Westcliffe and his companion.

Winifred was a little in awe of the former. He was a rather quiet, serious gentleman with hard, grey eyes, although they always gentled when they fell upon his wife. Other than that, his appearance was rather ordinary. He was of average height, barely a head taller than Lady Westcliffe, and although there was nothing objectionable in his features, they were of the sort that were easily forgotten. She imagined that he could easily make himself inconspicuous if he so wished. If, that is, one did not look into those eyes. When they fell upon on her, she always felt a little unnerved. She forced herself to meet them as he observed her approach.

"Ah, Miss Emmit, allow me to introduce you to Sir Nathaniel Conant."

She regarded the respectable-looking, elderly gentleman and executed a neat curtsy.

"Good evening, sir."

He took her hand and bowed. "It is a pleasure to meet you, Miss Emmit. Allow me to escort you to the dining room."

He treated her with such old-fashioned courtesy that she soon relaxed. He asked her several innocuous questions about her childhood and shook his head sadly when she told him her mother had died when she was sixteen.

"It is always sad to lose a mother, but to do so on the verge of womanhood is especially so, for who is better situated to present you to the world and guide you through its many pitfalls?"

"Indeed," she said. "My mother was a gentle, kind woman with a great deal of common sense."

"Ah," he said, smiling gently. "Then I see you resemble her."

"I hope so," she said softly. "And at least I was old enough to offer my younger brother some comfort. He was but nine when we lost her."

"You two were close?"

"Very," she said, a wan smile touching her lips. "At least, until he turned thirteen."

Sir Nathaniel nodded. "Boys can become a little rebellious at that age. They feel they are no longer a child and often wish to be guided by a man rather than the gentler sex."

"Yes, of course," she said, her chest suddenly tight.

She was grateful that Lady Westcliffe rose at that moment, giving the signal for the ladies to retire to the drawing room.

"Thank you, Miss Emmit, for listening to the ramblings of an old man."

She shook her head slightly. "I enjoyed speaking with you, sir."

The gentlemen did not join them when the tea tray was brought in.

"They have much business to discuss," Lady Westcliffe explained, handing her a cup of tea and a long, thin parcel.

"What is this?" Winifred said.

"You did not think I would forget that today you are one and twenty, surely?"

"I also have something for you," Lady Amabel said, rummaging in her reticule.

A blush infused Winifred's cheeks. "You shouldn't have, either of you."

"Nonsense," Lady Westcliffe said. "It is an occasion to be marked, even if only in a small way."

She unwrapped the parcel to discover a single string of pearls. She blinked rapidly as sudden tears sprang to her eyes.

"And here is mine," Lady Amabel said, handing her a small box.

Inside were matching pearl earrings.

"Thank you, you are too kind."

Lady Amabel passed her a handkerchief. "Dry your eyes, Miss Emmit. Today is a very special day.

Not only have you reached your majority, but you are old enough to be granted guardianship of your brother, who, by the way, is perfectly safe."

Winifred lowered the handkerchief. "How do you know?"

She smiled. "Because he is being tutored by a cousin of mine, Mr Jasper Landers, who takes very good care of him, I assure you."

Winifred blinked slowly. "Tutored?"

"I did not mention it before, Winifred," Lady Westcliffe said. "But Mr Emmit removed Adrian from school some months back."

Winifred gasped.

"Yes, I knew that would worry you, which is why I did not say anything. It was not Mr Emmit's idea, however. The school requested that he be removed. It appeared Adrian was not happy, and he had got into several fights. Before he did so, your uncle asked for recommendations for a tutor."

Lady Amabel took up the explanation. "As I fund a scholarship for intelligent boys who have not the means to attend Harrow, I have some influence with the dean. I asked him to keep me closely informed on Adrian's progress, and so I was able to let him know who I would like him to nominate as tutor."

"I wish I could see him," Winifred said longingly.

"And so you will," Lady Westcliffe said. "Mr Landers and Adrian will follow Mr Emmit to London. They are likely to arrive any day now."

"That," Winifred breathed, "is the best present yet. Again, thank you, both of you."

"But first," Lady Westcliffe said, "we must expect a visit from Mr Emmit."

Winifred paled. "Do I need to see him?"

"Perhaps, but you will not be alone, I assure you, and I think you will find that when he leaves this house, his destination will be Newgate."

"But do we have enough evidence?"

"I believe so."

"But how will he know I am here in Berkeley Square?"

Lady Westcliffe smiled. "He is to stay at The Pulteney. Finn will know when he arrives, and then we can make our arrangements. Do not fret about anything but go to bed. You look worn to a thread."

Winifred did not need to be asked twice. She took her leave of Lady Amabel and retired. Although she was exhausted, she found it difficult to sleep. Soon, the day she had long awaited would arrive. The thought was both exhilarating and frightening. Despite Lady Westcliffe's assurances, she could not help but be anxious. Her mind drifted to Oliver. How she wished he could be by her side when she faced the man who claimed to be her uncle. Her eyes drifted shut. No, perhaps that was not such a good idea, she had not forgotten how he had used the marquess when he had treated her badly. At the time, she had been incensed, but now a small smile curved her lips at the recollection, and she fell into a deep sleep.

# CHAPTER 20

Oliver had been both surprised and delighted to discover that Robert had married Lucinda Ashton, the younger sister of Freddie. She had been fourteen the last time he had seen her, and bidding fair to become a beauty even then. She had gone to him laughing and holding out her hands when Robert had taken him to her that first evening.

"Yes, you may well look surprised, Oliver. You and Robert always saw me as the annoying younger sibling who would tag along uninvited when you came to visit. Only dearest Freddie did not mind. I was always in love with Robert, you see, and fully intended to marry him one day."

"I was a marked man," Robert said, pretending to shudder. "Only I did not realise it."

"You were very fortunate I waited for you," Lucinda said archly. "I had received four offers of marriage and attained the grand old age of three and twenty before you realised what you had been missing."

"In my defence," Robert said, "it is quite difficult to see a girl you have known since a small child in a romantic light."

"What made you wake up?" Oliver asked.

A hint of colour brightened Lucinda's fair cheeks. "I had not yet turned down the fourth offer I had received from a very pleasant gentleman; a girl cannot wait forever, after all, when I saw Robert at Vauxhall. I had perhaps had a little too much punch and decided that if I was forced to marry elsewhere, I must at least have one kiss from Robert. I had the vague thought that if it was terrible, I would be cured of my unrequited love."

Robert grinned. "She dragged me down one of the darkened walks and pretended she wished to whisper something in my ear, but when I leant down, the hussy kissed me!"

"And it wasn't terrible," Lucinda put in smugly.

"Far from it," her husband agreed. "And although I was not suddenly blinded by love, I did begin to see her in a different light."

"And within three weeks he had proposed. I put my suitor out of his misery at once, of course. Even if Robert hadn't fallen in love with me, I could not have married another so soon after that kiss."

Despite the seriousness of the situation which had brought them together, Oliver had enjoyed the last few days. They had spent it reminiscing over old times and catching up on recent ones. Tonight, they had gone over the final part of the plan that would hopefully prove Mrs Thruxton a liar. There only one thing lacking, and that was what kept them from seeking their beds.

Dinner had long since finished, and Lady Lucinda Kirkby seemed completely unperturbed to be sitting at the table long after a lady would usually have withdrawn. Perhaps this was not surprising as all of the guests were known to her, although Viscount Crosby not as much as the others.

Freddie's actions had unwittingly changed Crosby's plans for the better. He had admitted to Oliver that he had intended to woo Mrs Thruxton until he had her trust, and then lure her to a secret rendezvous where she would find Oliver.

"And I'm extremely glad I didn't have to do it. I knew, of course, as soon as I met her, it was entirely achievable; she is a flighty piece, but I discovered I didn't have the stomach for it."

Oliver had looked sceptical. "Becoming straight-laced, Richmond?"

To his surprise, he had not taken offence but laughed. "More than you know, brother. And that was part of it. You are my brother, after all, and I found myself damned angry that she had put both of us in this situation."

Again, Oliver had been surprised, but then a memory had resurfaced. One of Richmond's friends had tried to follow his lead and make Oliver feel small, but his brother had said something cutting to him. Apparently, Richmond had allowed only himself the privilege of denigrating him.

"Anyway," he had continued, "I am glad Kirkby had the sense to bring his wife, and that Ashton insisted on coming. I was dubious about him, but him knocking into Mrs Thruxton made everything so much simpler."

Richmond had refined his plan. Lucinda had paid Mrs Thruxton a visit, ostensibly to satisfy herself that her brother's clumsiness had not caused her any injury. She had then invited Mrs Thruxton to come for tea one afternoon. Fortunately, her mother had been from home and had not needed to be included in the invitation. Unfortunately, Mrs Thruxton had insisted that her husband could not possibly accept the invitation that Lady Kirkby had so kindly extended to him, as apart from Sundays, he was allowed but one day off a year.

Mrs Thruxton was to come the following day.

"So," Robert said, yawning. "It is all set."

"Almost," Richmond allowed.

Lord Eagleton was announced. His arrival in Town had been unexpected, and the knowledge that Emma was only a few minutes away, both comforting and frustrating. It had, however, banished any qualms Oliver had at luring Mrs Thruxton in such an underhand way.

The marquess was dressed with none of his usual elegance. His coat was plain, his neckcloth simply tied, and he wore a hat that had seen better days.

"Did you find Thruxton?" Richmond asked.

Alexander removed his hat and handed it to the hovering butler. "Dispose of it, will you?"

"It would be my pleasure, my lord."

He seated himself at the table. "I would hardly be so late if I had not."

"A glass of port?" Robert offered.

"No," he said, his lips twisting. "I have had quite enough. Mr Thruxton is an unhappy man who has learnt to hold his drink. He let enough slip, however, for me to ascertain that his wife is largely the cause of his despondency. Neither does he enjoy his employment at Leadenhall Street. Apparently, things were much easier in India; his board and lodgings were provided, servants were cheap, and his hours less onerous. Now he finds himself stuck in a dim office for all the daylight hours, mindlessly copying the same document up to five times." He sighed. "One can sympathise, of course. His wages have hardly risen whilst his household expenses have considerably, and as you discovered, his wife likes to shop." He sighed. "He is certainly worried about what she gets up to when he is slaving away at the company offices, but when I suggested he plead illness and discover for himself, he would not hear of it. His financial difficulties make it impossible for him to risk losing his job."

"It would be better if he were here," Richmond said. "But perhaps not imperative. There will be enough witnesses, and surely he would not disbelieve us all."

"It is not enough," Alexander said. "There are a few holes in your plan. However unhappy he might be, Mr Thruxton is unlikely to clear Carne's name if it means muddying his own. For this to work, both he and preferably one of the directors of the company should hear what Carne can drag out of Mrs Thruxton. Otherwise, you can only counter one rumour with another. We are, after all, Carne's friends. Besides, the board of directors need to also absolve him of any wrongdoing for him to be free and clear."

"If there are any rumours," Richmond said thoughtfully. "We only have Sir Laurence Granger's word for that. Neither I nor anyone else has heard any whispers."

"I cannot see why he would lie," Oliver said. "Nor why he would take the trouble to pay a visit to my father's club when, if I am not much mistaken, he is suffering from consumption."

A rather gloomy silence fell on the company.

"Is it possible that we might persuade one of the directors to come here on such short notice, and perhaps bring Mr Thruxton with him?" Lucinda asked.

"I think it might be," Alexander said thoughtfully. "There are twenty-four of them, after all. It would perhaps be better to target one of the most newly appointed. Leave it to me. I have a considerable number of shares in The East India Company. My man of business will know who I should target." He got to his feet. "I am ready for bed. I am afraid I will not be present for the curtain call; I have other things to attend to tomorrow afternoon, but I will send word when all is arranged."

Robert got to his feet. "I think it is time we all retired."

He shook awake Freddie, who had long since fallen asleep, his head resting on his hands. No one had bothered to wake him, for it had been agreed that he would take no part in the morrow's events. Not only might he inadvertently alert Mrs Thruxton that all was not as it seemed, but he did not have the heart for it.

As everyone rose from the table, Richmond said, "Stay a moment, brother. I have a few things I would like to discuss."

Oliver sank back down. "Very well."

Richmond reached for the port and refilled his glass whilst everyone left the room. His hand was a little unsteady as he brought it to his lips. Eventually, he said, "I am glad you have such good friends. I was always a little jealous of the close relationship you had with Kirkby and Ashton." His mouth curled in self-derision. "To be honest, I was jealous about a lot of things."

Oliver frowned. "But why? You were the apple of Father's eye, not I."

Richmond's lips twisted. "I did everything to be his favourite because you were Mother's."

Oliver drew in a sharp breath. "She loved us all."

"Probably, but both Francis and I knew you had a special place in her heart. Her face lit up for you in a way it never did for us. He was philosophical about it, but I could not be."

"I never guessed it," he said softly.

Richmond took another sip of port. "You wouldn't have, of course. You never were very good at reading between the lines, and you were young when she died." He paused, his fingers curling loosely about the stem of his glass, and his eyes fixed on its contents. "The night before we went to school, I overheard Mother and Father having a terrible row. It was then I learnt you were only my half-brother, and that my uncle was your father." He sighed heavily. "I knew she was being sent to Farnham for the foreseeable future, and I didn't say goodbye. Part of me wished to; I loved her. But part of me was so angry that I was glad. And then she died."

Those stark words hung between them for a

moment. Oliver sucked in a deep breath. Richmond had been only thirteen. "And you felt guilty?"

His brother gave a ragged laugh. "I felt any number of things I did not know what to do with. Guilt, certainly, disgust also. My image of her had been shattered."

Oliver understood that, at least.

Richmond drained his glass. "I am not proud of it, but I blamed you. I told myself that if you did not exist, did not look so much like my uncle, then she would not have been sent away, and she would not have died. I told myself I hated you." He smiled wryly. "But the strange thing is, I never did. Resented you, yes, but that was all."

Oliver's eyes grew distant as he tried to reassemble his perception of the past, very much like moving the pieces of a puzzle into the right place when they have been forced into the wrong ones. "I am surprised you didn't taunt me with the truth long before I turned eighteen."

"For a long time, I couldn't bring myself to talk of it. I eventually confided in Francis." He laughed gently. "He was a hey-go-mad creature, wasn't he?"

Oliver smiled. "Yes."

"He promised all sorts of dire retribution if I dared breathe a word of it to you." He picked up the decanter again, but then thought better of it and replaced it on the table. "That is not why I did not taunt you, of course."

Oliver leant forward, placing his elbows on the table. "Then why?"

"What do you see when you look in the mirror, brother?"

He winced. "I try not to, for I see my uncle… or rather my father."

"Ah," Richmond said. "You were as appalled at our mother's defection as I and must have abhorred my uncle's way of life."

Oliver said nothing. His feelings for his true father had become rather confused. He had provided him with the means to live another life, to support a wife, and he was grateful to him for that, at least.

"Your hair and features are very much my uncle," Richmond continued, "but your eyes are all our mother's."

Were they? Oliver had only been eight when he had last seen her, and although he remembered them to be blue, the exact shade eluded him.

"And every time I looked into them, I saw her. Flinging the truth at your head would have been like flinging it at her, and I could not do it."

"Then why did you eventually do so?"

Richmond briefly closed his eyes. "My damnable temper got the better of me. I had just had a blazing row with Father about my allowance. He had informed me that as he had to pay your fees for Oxford, he would have to reduce it. He raked me down thoroughly, saying that you, at least, would not waste your time there. The green-eyed monster once more reared its ugly head, and the rest is history." He looked directly at Oliver. "When I saw the expression in your eyes, I instantly regretted it, and even more so when you threw your future away, or so it seemed to me at the time."

Oliver picked up his glass. "I wanted nothing to do with you, Father, or Mr Cedric Carne. I knew that becoming a surgeon would choke Father, and I rejoiced in the fact. But I was happy in my chosen profession until…"

He trailed off.

Richmond rose to his feet. "Yes, well, hopefully that will all be a thing of the past very soon. When I first heard of the oncoming scandal, I was furious with you, because I had finally thought I was getting somewhere with Amabel. I have since realised it was not your fault, that nothing was ever your fault, and as inadequate as it seems, I apologise. I would like to start afresh whatever happens. I have already lost one brother, as you have, and I don't wish to lose another."

Oliver pushed back his chair and stood. He held out his hand. "Let us shake on it."

# CHAPTER 21

W inifred found herself being shaken gently
awake.

"It's almost ten o'clock, Miss Wy… Emmit."

As Lizzie was to remain as her lady's maid, and
she had to give her some explanation for using a false
name, Winifred had admitted her some way into her
confidence. To say she had been shocked was an
understatement. The maid had also been incensed
and called Mr Emmit a string of impressive expletives.
She had then had to be reminded that the dress she
was meant to be carefully putting away was now but a
rag in her hands.

She smiled at the recollection, stretched, and
yawned. "You may still call me Miss Win, Lizzie. It is
what my maid called me when I was a child, for my
first name is Winifred, only with an i not a y."

"Very well, Miss Win, but get up do. There's a Sir
Nathaniel Conant downstairs as wants to see you."

She frowned. What on earth could that kindly, old

man want with her at this time? Admittedly she had slept in, but most people would be sitting down to breakfast about now, not paying morning calls.

"Very well, Lizzie."

She quickly washed and dressed, and enjoyed a cup of tea and a slice of toast as the maid arranged her hair. Lady Westcliffe's butler was waiting for her at the foot of the stairs.

"They are awaiting you in the library, Miss Emmit."

She entered the room to find Sir Nathaniel, Lord Westcliffe, and Lady Westcliffe in hushed conversation. Sir Nathaniel stood and offered her a bow, his face worryingly grave.

"Good morning, sir," she said. "I am very happy to see you, although I did not expect to have the pleasure quite so soon."

A hint of a smile curved his lips. "Your manners are faultless, Miss Emmit, and the feeling is mutual. However, it appears events have progressed more swiftly than expected."

"Events?" she repeated stupidly.

"We had word, very late last night, that Mr Emmit has arrived in Town, my dear," Lady Westcliffe said. "Lord Eagleton was on his way to an engagement when he came across Finn on his way here to inform us of it. He and Finn will bring him to us this afternoon, but we thought it best that we prepare you for what to expect. We are just going over all the evidence."

"The law courts have shut for two weeks as a mark of respect for the princess," Sir Nathaniel said. "So I have come to you."

Lady Westcliffe smiled. "Perhaps I should have mentioned that Sir Nathaniel is the chief magistrate at Bow Street. He has several times worked with my husband on various cases."

Sir Nathaniel chuckled as Winifred's mouth opened on a gasp. "Yes, I know it is hard to believe that someone of my advanced years could be of use, but I assure you my brain is as sharp as ever."

"I am sure it is… I did not mean…" She gave up trying to explain herself and glanced at Lord Westcliffe. "And you, sir? In what capacity do you work with Sir Nathaniel?"

A brief smile flickered on his lips. "I occasionally carry out work for the Home Office, especially in sensitive and difficult cases. Protecting the rights and liberties of individuals is part of their remit. I have no position, however, and my role is unofficial, you understand."

She was not sure that she did but felt it would be rude to enquire further.

"I am not here to try and convict the man who claims to be Mr Emmit," Sir Nathaniel said. "Only a jury can determine his fate. I merely intend to explain to him what we know and that there is enough evidence to arrest him. He will then be escorted to Newgate until a date for his trial at The Old Bailey can be arranged. There will, of course, be a backlog in the courts, so that might not be until sometime next year."

Winifred paled. "Will I still be able to take charge of my brother in the interim?"

"I do not see why not. You are the natural guardian of nurture, and your father expressed in his will a desire for you to do so. I have read the doctors' reports, and the support statements from Lord and Lady Westcliffe, and The Marquess of Eagleton. I have also had the privilege of meeting you myself, and I am in no doubt of your sanity, Miss Emmit." A satisfied smile crossed his face. "I am also in possession of enough facts to prove that you were not imagining things when you intuited that Mr Emmit was not, in fact, your uncle. I thought, however, that if you were made aware of these facts, your mind might be set at rest. Lady Westcliffe has said that you sometimes doubt yourself, and I wished to remove that doubt. There will be no need for you to do anything but identify the man calling himself Mr Emmit as the person masquerading as your uncle. Then you may go and leave the rest to me."

"Sit down, Winifred," Lady Westcliffe said gently. "My husband will explain what we know thus far."

Lord Westcliffe opened a buff file and began to read. "Mr Alfred Emmit sold his tea estate to the East India Company in August of 1815. He left on an East Indiaman on October 10th, 1815. He disembarked at the West India Docks on the 14th of May 1816. He appeared to be travelling alone as there is no record of any servant travelling with him. We have located all of the other civilian passengers apart from one. We did, of course, ask them for a description of Mr Emmit, but the answers were vague. Unfortunately, he was ill on the journey; he suffered from terrible seasickness, and so they rarely set eyes on him. We have been unable to question the ship's surgeon, who looked after him with the help of another passenger, one Mr

Jeremy Garforth, who appeared to be a friend of your uncle, both of whom might easily identify him. The ship was wrecked off the coast of South Africa on the return journey, and the surgeon perished. We have not been able to locate Mr Jeremy Garforth, whose profession was recorded as private merchant." A wintry smile touched his lips. "We have not been able to discover that anyone by that name traded out of India."

Winifred's brain scrambled to keep up with all this information. "Do you think it is Mr Garforth who pretends to be my uncle?"

"That is our suspicion, although I doubt his name really is Mr Garforth. One often finds that a person who commits fraud has many identities. They are also generally very good at impersonating another's handwriting once they have the chance to study it. As you had the foresight to hide the letters Mr Alfred Emmit wrote to your family when you began to suspect something was amiss, which, by the way, have been found and sent to us, and the man posturing as your uncle – let us call him Mr Garforth from now on – has several times written to Mr Leighton, your father's man of law and your brother's trustee, we have been able to set our best men on to compare the scripts. There are several minor discrepancies, which may or may not be enough on their own to convict him of fraud, but with other evidence, will be found to be damning."

Sir Nathaniel added, "I do not know if you are aware of it, Miss Emmit, but fraud alone is a hangable crime." He steepled his hands and frowned. "To forge a document is a serious enough offence, but to steal someone's identity is unpardonable. It is a danger to the very fabric of our society."

She nodded, her eyes returning to Lord Westcliffe. "What is the other evidence you speak of?"

He smiled grimly. "I believe you are aware that I was awaiting a reply from an acquaintance in India who I asked to instigate some enquiries on my behalf."

"Yes," Winifred said. "Has it finally come?"

"It is better than that. He has come. He sent a letter ahead of him, so I knew to expect his arrival. Fortunately, no ill wind delayed the ship, or we would have had to delay our plans. Mr James Clyde has spent the last few years in India, primarily at the Calcutta Botanical Garden, but he has also made several trips to various parts of the country to collect plants. At my request, he made a trip to your uncle's tea plantation, and brought back something that might interest you."

He went to his desk and withdrew a jar and a small box. "Come, Miss Emmit, and observe their contents."

She first looked in the jar, and then the box. "They seem to be seeds of some sort, and they appear to be identical."

"That is because they are," Lord Westcliffe said with a wolfish grin. "The jar was discovered on a shelf in Mr Garforth's closet. The box was brought back to England by Mr Clyde. They are of the *Ipomoea* family and are known to cause hallucinations."

Winifred's hand flew to her cheek. "He did drug me."

"It would appear so. We believe Mr Garforth visited your uncle. We intend to test their efficacy on him. The two doctors who interviewed you will be present, of course."

"But not," Sir Nathaniel said, "before he has had time to listen to the allegations made against him and respond to them."

"Of course not," Lord Westcliffe agreed. "If there is the remotest chance he will make a confession, and I do think it extremely remote, we do not wish him to be able to accuse us of extracting it by nefarious means."

Winifred shivered. His eyes were granite, and she had the distinct impression that he would like to get a confession from Mr Garforth by any means.

She picked up the box. "Is this what you had been waiting for?"

"Whilst the seeds are valuable in explaining what happened to you, Miss Emmit, they do not help prove that Mr Garforth is an imposter. The other things Mr Clyde brought back from India are more valuable still."

"Other things?" she queried.

"It appears that you are not the only person to suffer from your uncle's murder," Lady Westcliffe said gently.

Winifred's hand again flew to her cheek, and she gasped. "I knew, of course, that he must have been disposed of if my theory was true. It is just that I did not like to dwell upon that fact."

Sir Nathaniel offered her a sympathetic smile. "I completely understand. But you were correct, however; we must assume that in order to take his place, Mr Garforth must have murdered your uncle."

"It could have happened anywhere between

London and Yorkshire," Lord Westcliffe said. "You must resign yourself to the fact that his remains may never be discovered."

Winifred nodded and regarded Lady Westcliffe. She forced words past the lump in her throat. "You were saying that I was not the only one to suffer from my uncle's death?"

"Indeed." She regarded her husband, and that gentleman left the room for a few moments. When he returned, he had a small, dusky-skinned woman with him. It was difficult to determine her age, for although her black hair was streaked with grey, her face remained smooth, marked only by the finest of lines. She was exotically beautiful, with large black eyes that held a wealth of sadness, and ruby lips. She was extremely slender and petite but held herself with a quiet dignity.

Winifred rose to her feet and smiled uncertainly at the woman.

"Miss Emmit," Lord Westcliffe said, "allow me to introduce you to Mrs Sita Emmit, your aunt."

The lady brought the palms of her hands together and offered her a small bow.

Winifred stood frozen for a moment and then went to her and took her hands, tears starting to her eyes. Words tumbled from her mouth. "Oh, how can this be? Why did not my uncle speak of you in his letters? He must have been so proud to have such a beautiful wife! How sorry I am for you, and yet so glad to meet you."

Lord Westcliffe moved away to give them a moment of privacy.

The woman regarded her seriously for a moment and then smiled. "And I am glad to meet you, Miss Winifred. Your uncle often spoke of his family. I was for many years his servant, his housekeeper if you will, but I was also his friend, and just before he sold the tea plantation, he married me. He wished to make sure I was secure. He did not bring me to England immediately in case his brother disapproved."

Winifred's brow wrinkled. "I do not think that he would have, but surely my uncle would not have abandoned you if he had?"

The woman's eyes filled with anguish. "I had not thought so. He left me with my sister in Calcutta, promising to send for me if all was well, or to return if his brother could not accept me. But then I received a letter from Alfred saying that his brother had died, and he could not leave his children. It saddened him that I could not join him, but he had realised that I would never be accepted in England. He promised to send me a few hundred pounds a year. My heart told me it could not be true, and yet I had his letter."

Winifred took her arm, her heart aching for her. "You look a little weary, Aunt Sita, come and sit with me."

She smiled gratefully. "I have only recently arrived and still feel as if the earth is moving beneath my feet. It is a hard journey. I now understand why Alfred was so reluctant to return, but he was determined to see his brother one last time." She squeezed Winifred's hand. "I am so sorry for all you have suffered."

"I will ring for some tea," Lady Westcliffe said.

Lord Westcliffe cleared his throat. "Mrs Emmit

can, of course, identify whether the man claiming to be Mr Emmit is her husband. If any doubt was to be cast upon her testimony, she has her marriage lines, a letter written by the vicar who married her and Mr Alfred Emmit, and one other item."

Mrs Emmit opened the red silk purse she carried and withdrew a miniature. She traced it with her finger, a soft sigh escaping her, and then passed it to Winifred.

She glanced down into the face of her uncle and smiled gently. She could immediately see the differences between him and Mr Garforth. His eyes were kinder, his lips fuller, and his nose longer. This was the man in the portrait at Emmit Grange. "Hello, Uncle Alfred," she murmured. "I so wish I had had the opportunity to meet you."

Lady Westcliffe rose to her feet. "Now, why don't we leave the gentlemen to discuss matters, and you two can get to know each other a little better."

Lord Westcliffe cleared his throat. "One moment, my lady. There is the matter of the fire."

"Oh, but my dear, do you think it really necessary?"

"I do. We agreed that Winifred would be told everything on the day Mr Garforth faced justice."

Winifred stared at him. "The fire?"

His grey eyes darkened. "It was not an accident, Miss Emmit."

Her throat constricted and her heart began to beat faster. Her knees buckled and she sank once more into her chair. "Mr Garforth intended me to burn in that fire?"

"I am afraid so. Neither Doctor Ogilvy nor his

partner, Doctor Stevens, gave Mrs Kirk the order to shackle you; she did so on her own initiative. She then ensured that everyone apart from you escaped the fire."

"I thought I had been forgotten, or at worst that Mrs Kirk had panicked and thought it would take too long to unshackle me."

Her aunt took her hand and put a slender arm about her waist. Winifred smiled wanly and straightened her spine. "When did you discover this?"

"We suspected it from the outset," Lord Westcliffe said. "But we could not prove it, nor could Doctor Stevens credit it. Mrs Kirk had worked at the asylum for ten years and had given them no cause for concern. She left York soon after the fire, and we could not locate her. And then, only two weeks ago, she wrote to Mr Garforth. He had paid her two hundred pounds to set the fire and ensure that you did not escape, but it appeared she wanted more. She asked Mr Garforth to send a similar sum to a house of ill repute here in London."

"Greed is a terrible thing," Sir Nathaniel murmured.

"Indeed," Lord Westcliffe agreed. "Your uncle had already acquired a reasonable fortune by assuming your uncle's identity, and yet he wanted more."

Winifred felt a sudden blaze of anger. "You said that it was me he wanted out of the way because I had begun to guess he was not who he appeared to be, that he needed to discredit me. You assured me that my brother was safe, and that my uncle would have no reason to move against him if he thought me dead. But he is worse than I thought, and every inch the monster I saw in my hallucination. How did you know Adrian was not in danger?"

Lord Westcliffe was unmoved by her outburst. "Mr Garforth would not be so stupid as to attempt to get rid of your brother so soon after dispensing with his sister. Not only has Mr Landers watched over your brother, but we planted a footman in Emmit Grange. He has watched Mr Garforth very carefully. And as he fetches the post, he has read every letter that has crossed the threshold. He made a copy of Mrs Kirk's letter and kept the original. We knew, of course, that this time Mr Garforth would leave nothing to chance but would come to London and attempt to silence Mrs Kirk. He sent a note to that lady soon after he arrived, arranging to meet her at a tavern in Covent Garden not far from her establishment." He paused, and then said with ominous emphasis, "And very close to the river."

Winifred gaped at him. "But how do you know all this?"

"It is better that you do not know, Miss Emmit."

"Nor I," Sir Nathaniel murmured.

She accepted this but was still not satisfied. "But surely she will not be stupid enough to go?"

"She will go, but she will take two thugs who protect her ladies with her. They will be dealt with. Mrs Kirk, who now goes by the name of Madame Celeste, will be locked up and dealt with later. Mr Garforth will be brought here by Finn and Lord Eagleton."

It all sounded very dangerous. "Why would Lord Eagleton involve himself?"

"Because he promised Mr Carne to offer you any aid he could."

The glint in Lord Westcliffe's eyes made her shiver.

"He agreed to keep Mr Carne in ignorance of what is planned, but I suspect he will do what that gentleman would wish to do in his stead."

"I did not hear that," Sir Nathaniel muttered.

# CHAPTER 22

Oliver awoke with a sense of anticipation. It was still dark outside, the sky bruised and puckered by intermittent clouds. There were several hours to occupy before he must face Mrs Thruxton. Feeling restless, he washed and dressed before slipping out of the house. He walked the streets, trying to formulate what he would say to her, but his thoughts proved nebulous, refusing to coalesce into a reasoned argument.

Although he had not been consciously thinking about where he was going, he found himself in Berkeley Square. He paused outside number 44, which he knew belonged to Lord Westcliffe, his eyes going to the upper windows, wondering which one Emma lay sleeping behind.

"Only a few more hours," he murmured, "and then I will ask you to be my wife, my darling Emma."

He turned away and began to swiftly retrace his steps. That could only happen if he could persuade Mrs Thruxton to confess. He must sit down and try to organise his arguments on paper. Slipping quietly back into his room, he lit a candle and placed it on the desk. He pulled open a drawer to find some paper and saw the letters he had brought with him. He picked them up and dropped them in the basket next to the desk. There was no point in reading them now; he had caught up on all his friends' news, and he would soon ask them what they knew of Emma's uncle. Once his own business was concluded, he fully intended to interest himself in hers.

Putting her from his mind as best he could, he took several sheets of paper, dipped the quill in a pot of ink, and began to write. The pen scratched the paper with increasing rapidity as he allowed his thoughts to flow freely. When they dried up, he took a clean sheet and began to summarise the key points. When he had finished, he read them through, scrunched up the paper, and threw it on the floor along with his first efforts. Putting down the pen, he rested his elbows on the desk, pushed his hands into his hair, and swore softly in frustration.

A rustle beside him made him turn his head, and he sat back as he saw Steen picking up the sheets. The valet glanced at them and placed them in the bin.

"I'm sorry for making such a mess, Steen."

"Not at all, sir. It is a difficult task for someone as straightforward as you to understand how to persuade a conscienceless woman to give up her secrets."

Oliver raised an eyebrow. "Have you been listening at keyholes, Steen?"

The glimmer of a smile touched his lips. "A good valet should always know how best to help his master."

Oliver realised that although Steen had been his

valet for a year, he hardly knew the man. He had been afraid to encourage any sort of intimacy between them. He had not wished to discuss his past with the man, nor had he wished to hear of the valet's previous existence, for if the valet spoke of his past, he must speak of his time with Mr Cedric Carne, Oliver's father. His eyes sharpened as a thought occurred to him.

"Perhaps you *can* help me, Steen. How would my father have dealt with this? He was one for the ladies, after all."

The man did not pretend to misunderstand him. "He would not have tried to use logic or appeal to a better nature that did not exist. I believe your best course is to lure Mrs Thruxton into a false sense of security, assure her you mean her no harm, and perhaps try to charm her a little. If that doesn't work, I'd try to make her angry. A scorned woman has a hot tongue and little discretion."

He once more set pen to paper. "Thank you, Steen."

The valet cleared his throat.

"Yes?" Oliver said absently.

"I'm not sure writing it down will help, sir. You will not have the paper to hand when you speak with her, and you do not know how the conversation will go, after all."

Oliver threw down the pen. "Then what do you suggest?"

"I suggest that we play act the conversation, sir. I shall take the part of Mrs Thruxton."

Oliver glanced at the dignified valet and laughed. "You, Steen? Take the part of Mrs Thruxton?"

"Certainly, sir," he said. "Mr Cedric and I often enlivened a dull winter evening by reading one of Shakespeare's plays. I think my favourite was *Much Ado About Nothing*. Amongst other roles, I played the part of Beatrice. I also played Kate in *The Taming of the Shrew*."

Oliver was momentarily lost for words.

The valet smiled. "*Cucullus non facit monachum.*"

Oliver grinned. "The cowl does not make the monk, spoken by Feste in *Twelfth Night*, I think."

"That's it, sir. Now, you station yourself by the fire, and I shall enter the room."

The following hour was both exhilarating and exhausting. Steen threw himself into the role, adopting the poses and mannerisms of a lady effortlessly until Oliver stopped feeling foolish and applied himself whole-heartedly. He went down to breakfast feeling far more confident. All eyes turned on him as he entered the room.

"I say," Freddie said. "Are you feeling quite the thing, old fellow? I am sure I heard you shouting at your valet, or was it the other way around? Either way, not good form, you know, particularly before breakfast."

Robert smiled. "Practising, Oliver?"

He grinned sheepishly. "Something like that. Steen has hidden depths I was unaware of."

Lucinda gave him an approving look. "That was a very good idea."

"Yes, but his not mine."

For once, Freddie followed the conversation without difficulty. "A bit premature to be practising, isn't it? Mrs Thruxton's not due until tomorrow, and you might forget it all by then." He looked troubled. "I hope you won't shout at her like that, not at all gentlemanly."

"I have no intention of shouting," Oliver assured him.

A footman entered bearing two notes. The first he gave to Oliver, the second to Robert. Oliver's was merely a brief few lines.

*All set. Expect Mr Campbell and Mr Thruxton at 12:30. Mr Campbell will pretend to be an acquaintance of Lady Kirkby and inform Thruxton that she has expressed a desire to meet him as she knows his wife. That should inculcate a little anxiety without rendering him completely witless. I have also sent a note to Crosby. Eagleton*

He looked up, met Robert's eyes, and nodded. That gentleman then made a show of looking crestfallen. "What a pity," he said.

"What is?" Freddie asked.

"There's to be a prize fight in a warehouse in Covent Garden, but I can't go. I promised to take Lucinda for a drive around Hyde Park."

Freddie's eyes lit up. For all his gentle ways, he was a keen pugilist. "Well, if you promised her, you'll have to do it. Dashed shame though." He glanced at Oliver. "Makes you glad you've not been caught in Parson's Mousetrap, doesn't it? Coming, old fellow?"

"It's not quite in my line, Freddie," he said.

"It's not? Well, never mind. I don't need an escort. What time does it start?"

"Midday," Oliver said.

Freddie went off with a spring in his step just after half past eleven. Richmond arrived shortly before midday, and to everybody's surprise, he had a lady on his arm. He introduced her as Lady Amabel Kingston.

When they were settled in the drawing room, he smiled wryly.

"I took Lady Amabel for a drive this morning, and she wormed everything out of me."

"Wormed, Crosby," she said, "is a terribly inelegant expression. I would rather say, I coaxed everything from you."

She turned her turquoise eyes on Oliver. "I am very glad to meet you, Mr Carne. It is a shame it is in such trying circumstances. Although," she added thoughtfully, a hint of mischief in her expression, "those circumstances have brought several interesting things about your brother to light."

"Oh?" he asked.

"Indeed," she said, giving Richmond a sideways glance. "Although his hand in this affair is a little amateurish, it does show promise and a reasonable degree of intelligence."

"I am not stupid, I believe," Richmond said dryly.

"No," Lady Amabel agreed. "And, of course, it is charming that he has worked so hard to save his family's reputation and yours, in particular."

A hint of colour rose in Richmond's cheeks. Oliver began to be amused. "I am very grateful to my brother and glad to have this opportunity to become reacquainted with him."

She smiled. "That is the most charming thing of all. Your brother, Mr Carne, has a great many bad habits to unlearn."

Oliver's lips twitched as Richmond crossed and recrossed his legs. "I believe he has made considerable progress in that direction, Lady Amabel."

"Yes," she said thoughtfully. "So do I."

"I do not mean to be rude, Lady Amabel," Lucinda said, glancing at the clock. "And in normal circumstances, you would be welcome to stay as long as you desired, but——"

"I know what you are going to say," she said. "And I quite understand, but I think I will stay. You see, in my experience, the best laid plans often have hiccups. If one is not adaptable, things can very quickly get out of hand."

"Oh," Lucinda said. "And you are adaptable?"

"Very," Lady Amabel assured her.

"Nothing ever discomposes her," Richmond said, admiration in his tone and gaze.

"That is true," she said. "And I do enjoy a little subterfuge if it is in a good cause. I have an eye for all those little details that are so often missed." She got up and crossed the room to a pair of double doors that led into the dining room. She opened them and glanced inside, before turning back. "So, as I understand it, Mr Thruxton, Mr Campbell, and the rest of us, apart from Mr Carne, will be in here, with the door ajar."

"Yes," Richmond confirmed.

"In that case, Mr Carne, you must make sure you remain between Mrs Thruxton and this door. The other, of course, must be locked after she is shown in." She glanced at Lucinda. "Will your butler blink at doing such a thing?"

"I do not think so, but I am not at all sure where the key may be."

It was Lady Amabel's turn to look at the clock. "I suggest, then, that you go and find it."

She regarded Robert. "I assume all your servants are to be trusted?"

"I believe so," he said.

"As my valet is fully aware of what is afoot, ma'am," Oliver said, "and I had not informed him, I suggest that they likely already know what is planned."

"Very well." She glanced at Robert. "Where and how do you intend to entertain the gentlemen until Mrs Thruxton arrives?"

"I thought we might start in here, and then move into the dining room for a light luncheon," Lucinda said, coming back into the room.

"Messy," Lady Amabel said. "I suggest that you take them straight into the dining room. You may make some excuse about this room needing redecoration. Only you and your husband should be there until Mrs Thruxton arrives, and then Richmond and I will join you. In the interim, we will wait in the little parlour across the corridor." She smiled. "There, I think that is everything. Oh, apart from one other thing. Poor Mr Thruxton is going to be in a very difficult position, and it is entirely possible he might try and warn his wife. Perhaps it would be better if a gag was to hand."

Oliver met his brother's twinkling eyes. They seemed to say, *see, didn't I tell you she was remarkable?*

"I will be prepared for that eventuality," Richmond said, "but I have a suspicion he will be more in awe of Mr Campbell than his wife."

Oliver hoped that he was right, and as they disappeared to take up their stations, he paced the floor, forcing his limbs into a chair when he heard voices in the hall, and then in the dining room. He spent the fifteen minutes until Mrs Thruxton's arrival replaying his and Steen's roleplaying that morning. He brushed his clammy hands on his trousers and rose to his feet as he heard more footsteps outside. He froze as he heard several female voices. He was sure one of them belonged to Mrs Thruxton's mother; it had a nasal inflection that was hard to forget.

He crept a little closer to the door and heard Lady Amabel's bright tones.

"Do not concern yourself, Mrs Ripley. I am sure your lack of an invitation was a mere oversight. I am Lady Kirkby's good friend, Lady Amabel Kingston. Lady Kirkby has been detained for a moment but will be with us directly." She gave a little cry. "Oh, how clumsy of me. I don't know how I came to step on your dress, Mrs Ripley, but if you step upstairs for a moment, Crimble will show you to a room where you may mend your torn lace in a trice. Mrs Thruxton, you go into the drawing room and make yourself comfortable."

Oliver retreated towards the dining room doors, reflecting that his brother was right. Lady Amabel was remarkable, although rather too managing for his taste. That did not detract from the fact that she had earned his gratitude that day. The door opened, Mrs Thruxton tripped into the room, and the door closed behind her. Her dark eyes began a slow, interested appraisal of the furnishings in the room. She removed her bonnet as they did so, revealing glossy black ringlets. And then her eyes fell on him. They widened, and she gasped.

Three phrases echoed in Oliver's mind. *Assure her*

*you mean her no harm, charm her a little, make her angry.* He took a step towards her.

"Do not be alarmed, Mrs Thruxton. I mean you no harm."

Her eyes narrowed. "Then why are you here?"

"Lord Kirkby is a childhood friend of mine, one of the few I have left, and when I heard you were to visit, I had to see you." He hoped his smile did not look as stiff as it felt. "You are as pretty as ever, I see."

Her chin tilted a little. "You never found me at all pretty."

He pressed on. "That is not true. I did not show it because it would have been inappropriate. I cannot believe, Mrs Thruxton, that one bearing so fair a face could malign me without a very good reason. It might help me to come to terms with the shame of losing my position if you would explain to me why you felt forced to cast me as such a villain."

"I did have a reason," she said, her smile as false as her character.

"What was it?"

She stepped towards him, her eyes suddenly bright with spiteful cunning. "You do know that I will deny whatever passes between us in this room? And if you should try and start any malicious rumours about me, I might be forced to report you to the authorities. That would bring you more than shame."

"I am fully aware of it. What was your reason?"

She gave a brittle laugh. "You brought it on yourself. You were so self-righteous and judgemental, merely because I asked you to help me get rid of the child."

"To take a life is a grave sin, Mrs Thruxton. I could not condone it."

Her eyes suddenly flamed, and her voice rose. "It was not your place to condone or not condone it. Your place was to do what I asked of you. Not only did you refuse to do what I requested, you threatened to tell my husband if you ever suspected I had got rid of the child!" She gave a wild little laugh. "But I dealt with you, and the babe after you had gone."

"But why?" he asked appalled. "Did your husband insist on it?"

"No," she said bitterly. "My husband was quite prepared to bring up another man's child. Pitiful, isn't it?"

His mind tried to grapple with what she was telling him. "Mrs Thruxton, if you were raped, I can under-stand why you would wish to give up the child, but there were other ways."

"You really are stupid, aren't you?" she hissed. "I was not raped. I made a bargain. In return for my favours, I secured a promotion for my husband in the company offices in London. I hated India, but for some inexplicable reason, Mr Thruxton liked it. He kept saying that I would get used to it, to give it time. But I wouldn't have. When the offer came, I told him he could take it, or I would return to England without him."

A dull voice came from behind Oliver. "I wish you had. I wish I had never met you."

Oliver stepped aside, revealing a bespectacled man standing in the doorway. His face was ashen. Mrs Thruxton's eyes widened, and she retreated until her back pressed against the locked door.

"You don't mean it, Lucius. And neither did I. Seeing Mr Carne after all this time disordered my senses." Her hand slipped behind her back. "I am going to find Mother; she will not let you speak to me so." She stepped away from the door and tugged on the handle. When it did not open, she looked over her shoulder, fear in her eyes.

Mr Thruxton walked slowly towards her as if in a trance. "We have done Mr Carne a great wrong. Who recommended me for the position, Alice?"

She turned towards him. "Do you not see, Lucius, that I have been tricked?"

"Who, Alice?" he said implacably.

"Sir Laurence Granger," she whispered.

An irate voice was heard in the hall and the door behind Mrs Thruxton opened.

"Alice," Mrs Ripley said. "We are leaving. Would you believe I have been locked in a room upstairs, and no matter how much I shouted no one came?"

Lady Amabel answered her, her tone placatory. "You are mistaken, Mrs Ripley. It is just that some of the doors in the house are warped and they stick."

Mrs Thruxton turned and threw herself into her mother's arms. "Take me away, Mama."

She glanced over her daughter's head, her eyes colliding with her son-in-law's.

"Lucius?" she said uncertainly.

"Take her home," he said, his tone steely. "And then pack both your bags. You have a perfectly good house of your own. If either of you are there when I get back, I will not answer for my actions."

She opened her mouth to protest, but something

in his expression changed her mind. "Come, dearest," she said, shepherding her daughter away.

Oliver collected the hat his nemesis had discarded and handed it to a footman who hovered in the hall. "Give this to Mrs Thruxton. We don't wish to provide her with an excuse to come back."

Mr Campbell spoke. "Mr Carne, you have been badly treated, indeed. I will pay Sir Laurence a visit myself this very day, and I will call a meeting of the board. I am sure they will restore you to your position if you so desire, or perhaps offer you some compensation."

"I want nothing but my good name restored," Oliver said.

"Please, Mr Carne," Mr Thruxton said, "accept my apologies, although I know them to be woefully inadequate."

"You were a victim in this as much as me, sir," he said gravely. He glanced again at Mr Campbell. "Actually, there is something I desire. I would not like Mr Thruxton to lose his position merely because he had the misfortune to marry unwisely."

"I shall certainly make your feelings known, Mr Carne." He placed his hand on Mr Thruxton's shoulder. "Come along, now. You can't go home yet, so you may as well go back to work."

As the door closed behind them, Richmond surged forward and shook his brother's hand.

"Oliver, you were outstanding. Well done."

"It is rather my valet you should praise; without his advice, I would have floundered." He smiled at Lady Amabel. "And you, of course. How did you know Crimble would understand you wished him to lock Mrs Ripley up?"

She smiled. "All good butlers know how to interpret a look, Mr Carne. I took the key to the drawing room door from his hand and raised my eyebrows. It was enough."

Running footsteps were heard, and Freddie appeared. He leant his hand against the wall and bent over panting.

"This is my brother, Frederick Ashton, Lady Amabel," Lucinda said.

"Ah, yes," she said. "The cherub."

Freddie raised his head. "Pleased to see you, Lady Amabel, but please don't call me that."

"Very well," she said. "If you will tell me why you are so out of breath, I won't."

His blue eyes grew round. "Dash it, I almost forgot. Thought you'd want to know, Oliver, as he's a friend of yours."

"Know what, Freddie?"

"I was coming away from the fight when I heard a scuffle in an alley. That's not an unusual occurrence in Covent Garden, I'll admit, but I thought I'd better take a quick look. There might have been a lady in the case."

"How very chivalrous of you," Lady Amabel said.

"What? No. I don't think I am. But got to protect the ladies. Anyway, there weren't any. Ladies, that is. I saw Eagleton plant the flushest facer it has ever been my fortune to see. The other fellow went down like a stone. The big bruiser of a man who was with him, threw him over his shoulder, bundled him into a hackney, and climbed in after him."

The hairs on the back of Oliver's neck prickled. "Where did they go?"

"Thought you'd want to know, so I set off after them. Couldn't get a hackney so I had to run. It turned into Berkeley Square."

"Thank you, Freddie. Now, if you'll all excuse me, there is somewhere I need to be."

"We'll come with you," Richmond and Robert said in unison.

"No, I don't think you should do that," Lady Amabel said, adding when Oliver looked at her, "I meant the others, not you. There is no need for you to go hot foot, however. I believe Lord Eagleton has acted in your stead already."

"It is Emmit then?"

"Well, no, it is the man masquerading as Emmit. Everything is well in hand there. You have nothing to worry about, I assure you."

"Emmit?" Freddie, Oliver, and Richmond said in unison.

Ignoring them, Lady Amabel regarded Oliver. "I met Winifred last evening, and she is perfectly well. I thought her charming."

"Winifred?" he said. "I should have guessed, of course. I am so used to thinking of her as Emma, it will be odd to address her by a different name."

"What's in a name?" Lady Amabel said smiling.

"Quite a lot if they call you, cherub," Freddie said. "I can't follow any of this at all. Care to explain?"

"As Lady Amabel is so well informed, she can tell you. I'm off to see Em… Winifred."

# CHAPTER 23

Winifred jumped as a knock fell upon her door. Lizzie came into the room.

"It's time, Miss Win. I'd tell you to give him a poke in the eye, but it looks as if he's already had one."

She nodded, her nerves jangling, and began to walk towards the door. She suddenly stopped. "Lizzie, could you bring me the topaz pendant? It is a lucky charm."

Lizzie did as she was bid. It was a measure of the girl's growing confidence that when she fastened it about her mistress's neck, she murmured, "I thought you didn't hold with superstitions."

Despite the unpleasant sensation in the pit of her stomach, Emma smiled. "I don't, but it will make me feel a little braver, nonetheless."

"You've no need to feel scared. Lord Westcliffe won't let any harm come to you, and neither will Lord Eagleton."

"Thank you, Lizzie."

Her aunt was waiting with Lady Westcliffe outside

the library door. The latter sent her a reassuring smile. "It will take but a moment, and I will come in with you if you wish it."

Winifred took her aunt's hand. "No, it is quite all right. We will do this together."

They entered the room to find Sir Nathaniel behind the desk, a clerk at his side, quill at the ready. Lord Westcliffe stood a little behind them. Lord Eagleton sat on a sofa, his legs crossed, and an arm laid casually along its back as if it were a social gathering. Winifred was not fooled, however, there was an intensity about him that suggested he was quite ready to spring up at a moment's notice. She saw his knuckles were grazed. Finn stood behind the chair upon which Mr Garforth sat. His eye was swollen and purple, and when his mouth fell agape at sight of Winifred and her aunt, it could be seen that he was missing a front tooth. The gentlemen rose to their feet as the ladies entered, but when Mr Garforth attempted to follow suit, he was pressed firmly back down.

"Winifred—"

"Don't say a word to either of the ladies, or I will do some of the things I promised earlier."

Winifred had never heard the marquess speak in such a soft, malevolent tone, and it had its effect. Mr Garforth looked as if he were about to be sick.

"Miss Emmit," Sir Nathaniel said. "Is this the man who claimed to be Mr Alfred Emmit?"

She did not turn her eyes to him again, but said, "Yes."

"And, Mrs Emmit," he continued, "do you recognise this man?"

Winifred glanced at her aunt and squeezed her hand. Her eyes had narrowed almost to slits. "Yes," she said, her voice hard and bitter. "He came to the plantation not long before we left for Calcutta. He called himself Mr Garforth. We offered him our hospitality, and this is how he repaid us. If you had not assured me that he will hang, I would kill him myself."

Sir Nathaniel met his clerk's eyes and murmured, "You may ignore that last comment." Then, regarding the ladies, he said more clearly, "Thank you, Miss Emmit, Mrs Emmit, that will be all."

When they stepped back into the hall, Lady West-cliffe put a hand on each of their arms.

"There, nothing more can be done until it comes to trial. Let us—"

She was interrupted by the sound of the door knocker being plied repeatedly and forcibly. She seemed unperturbed; indeed, a hint of a smile touched her lips. She nodded to a footman, and as he went to answer the summons, said, "I think you will find, Winifred, that Mr Carne is eager to see you. Lady Amabel could not resist taking a hand in Mr Carne's affairs, which of course, gave me every confidence of him succeeding."

Winifred's breath caught in her throat, and she moved towards the door. There were a few words exchanged and the footman stepped back. Oliver strode into the house, his eyes immediately finding her. For a moment, their eyes drank each other in, and then, with no thought to decorum or who might be watching, they surged towards each other. Winifred found herself almost lifted off her feet as he held her to him.

"It's over," she murmured.

"Yes," he sighed. "It is."

She drew back so she could gaze into his face. Motes of light flickered in his cobalt eyes like flecks of sun on a deep ocean. The unpleasantness of the last few moments receded, and the heaviness in her heart lightened. He lowered his head and she tilted hers to receive his kiss. His lips paused above hers as a crisp voice cut through the warm bubble that enveloped them.

"Mr Carne, I presume?"

He smiled ruefully and drew away. Winifred stepped back, colour flooding her cheeks.

"Mr Carne, allow me to present you to Lady Westcliffe and Mrs Emmit, my aunt."

Oliver bowed. "Forgive me, ladies. Lady Westcliffe, I have long wished to meet you, and to thank you for all you have done for Em… Winifred." His gaze moved on to Mrs Emmit. He stared at her, a look of recognition coming into his eyes. He bowed his head, pressed his hands together, and spoke rapidly in a language Winifred did not comprehend. Her aunt smiled and answered him in kind, before turning to her niece.

"Winifred, I have met Mr Carne before. We heard of a surgeon travelling through the mountains, and when Alfred fell ill, we sent for him."

Winifred's eyes widened. "But you said you had not met my uncle."

Oliver smiled ruefully. "I said I did not think so. I am very good with faces, but I am terrible at remembering names unless I see a person regularly. I believe Mrs Emmit, who was then your uncle's housekeeper, generally referred to him as Mr Alfred. I heard his name but once."

"It is true," Mrs Emmit said.

He raised his hand, and Winifred saw he held a slim, black volume. "I refreshed my memory before I came. Mr Emmit had a putrid sore throat. I noted that he had a small birthmark on the side of his neck in the shape of a crescent moon. I thought the information might prove useful."

"How interesting, Mr Carne," Lady Westcliffe said, holding out her hand. "I will take that notebook. I am sure my husband will wish to speak with you, but he is rather occupied at the moment. I suggest you take Winifred for a walk in The Green Park. Run up and get your cloak and hat, my dear."

"There's no need, Miss Win."

She glanced up to find Lizzie running down the stairs with the desired objects. She took the hat and as the maid fastened her cloak, murmured, "You really must stop eavesdropping, Lizzie."

The maid grinned as Oliver winked at her. "You were right, ma'am. That necklace has brought you good luck."

Winifred smiled and gently extracted the pendant from beneath her cloak. She fingered the three topaz stones for a moment before letting the pendant fall. "Yes, Lizzie, I think you are right." She turned to take her leave of Lady Westcliffe and her aunt, but they had already entered the parlour on the other side of the hall. She smiled as Oliver offered his arm and they left the house. It was a short step to the park, and they did not speak, content to simply be in each other's company.

The overcast sky and chill breeze had discouraged visitors, and as soon as they neared a stand of skeletal trees, Oliver guided her between them, leant his back against the nearest trunk, and pulled her against him. She smiled, a sudden rush of love causing her heartbeat to quicken. There was nowhere else she would rather be than locked in his arms. She wrapped hers about his neck.

"I have long wished to embrace you properly. The doctors who interviewed me were most impressed with your work. They asked me to pass on their compliments."

"Shh," he murmured. "We will speak of that later, of everything later, but let nothing intrude on this moment. To know you were so near and not be able to see or communicate with you was torture."

He kissed her lightly.

"I know. I felt the same."

A crooked smile twisted his lips. "I stood in the square before it was light, looking up at the windows, wondering which one you slumbered behind."

She sighed. "I wish I had known. How much I wished to see you, but my room looks over the garden."

He gently moved her a few inches away and took her hands, raising first one and then the other to his lips. "I owe you so much, Winifred. I was lost, unhappy, and lonely, but you gave me a reason to come out of the dark, to move forwards. I have not known love since I was a small child or felt a sense of belonging anywhere, but that has all changed. I belong with you. You fill my thoughts, and your happiness is more important to me than all else. Do you think I can make you happy? Will you do me the honour of becoming my wife?"

She sank into the blue waters of his eyes, sensing depths to him she had not yet imagined, her heart filling with joy at the prospect of discovering them over the coming years.

"You do make me happy, and you will continue to do so. I have sorely missed you, and the prospect of perhaps never being with you again has haunted my dreams. I have prayed every night that you would succeed and reclaim your honour, for your sake and mine. I will marry you, Oliver Carne, because I love you and will always love you."

Her smile was gentle, her eyes glowing softly with love, faith, and trust. Oliver pulled her back into his arms, kissing first her forehead, then the tip of her nose, and finally her lips. He had kissed her before, but this felt different. This time he was not hindered by fears that he was unworthy of her. His love was unfettered, as was her response to his kiss. She pressed closer to him, aware only of his smell, his touch, and the sweet turmoil he was generating inside her. An army could have marched by its bugles sounding, and she would not have noticed.

When he raised his head, she stood on her toes and tried to pull it back down. He chuckled softly and put her gently from him.

"There is nothing I would like more than to carry on kissing you, my dearest love, but someone might come upon us at any moment. We have only just salvaged our reputations, let us not once more put them in jeopardy."

She blushed and nodded. "When you kiss me, I

am not sensible at all. It is as if the world fades into shadow and there is only you, a bright, shining beacon that draws me like a moth to a flame."

He groaned. "And you inflame my senses, but it will not do, not here, not now."

His eyes were dark with passion, and her mouth opened on a gasp of delight at the thought that she, who was not a beauty, but merely the practical daughter of a wool merchant, could inspire such feeling in the gentleman standing before her.

"Very well. Perhaps we should return then."

As they walked along the path, she saw another couple coming towards them and was glad of his restraint. As the way was narrow, they stepped onto the grass to allow them to pass. The woman turned her head and glanced at them. Winifred smiled and stepped forward.

"Lucy? This is a surprise."

The words had left her mouth before she realised the unlikelihood of her being the youngest resident of Ashwick Hall, yet everything about the woman mirrored Lucy's looks, apart, she realised, from the hard look in her eyes. The lady's chin tilted, and her fine eyebrows rose a fraction.

"You are mistaken, ma'am, my name is not…"

Winifred's mouth went dry. She knew she had made a grievous mistake. The woman was staring at the pendant around her neck. She forced a smile to her lips. "No, I see I was mistaken. You must forgive me; I am a little short-sighted."

The woman's gaze remained riveted on the necklace. "That is a pretty piece of unusual design," she said. "Would you mind telling me where you purchased it?"

"I cannot tell you that," she said, "for it came to me through my mother. I cannot remember a time when she did not have it."

"Come along, Abby," the dark-haired man at her side said. "We will be late."

They moved off, the woman sending one last glance over her shoulder.

"I did not know you were short-sighted," Oliver said. "It explains, of course, why you find me so devastatingly attractive."

"I'm not," she said. "And neither was this necklace my mother's. It belongs to one of the other ladies Lady Westcliffe takes care of. That must be her twin sister, for they are identical. We must hurry back. I need to tell Lady Westcliffe what I have done."

"Very well," he said. "But there is no need for all this panic. You carried it off very well."

They found Lady Westcliffe in the small parlour. She rose gracefully, a smile playing about her lips. "Am I to take it congratulations are in order?"

Oliver grinned. "Yes, thank you, ma'am."

She regarded Winifred. "Then why do you look so downcast, my dear?"

When she had explained, Lady Westcliffe took the same view as Oliver. "It is unfortunate that Lucy should have given you her necklace, but you did very well, Winifred. Your explanation for mistaking her likeness was inspired, and it is very rare, you know, that a piece of jewellery is wholly original. Do not let it trouble you."

She sagged in relief. "Oh, I am so glad."

"And so you should be. It is a special day. You will be pleased to know that Mr Garforth is no longer here, but there are one or two visitors upstairs in the drawing room who wish to see you."

Oliver looked a little crestfallen. "Then perhaps I had better go."

"Not at all, Mr Carne," she said, ushering them from the room. "I believe your presence is also required."

They exchanged a confused glance.

"Perhaps Lord Westcliffe wishes to speak to you about what is in your notebook," she murmured.

Lady Westcliffe entered the room first, saying, "All is as we hoped."

Winifred and Oliver entered to a round of applause and the sound of champagne corks popping. Lady Amabel made her way through a throng of people, flashed a smile at Oliver, and kissed Winifred on the cheek.

"I hope you don't mind, my dear, but I think special occasions should always be celebrated."

Richmond appeared at her side and bowed. "Miss Emmit, please accept my humble apologies. When last we met, I was unforgivably rude."

"It is forgotten," Winifred said. "Apart from on that one occasion, you were always gentlemanly."

He smiled. "You are too kind."

"Undoubtedly," Lady Amabel said dryly.

Ignoring this aside, Richmond turned to his brother and clapped him on the shoulder. "Accept my heartfelt congratulations, Oliver."

He grinned. "Certainly. Am I to also offer you mine?"

"Not yet," Lady Amabel said. "And only time will tell if you will ever get the opportunity to do so."

Her words were softened by the humorous twinkle in her eyes.

Winifred sensed Oliver tense as Lord Painswick approached, but it seemed he was in a buoyant mood.

"Well done, my boy. Richmond tells me you carried the thing off with panache." He turned to Winifred. "I'm pleased to welcome you to the family, Miss Emmit. I always thought you were a good girl. Glad that other business has been cleared up too."

"Thank you, sir."

Oliver was suddenly engulfed by his friends, and Winifred found Lady Westcliffe's hand on her arm.

"Follow me, my dear."

She led her to the back of the room, and through a door into an adjoining parlour. There, sitting quietly on a sofa was a dark-haired young man. Tears sprang to Winifred's eyes, and she stumbled forward.

"Adrian!"

He rose and embraced her. "Win, oh, Win! How I have missed you."

She held him close, her happiness complete.

# CHAPTER 24

*arne Castle, August 1818*

C Oliver sat with his back against the trunk of an ancient oak, Winifred's head in his lap. His gaze was fixed on the river, and there was a contented smile on his lips.

"I shall miss Aunt Sita," Winifred murmured.

She had sailed for India at the beginning of July, Mr Garforth having been tried and sentenced to hang the month before. The trial had caused a sensation and been reported in all the papers, thus alerting a certain man of law to his duty. It had transpired that Mr Alfred Emmit had had the foresight to send a copy of his will to a solicitor in Leeds before leaving India in case of accident at sea. He had contacted Winifred and her aunt, informing them that Mr Emmit had split his fortune between his wife, nephew, and niece. His spouse received half of it, and the remaining fifty per cent had been split between Adrian and Winifred. She had protested that they had no need of his money and had wished to gift it to her aunt, but Mrs Sita Emmit would not hear of it.

"I have far more than I will ever need," she had said. "I will be able to support myself, my sister, and her children forevermore in comfort."

"I am glad you and Adrian were able to know her," Oliver said, stroking a curl from her forehead. "But she will be happier with her sister, I think. She thought England far too cold."

"True," Winifred said, grasping his hand and laying it against her cheek. "I am glad you introduced her to Mr Thruxton. It will be good for her to have some company on the journey."

"It will be good for them both," Oliver said. "I am glad that the company saw the sense in granting his wish of returning to India in exchange for him not suing for a legal separation. The sordid details of such an eminent employee as Sir Laurence Granger using his position of power to corrupt the young wife of another employee, would not have reflected well on the company."

Winifred sat up. "I believe," she said dryly, "that it was rather Mrs Thruxton who corrupted Sir Laurence. Did his letter not make that clear?"

When Oliver and his friends had returned to Green Street after celebrating his engagement, two letters had been waiting for him. The first had been from Mr Campbell.

*Mr Carne,*

*Sir Laurence lost his life to consumption in the early hours of this morning. He had left instructions for a letter to be delivered to the directors of the company in the event of his demise. I have had a copy made for you, and a meeting of the board is to be convened first thing in the morning.*

*It appears that the scene enacted in Green Street was not at all necessary to restore your honour, but I cannot help but feel that it benefited Mr Thruxton. It appears he has always been a hard-working, diligent employee, but it has been noted that a few uncharacteristic errors have begun to creep into his work. The shock of having his wife's true character revealed in such a way has been great, but I believe that when he recovers from it, he will be relieved to be rid of her.*

*Mr R Campbell*

Oliver had quickly turned his attention to the other missive.

*12 Gracechurch St, 8th November 1817*

*Dear Sirs,*

*It is with great regret and shame that I write this letter. It is a shame I cannot bear to face in this life, and so you will receive it after my death. It will not be long now, I think.*

*You will be aware that Mr Oliver Carne, a former surgeon working for the company in Calcutta, was accused by the wife of Mr Thruxton, a clerk then working in that city, of raping her and getting her with child. Mr Carne denied the charge which could not be proven, but due to the circumstantial evidence of her pregnancy being confirmed and Mr Thruxton finding her half-swooning in his arms, a promising and talented surgeon lost his employment, his right to practise medicine, and his honour.*

*There was no rape, and Mr Carne, a profoundly moral young man, never laid a finger upon Mrs Thruxton. Whilst I was treating that lady for low spirits, she began to flirt with me. I was not immune to her charms although I tried to conceal that fact from her. On my last visit, she had not risen from her bed. She dismissed her maid and threw back her covers, revealing herself to be quite naked. I turned my gaze away and asked her to don her nightgown, but she left the bed and threw herself into my arms. I am ashamed to say my resolve to fight my desire crumbled. After I had lain with her, I told her it had been a mistake on both our parts, and that I would arrange for another doctor to take over her case. How I wish I had done so sooner.*

*Mrs Thruxton smiled and said she perfectly understood, but unless I recommended her husband for a place in the London offices, she would cry rape. Self-preservation and a strong desire to have her far from me, ensured that I did so. I requested Mr Carne to take her as a patient, for I knew that he would never show such weakness as I had.*

*I had no idea that Mrs Thruxton was with child until she accused Mr Carne, quite falsely, of forcing himself upon her. I should, of course, have come forward then, but I was a coward. I justified my behaviour by telling myself that he was young, and that as his uncle had left him a property in Cornwall, he was not without means.*

*Not many months later, my sins found me out and I was afflicted with consumption. When I returned to England's shores, I made some enquiries and discovered Mr Carne had been grievously ill on the ship home, and that he had retreated to his estate and been heard of no more. I was conflicted. My actions appeared to have blighted his life, and whilst part of me wished to confess, part of me shuddered at the thought. I determined to leave it to fate.*

*I visited Mr Carne's father, The Earl of Painswick, at his club, and informed him of what his son stood accused of. I said there were whispers of it circulating in Town. I had heard no such whispers but hoped that his family might offer Mr Carne some support and even make an effort to restore his good name. I thought that perhaps they would be able to persuade Mrs Thruxton to confess.*

*I think it extremely unlikely that Mrs Thruxton will ever*

*admit to her wrongdoing, however, and so have written this letter. Every word of it is the truth, and I beg you all to exonerate Mr Carne and reinstate him if he so desires it. I have worked tirelessly for the company these thirty years, and it pains me to besmirch my record with so sordid an indiscretion.*

*Your loyal servant,*

*Sir Laurence Granger*

"His letter did indeed throw the blame on Mrs Thruxton," Oliver conceded, "but that is not how the public may have viewed it, and no matter the temptation, he should not have given in to his base desires."

"No, I suppose not," Winifred agreed. "Is Mrs Thruxton still living with her mother?"

Oliver cleared his throat. "I believe so."

Winifred's eyes narrowed. "Oliver Carne! I thought you disliked falsehoods."

He looked sheepish. "The truth is not for a lady's ears."

Winifred shook her head and laid her hand on her gently rounded stomach. "Do not be so ridiculous. I am no innocent but a married woman who is expecting your child. If you won't tell me the truth, I'll ask Freddie."

Oliver's gaze returned to the river as sounds of splashing and laughter drifted on the hazy, summer air. Freddie and Adrian were in the water, frolicking around with gay abandon. The former's sunny temperament and simple tastes exactly suited the fourteen-year-old.

"I beg that you won't," he said. "It would cause him great embarrassment."

Winifred picked up a slender twig and began to

prod him with it, scrunching up her face in a woeful attempt to appear menacing.

"Then you had better tell me yourself, before I turn you black and blue."

He laughed, reaching out a hand to gently catch a bee that hovered about her. He released it, and as it drifted off, said, "You, Mrs Carne, need a spoonful of Crawford's honey to sweeten your distressingly sour disposition."

She gave him one last prod. "And you, Mr Carne, need to open your budget."

He pulled her to him and kissed her. "Very well. Mrs Thruxton is no longer living with her mother. She has been set up in a nice little house in Hans Town."

Winifred wrinkled her brow. "Set up as what?"

Oliver gave her a meaningful look. She blushed. "Oh! Do you mean she has become some gentleman's mistress?"

"That is precisely what I mean."

"Poor Mr Thruxton," she said, dismayed.

"It need no longer embarrass him when he is in India, and neither will he need support her."

He stood and pulled her gently to her feet, as a bedraggled Beau raced up the lawn from the river, barking excitedly. "We have company, Mrs Carne, so try for a little decorum."

She glanced towards the house and saw Richmond, Lady Amabel, Nell, and Alexander strolling towards them.

"Oh, they have arrived at last. It is a pity that Lucinda and Robert could not come, but perhaps they will manage the journey next year. I am so happy that our babies will be born within a few weeks of each other. I am sure they will be the best of friends. Do you think you should tell Freddie and Adrian to make themselves respectable?"

"No," he said, smiling gently. "Although Adrian has done me the honour of accepting me as his guardian, I don't have Freddie's knack of making him laugh. It is good to hear him enjoying himself in such an unrestrained manner."

"Yes," she agreed. "So it is. Let us go and meet our guests. I will admit I am agog to discover if Richmond has finally persuaded Lady Amabel to accept him as her husband. He must have proposed a dozen times now, and yet has not swerved in his devotion despite all the rebuffs."

"Winifred," Oliver said as they made their way up the gentle incline towards the house, "you must not ask."

"Of course I won't be so blunt." She suddenly glanced up at him, the sweet smile that always took his breath away curving her lips. "I don't think I need to. Look."

He looked, and saw that Lady Amabel had a secret little smile hovering about her lips, and although Richmond was not one to wear his heart on his sleeve, when his eyes met his brother's, they also smiled.

"I think you're right," he murmured. "A constant love conquers all, it would seem."

He glanced down as Winifred put her hand on his sleeve. "Sometimes. But love can be constant without conquering. I wish you would read the letter your father left you. After all, we would not have met if he had not left you this property. Perhaps it is time for you to let go of your resentment and forgive him."

Although he had not known it, Mr Cedric Carne's letter had been amongst those he had thrown in the bin in Green Street. Steen had retrieved it, and he had returned home to find it laid neatly in the middle of the desk in his room.

He raised Winifred's hand to his lips. "You are ever the romantic, my love. I no longer resent him, but I am afraid that I will again if his letter is couched in the same terms as Sir Laurence's, putting all the blame on my mother. I would never be able to forgive him. She died alone and unloved."

"No, dearest," she said gently. "Alone, perhaps, but she was loved by all of her children, and perhaps even by your father."

He shook his head. "How is it you always see the best in people?"

"Because, my love, with one exception who we won't mention, people are rarely as black as they are painted."

"Well," Lady Amabel said as she came up to them, "Richmond has finally worn me down. I found I could not in all good conscience humiliate him any longer."

"In other words," Richmond said dryly, "I have finally paid my penance for succumbing to my father's order to offer for you, Winifred, after Amabel rejected me." He smiled and kissed Winifred's hand. "No offence meant."

"And none taken," she assured him.

"Congratulations," Oliver said, grinning.

Beau was eager to add his and raced around Richmond several times, occasionally stopping to give his wet fur a vigorous shake, before becoming very interested in the tassels hanging from his boots. Oliver called him off, the frown gathering on his brother's brow warning him that his patience was wearing thin.

"I'll take him into the house and ask Hurley to dry him off. I'll also send the footmen out with the food and blankets."

"Don't eat too much," Alexander said lightly. "We are to have a sailing race later, remember? I don't wish you to use the excuse that your overindulgence slowed you down when I pass the finish line without you in sight."

Oliver grinned. "Not a chance of it."

Nell exchanged a smile with Winifred. "Do you know, my dear, I do not think men ever really lose the boy in them."

"Let us hope not," Winifred said, smiling.

Much later, when his guests had returned home or retired for the evening, Oliver sat in his library, Mr Cedric Carne's unopened letter in front of him. He had a vague recollection of meeting him when he had been very small. He remembered a jolly laugh and a bluff manner, but nothing more. This man had been his father, and apart from his liking of Shakespeare, his acuteness in picking good men to conduct his business, and his love of wine and women, he knew little about him. Winifred had not pried, but she had, over time, asked gentle questions, and she seemed to believe he would not be disappointed. He had learnt to trust her intuition. Expelling a long, slow breath, he broke the seal.

*Carne Castle, October 1814*

*Oliver,*

*It was both your mother's and Painswick's wish that I did not contact you, although I will admit it was only your mother's wishes that carried any weight with me. As she died so soon after being banished to Farnham, I doubt very much you will ever know the truth if I don't take it upon myself to inform you of it.*

*First of all, I would like you to know that she did not die alone. I was with her. Painswick does not know, and I advise you never to inform him of it. Fanny, her lady's maid, was always in Alicia's confidence, and without her knowing, wrote to me when she lay in a dangerous fever. She died in my arms, and she was happy for it to be so. I imagine that this knowledge will make you simultaneously angry yet relieved.*

Oliver closed his eyes. His father was right. He felt both emotions. Relief had the upper hand, however, and so he read on.

*Painswick will tell you that his was not a love match, that he condoned Alicia having discreet affairs once she had presented him with two sons, but that her liaison with me was the ultimate betrayal. He may even have convinced himself that he believes it, and I did betray him, I suppose.*

*On your mother's side, it was never a love match. We had fallen in love before Painswick offered for her, but I was only a second son and at that time had no prospect of inheriting Carne Castle. It is not surprising, therefore, that your mother's father would not hear of the match. In those days, a girl did what she was told. I did not get on with my brother; our temperaments were very different, and he did not hesitate to offer for her, even though he knew I loved her.*

*I licked my wounds and threw myself into a life of overindulgence. It was only years later, when Alicia came to me and begged me to stop before I killed myself, that our love was rekindled. By then, I am convinced that Painswick really was in love with her. How could he not be? She was a remarkable woman with a wit as sharp as a razor, but a heart that was fierce in its affection for those she loved. Painswick must have* seen that in her affection for you and your brothers, and I can find it in myself to pity him that it was never directed his way.

It was not out of any spirit of meanness or malice that we rekindled our love; we were both miserable and were not strong enough to withstand temptation. Do not blame your mother. As a gentleman, and in the world's eyes her brother, I should have had strength enough for both of us. My life had been rudderless for so long, however, that I clung to her like a drowning man clinging to a piece of driftwood.

I saw the likeness between us long before Painswick. The last time I saw you, you had just turned five. Your mother had taken you for a walk in Hyde Park, and I came upon you by chance. She would never have arranged a meeting between us intentionally. She knew that your future happiness depended on Painswick never guessing. Your eyes were all your mother's, of course, but your hair and nose were already mine. I wished to pick you up, to cradle you in my arms, and tell you what a fine little man you were, but I could not. I think Alicia must have sensed what I was feeling, for she told me that we must never meet again.

I went to the dogs from that day forth, indulging in every excess apart from gambling. I was never so far gone as to lose sight of the fact that I must ensure you had something to inherit. I knew it was only a matter of time before Painswick saw beyond the end of his proud nose and discovered the truth. Do not judge him too harshly for sending your mother away; I am certain he would have forgiven her, if not me, in time. He could not have known that time was the one thing she did not have. She had rarely suffered a day of illness in her too short life.

I tell you all this not in the hope you will forgive the fact that I have most likely tarnished the picture you had of your mother, nor in the hope that you will understand, but because I wish you to know that however it must appear, there was never anything *sordid about our relationship. We loved each other completely and were fitting subjects for a Shakespearian tragedy.*

*That brings me to Steen. He is not merely my valet, but my trusted confidant and friend. He loves me, I believe, and I have entrusted him with the office of giving you this letter. It is time he retired, and I have provided him with the means to do so. I understand him well enough to know that he will not leave Carne Castle until he feels it is time. I think that time will be when you have read my letter. He will know that if my words cannot move you from the natural resentment you must feel towards me, nothing will. I understand it, of course, but his loyalty and love will lead him to hope that you might relent. You might even unbend enough to give him that impression whether it is true or not.*

*All that remains to be said is that I have, through various agents, kept abreast of your life, and I understand you to be a hardworking and earnest young man. I am proud of you, Son, and am sure you will make your mark in the world as a surgeon. I hope life treats you kindly, but none is more aware than me that it does not always turn out quite as we hope. I am certain you will not dance a jig when you discover I have left you Carne Castle, but it is there, nonetheless, and under the stewardship of Mr Grant, can but flourish. I know you won't want to hear it, but I love you, Oliver, and always have, even if only from afar.*

*Your father,*

*Mr Cedric Carne.*

Oliver was not aware of the tears running down his face until they smudged the ink of the letter. Winifred had been right. Mr Cedric Carne's love had been constant for both his mother and for him. His dissipated life had been driven by unhappiness as much as his unsteadiness of character. Apart from his mother, Winifred was the only person who had ever uttered the words *I am proud of you,* or *I love you.*

For the first time in his life, he wished he might have known his father. He could not bring himself to condone his actions, but he could accept them, for in the back of his mind a quiet voice whispered, *what would you have done if that had been you and Winifred?*

He rose from the desk, wiped his eyes, and went in search of Steen.

Lucy's story will follow in a few months.

# ALSO BY JENNY HAMBLY

Thank you for your support! I do hope you enjoyed What's in a Name? If you would consider leaving a short review on Amazon, I would be very grateful. I love to hear from my readers and can be contacted at: jenny@jennyhambly.com

### Other books by Jenny Hambly

# Confirmed Bachelors Books 4-6

# ABOUT THE AUTHOR

I love history and the Regency period in particular. I grew up on a diet of Jane Austen, Charlotte and Emily Bronte, and Georgette Heyer.

I like to think my characters though flawed, are likeable, strong and true to the period.

I live by the sea in Plymouth, England, with my partner Dave. I like reading, sailing, wine, getting up early to watch the sunrise in summer, and long quiet evenings by the wood burner in our cabin on the cliffs in Cornwall in winter.

Printed in Great Britain
by Amazon

37407587R00179